PRAISE FOR
Signs on a Page

"A recipe for an original novel: Start with an unconventional heroine. Add a seemingly innocent assignment. Mix with danger, intrigue, suspense, and historical events. Bring contents to a satisfying conclusion. You now hold an engrossing book that will leave you hungry for more."

—Edwin Goldstein, Reader

"Prepare to be captivated! *Signs on a Page* is a masterfully crafted mystery that will keep you on the edge of your seat till the last page. The intricate plot, vivid characters, and unexpected twists showcase the author's exceptional storytelling prowess. A must-read for mystery enthusiasts craving a thrilling and satisfying puzzle."

—James Petersen, Mystery Enthusiast

"Erik D. Weiss has written a compelling adventure through human history. He has managed to weave a tapestry of intricate clues that will keep you wondering how they fit together and where they will lead his heroine. Add in the life-and-death danger of the competing guide factions, and Dr. Weiss has created an enthralling page-turner."

—Derek Lee, Reader

"With *Signs on a Page*, Erik D. Weiss has created an intriguing, fast-paced mixture of mystery, discovery, and danger. Every chapter leads you further down a rabbit hole lined with enough well-researched history to make Dan Brown wonder, *Why didn't I think of that?* Following the thrilling journey of Molly, the book's tough-as-nails female protagonist as she unearths centuries-old secrets and mysteries, had me constantly wondering where the trail would lead next. Not only is this book entertaining, but I found myself wanting to further research some of its historical revelations, some of which I'd never heard of myself. It's an exceptional page-turner that leaves you mulling its contents long after you've put it down."

—Bradley McCaa, Reader

Signs on a Page

Signs on a Page
by Erik D. Weiss
© Copyright 2023 Erik D. Weiss

ISBN 979-8-88824-162-2

All rights reserved. No part of this publication may be reproduced,
stored in a retrieval system, or transmitted in any form or by any means—
electronic, mechanical, photocopy, recording, or any other—
except for brief quotations in printed reviews,
without the prior written permission of the author.

Published by

köhlerbooks™

3705 Shore Drive
Virginia Beach, VA 23455
800-435-4811

SIGNS *on a* PAGE

Erik D. Weiss

VIRGINIA BEACH
CAPE CHARLES

For my parents, Robert and Ilana,
with love—my first readers and greatest editors,
who always urge me to be better,
For my sister, Dana,
who always drives me to be better,
For my grandparents, Nathan and Jenny,
who always knew I could be better,
And for my wife, Ruo, and darling little ones, Alex and Abby,
with love, who inspire me to be the best I can be.

1

Her steps echoed through the nave as she approached the circulation desk. Part of a Gothic Revival–inspired campus, the 1930s-era university library emulated a cathedral of books, with transepts and large reading rooms on the right and left. No matter where her research began or where it directed her, she liked to start her work in this enclave of academia. She was inspired by the collected diverse knowledge of this place. It made her feel like she was following in the footsteps and thoughts of the scholars who came before her.

"Hello, Molly," the chief desk librarian greeted her while one of the student assistants brought over the books she had requested. "Hard at work again? It has to be at least a week since I've seen you in here!" Although she was no longer a student here, Molly's work required her to keep access to the book stacks.

"Hey, Frank. I was out of town at a meeting in Chicago. It was nice. I always like that city. There was a good symposium on Renaissance Italian lit, so I also gorged myself with Italian food! To get in the mood, of course."

Frank grinned. "The eating sure is good there. Well, here's most of what you asked for, although one of the older Rosicrucian texts is no longer in our collection, the one by Freedman."

"Ah, shoot. Have you heard anyone say that they have it? What happened to your copy?"

"Not sure; somehow these books just drop off the radar. You'd think with all our technology, we'd be able to keep closer tabs. Well, this may have been gone before that. I did phone around for you, though. Penn might have it, and U Delaware thinks they do."

Molly thanked the librarians as they swiped her library card and took the two books they were able to find.

What Molly enjoyed most about her work was that her mind was never idle. She had studied history and literature in college, but after (or even during) studying—reading, rote memorization—her mind was often unoccupied. She would write a long paper and then just sit and stare at a wall afterward. Or, more likely, drown her contrived thoughts with her friend Johnny Walker or Jim Beam.

Those were the days. College had been one of the best parts of her life. What she had enjoyed most about her studies was the research—the process of formulating a goal, a thesis, and then harnessing the resources to explore her topic. Books, manuscripts, and, perhaps the most disturbing and yet the most marvelous, the internet!

Following a short stint working for the National Security Agency in Maryland and for Google at their branch office in Boulder, Colorado, she took the saying "Do what you love" fully to heart, and when all her friends were cultivating their careers in med school or law school or Goldman Sachs, she made a career out of what she loved: research. A productive day for Molly involved roaming the Sterling stacks, sitting in the clean, white, sterile reading room at the rare-book library, and having the librarian carefully place an old original manuscript before her—or interviewing a live source on some projects, but there weren't too many of those left.

Molly McMurphy was a consulting researcher. If someone had a project they needed to explore, an old family photo they needed explained, a lost document they needed to find, a bit of arcane trivia they needed to answer, or a paper they needed to research for their company, Molly was their girl. For a rather handsome fee, she would comb libraries, travel to archives in distant cities, discover and meet with living sources, and hike to the tops of mountains (both literal and figurative) to hunt, isolate, and capture her prey: the details that fed a research project.

Her clients were too busy to do this legwork themselves and often too rich to ignore what they wanted to discover about the world. Whether it was the source of family heirlooms or the role of a certain assistant in Churchill's cabinet, however small the question, she would search and answer it. Her only scruple was that she wouldn't work for students, at any level. Students had to learn for themselves.

During her few years in practice, Molly had gathered a diverse series of contacts who helped facilitate her access to all sorts of human, technological, and archival resources. While she was an independent contractor, many of her assignments came from both US and foreign governments. Earlier that morning, she had met with a client at a coffee shop in New Haven and handed over a freshly printed paper summarizing the role his childhood next-door neighbor played in designing the Hubble Space telescope. That project had carried her to NASA headquarters in Washington and the Redstone Arsenal in Huntsville, Alabama.

She trudged into one of the large reading rooms and sat with her books about the Rosicrucians. Her personal research project had grown out of a junior-year course centered on the occult seventeenth-century philosopher Thomas Vaughn and his explorations of the esoteric remote past in the context of Rosicrucianism.

The larger chairs in this room were conducive to both reading and napping; she once awoke after a four-hour nap in the very same chair she now occupied. With about three hours to kill before meeting nearby with a potential new client, she would need to forbear this time. She often used the library's inner, tree-lined quad as a casual meeting space for clients, unless one (the haughtier variety) demanded that she come directly to their office in New York or Cincinnati or Stuttgart.

Three hours later, Molly packed up her backpack and trudged out to the courtyard to meet her newest inquisitor. This man—he'd sounded fairly young on the phone—had called her a week ago, referred by one of her former professors. Apparently, he was in the process of researching his ancestry, and the usual websites had only gotten him so far. This was a typical topic for her research. No history was more interesting to a person than that of his own forebears.

Ironically, Molly had never been able to uncover her own ancestry beyond her great-grandparents. They had emerged from almost entire darkness in various parts of Europe. It saddened her that her forefathers had lived (presumably) anonymous lives and gone to their graves with all their thoughts and pasts and memories locked in their inert brains, never to be revealed. Who were they? What had they done? What were their aspirations? Who had they loved?

"Good afternoon, Ms. McMurphy."

A short, thin redhead with a close-trimmed beard rose from one of the benches. He had been staring at the fountain when she walked in and wore a well-fitted suit.

She smiled. "Hi. Frank Samuels, I presume?" They shook hands. "Nice to meet you."

"Thank you for meeting with me."

She sat with him. Molly wouldn't take notes until she'd heard the basics of the job. There was no point wasting her time if the proposed project was impossible or absurd. Luckily, she could afford to turn down a project here and there.

But this client seemed like an honest, friendly sort, and she quickly knew she wanted to help him.

"You see, Ms. McMurphy, I've been researching the English side of my family. The farthest I've been able to uncover is my great-great-grandmother, who was born in Cornwall in 1869. Her legal marriage certificate in 1891 states her age at that time as twenty-two. But looking in birth registries in Cornwall from the late 1860s, I can't find anything of her birth or who her parents were."

"I see. Do you have any idea what sort of social status they had? Are you sure they were in Cornwall when she was born? Was she an Anglican? You've inquired at the Anglican churches there?"

"Eh." He looked down and laughed a bit. "I haven't gotten that far. That's why I'm hiring you, remember?" He looked her in the eye for just a touch too long. "She's on my mother's father's side. So, she'd be my grandfather's maternal grandmother. I know my grandfather's maternal grandfather's last name was Horace. His profession is unknown, and I'm not sure of his wife's maiden name, but her first name was Victoria; I'm sure of that."

"Any recollections you have from your grandfather? Maybe he told you something about his family?"

"He died when I was young. All I remember from him was a story he used to tell me and my younger brother, about a caravan riding through Marylebone. I'm not sure where that is!"

"Okay, Mr. Samuels—"

"It's doctor, please."

"Okay, Dr. Samuels. I've been surprised at how many archives sometimes don't list maiden names on marriage registries, even as late as the late nineteenth century. If I find something in terms of birth, I will be sure to try to confirm her maiden name before she married Mr. Horace. Is the fee I emailed you acceptable? If so, I'm on the job."

"Very good. Thank you. Please, Ms. McMurphy, I trust you will stop at nothing to find them."

"I'm a very determined researcher, you'll come to find, Dr. Samuels. But I take my time. I don't rush. It'll take as long as it takes, and you'll have to cover all my travel expenses, of course."

"Of course. Money is no object, madam."

"Madam?" she laughed. "Please, sir, you're making me feel old!"

"I'm sure you never could seem old, young lady." He smiled—again, a bit too long.

Molly stood. "You have my contact information, and I have yours. I will begin at once and inform you on my progress. Hopefully I'll have an answer for you sooner rather than later, but as I said, I can't promise anything."

"I understand. Thank you."

They shook hands, and Dr. Samuels left the courtyard in a rush. Molly sat back down on the courtyard bench and began formulating a research plan on her phone. Too often, the instinct of young researchers was to attack projects with a random approach, a shot in the dark here and there, hoping to hit on something somewhere. She knew better. A cogent strategy was needed. She would spend days crafting that strategy if need be.

The 1891 marriage certificate was the obvious place to start, followed by a search of local businesses and town archives for both his known great-great-grandmother and her husband. Church records were often of key importance, and she would search these extensively in Cornwall and nearby. But Victoria could have come from elsewhere, even the continent or—if her father was in the military or East India Company, for instance—the Far East. An individual's origins could never be assumed.

2

WHILE IN NEW HAVEN, Molly never skipped tea at her old college club or a taste of the greatest pizza on earth (as far as she was concerned). Her heels clicked on the stone library floors, and she smiled and chatted a moment with the guard as he slid her library books over the scanner. She remembered him sitting at this same guard desk back when she was a freshman. Although she'd passed through this turnstile thousands of times over the years, he always greeted her like she was a totally new face. *He sees so many faces*, she figured, *how could he remember mine?*

Molly maintained only one friend in New Haven. Her college classmate, Samantha Cavitelli, worked as a nurse practitioner at the hospital, and the two enjoyed a pizza and pitcher of beer together that evening. Samantha was a short, bold-featured brunette, and beside the tall, thin Molly with her long, light-brown hair, pale skin, and greenish-gray eyes, the two ladies provided quite a contrast.

"How's it going, Molly? What's Rick up to? Speaking of, my last two dates were a mess, although one of the guys I think I'll see again. Maybe. Nothing else to do."

"Eh, bit of news there. Joker Rick jumped ship! Never thought that'd work, though. They never do."

"Oh, too bad, Molly. I thought you really liked him. This last date guy I don't really like, and we're likely not compatible at all, but might as well hit him up for another date, right? But one more time, and that's it; he's done."

"C'mon, Sam! That's not nice! Be honest with these guys, and they'll be honest with you. Actually, forget I just said that." They both giggled and poured more beer. "I thought Rick and I were honest with each other, and then I took a break from the head-games LSD and woke up. He couldn't stand all my traveling, just wasn't into my work and lifestyle. As Paul Simon wrote, 'stolen minutes of his time was all he had to spend.' He was fixated on his med residency and basically just looking for someone with a stationary, fixed job."

"Most people are, Molly." Samantha smiled and took her friend's hand across the table. "But it's good you're still so immersed in your work. I like mine too, no doubt, but when it comes to the dating scene, I must admit I don't prioritize work."

"Work going well?"

"Not bad. You remember I switched over to the transplant service about six months ago. New staff to get used to."

"That can be either good or bad, right?" They both grabbed another slice of white spinach pizza. The doctors and nurses at Samantha's hospital sounded like a sitcom to Molly—much more like *Scrubs* than *Grey's Anatomy* (she watched neither but knew the basic idea). "I'm off to England next. My new project will at least start there."

"Another adventure? How good is this one?"

"It's basic family history kind of stuff. The task is fun, at least. Haven't been to London in a few months, so I may catch a couple days there if I can. I think Stuart Whatshisname is still working there. You remember, the dork from Branford."

Samantha almost spit out her beer at remembering this long-lost character from college. "Physics, right?"

"J. P. Morgan. Scientist in college, graduated to moneyman in life."

Samantha smirked. "Not all of us can pursue academia or your brand of research academia. No jobs. I mean, whatever happened to my anthro courses? Great at the time—"

"And you had a crush on your sophomore advisor there, I remember."

"Ha! What I meant was I'm not sure any of that knowledge helps me in my work and life now."

"I'm sure it does, in ways you don't know. You read and perceive differently because of all that. Trust me. College kids who don't treasure their learning are missing out. It's a unique opportunity, at any school, whatever they're studying."

3

TWO DAYS LATER, Molly drove down to New York to board a plane for Heathrow.

Various sets of regional records had been transferred to the National Archives in London over the years, and she had found many sources that that the curators themselves were surprised to have in the first place. She preferred to first attack this large central repository and then move on to more local archives.

Cornwall was the second focus. Whether or not Dr. Samuel's target ancestor had been born there, this was the place to explore.

The frumpish woman at the National Archives entirely looked the part of a British librarian, complete with thick-rimmed glasses and a tight hair bun.

"Madam McMurphy, we have no documents from parishes as small as Cornwall. What I do have is the number over at their parish church, where I believe records would be kept. The 1860s is fairly recent for them, I'm sure, and unless records were destroyed or never deposited, I think you'll find them there."

Molly spent a couple of days combing the archives' catalogue herself, regardless. On these projects, she never simply followed guidance from others. Many of these documents were occulted within larger sets of manuscripts, so she searched through pages and pages of mid-nineteenth-century census data and birth records from throughout the country. She unearthed nothing.

It was time to make the trip to Cornwall. She rented a car in downtown London and headed out first thing in the morning, following an evening at a center-city pub. Although Molly enjoyed the English grub, the lukewarm beer wasn't to her Midwestern US tastes.

The drive took about two hours, but it was smooth with not a terrible amount of traffic. She had driven often enough in England to be comfortable. In fact, driving on the left made more sense, given the historical origin of the practice. In a violent, feudal society, driving a chariot or riding a horse on the left side of the road kept a man's right arm free to defend against an opponent advancing in the opposite direction.

Cornwall was a very small village and civil parish in West Oxfordshire. Although Google was generally Molly's closest friend on the road, the "man on the street" often stole its thunder when it came to smaller towns (she had been led in circles by the app too many times). She pulled off onto a shoulder and jumped out of her car to stretch her legs and hail an oncoming dog walker.

The young man was hauling a group of canines, both large and small, and was young enough to seem like he should be in school at this time of day.

"Excuse me." She beamed a smile in an attempt to brighten the dull, gray English day. "I'm looking for your local parish church. Or any other churches around, if you know."

"Certainly, miss, happy to help." The boy tied the handful of dog leashes to a nearby tree. "Let me show you, right around the corner."

Following a curious custom Molly had sometimes witnessed in England, usually in the smaller towns but often even in London, this young boy walked her to her destination himself.

"Thanks so much. This is the main church around here?"

"The only one, Anglican. If you mean just this village."

"Yes, the person who sent me here insisted his ancestor came from this specific village, in Oxfordshire."

"Then this is the church you're looking for. You want to see the priest? He lives just down the road."

"Well, I was more curious to see their birth records and other archives."

"Mmm, you're studying something? He may not be in right now, in the midafternoon. You wait here, and I'll run down and see if he's at home."

"Oh, thank you so much for your help. All my work would be so much better with chaps like you around!"

He led her to the church's porch to wait. She knocked on the locked door just in case, but no one answered. As the boy headed off down the street, Molly quickly strolled the perimeter of the church. She always explored each destination as fully as possible and made every professional connection she could. There was no telling how some remote knowledge might come in handy later on. She made bridges and tried not to burn them. After all, the world was sometimes smaller than it seemed.

She made particular note of an old sundial on the porch, taking a picture with her phone as she stood over it. *Sort of an old relic for a nineteenth-century building.* She had read earlier online that this parish church of Saint Peter was originally a Norman church, with a chancel arch surviving from that time. So much history was held within architecture.

"Good day, miss." A gentleman with gray beard and balding head approached up the road, accompanied by the helpful boy. "So glad to have a visitor! Between Sundays, it's awful quiet around here."

He thanked the boy and offered him a coin or two, which the boy declined.

"Happy to help." He nodded and waved at Molly and strolled back to his dogs.

"Arthur tells me you're looking for archives. What's the interest?"

"Nice to meet you." Molly brushed the dust she had picked up from the sundial mount from her skirt and endeavored to be both friendly and authoritative in her approach and handshake. She'd retained remnants of lessons from a casual after-hours class she once took on manners to get ahead in business. The class seemed silly at the time, but body language and posture and verbiage went a long way, she had found. Some sources were harder to cultivate. Many places, especially the more tightly run government ones, were less helpful to someone who seemed like a dilettante.

"Yes, Mr. . . ."

"Stevens, miss."

"Yes, Mr. Stevens. I'm a consulting researcher from the States. My name is Molly, and I've been hired to research family forbears of an individual back on the East Coast."

"Consulting researcher? What sort?"

"Most of my cases involve historical, political, diplomatic, or literary research. This is an ancestry probe, a common theme. I'm looking for birth registries from Cornwall. My client believes his ancestor was born here in the late 1860s, likely 1869."

Mr. Stevens nodded thoughtfully. "Come inside and let's talk."

They entered through the south-facing door, behind the sundial.

"This church underwent renovations in 1830 and 1882. Although it maintained its Anglican mission during those times, many activities were relocated to local homes and businesses and sometimes schools in the area," he began.

"They must have rebuilt a lot over the years. I read this was originally from Norman times."

"Indeed. The precise year is unclear, but it has no doubt seen many changes. The thing is, while the archives are still mainly located in the basement"—he led her to a small back stairway—"which you can look through, one of those ancestry websites digitalized these records a few years ago. Yet you've found nothing there?"

"I took a survey of the most wide-reaching sites, and I found nothing, and apparently my client looked and also found nothing."

"Ms. . . ."

"McMurphy."

"Ms. McMurphy, I know that some of the archives may have been relocated, but I'm not sure where."

"Ha, construction and reconstruction once again trying to foil us! But it will not succeed. Do you have records of any reconstruction details? I'll take a look through these archives first, but then I'll have to see if we can find what happened."

The priest smiled as he opened a modern-looking cabinet (looked like Ikea) and pulled out three large, leather-bound books.

"Well, you can take all the time you need, at least until nightfall. I lock up the church then. You're welcome to come back in the morning as well, of course."

"Thank you. I may need that time!" She smiled, preemptively had the minister show her where the restrooms were, and sat down for a few hours of sifting through sheets and sheets of names. She had sometimes found names in physical records that did not make it onto the digitized archival websites. She wasn't sure how that happened and wished she could ask one of the researchers. Ultimately, she never figured that her work was done when she had fully explored an online site. They often provided only images of the real sources, and she even vetted the quality and thoroughness of those images.

Sure enough, Molly's work carried her into the next day, and the next. She joined the priest for lunch one day, at a pub down the road where they proudly displayed banners from NFL teams back in the States. Nowadays she never really felt like she left home, despite all her travels. US culture had spread around the world in more than just word. She could enjoy a Big Mac in Bangladesh and the Yukon.

During the course of three full days at the books, Molly found two birth records for women named Victoria, both from the 1840s, and one listed as only "Vic" from the 1820s. She took down the names just in case they matched the maiden name she hoped to find in a more thorough search for Mr. Horace, whose location was unknown, and also stored pdf images of the entire archive on a small laptop.

She intended to develop her own digitized archives, perhaps more focused and thorough than the commercial sites. She was sure she'd spent more physical time with these manuscripts and archives than a large company that was intent on selling and distributing large caches of data.

"So you know of no record of any replaced or moved archives from here, Mr. Stevens?" she asked the minister on the third day.

"Unfortunately, no, but I'm sure they must exist. It's a pet project of mine to find them. I know those ancestry-site researchers were here for a day or so and then left. The previous deacon brought them in."

"Is he around?"

"She. She died a few years ago. That's when I took over. She was a true student of the church, from a more academic background. She studied theology and English history at Bristol before settling down here. Became a student of this particular church, even."

"Did she write anything? Any surviving text from her records? You presumably work in her former office?"

"She actually maintained an office at home. That's been sold off, I think. She never had any children, and never married."

"She was a scholar, though, it sounds like. You're sure she didn't write anything, nothing even for internal perusal, like for your own church records?"

"She did teach a short class at the high school. I think it was about the Anglican church in general, but maybe she touched on this church's history."

Molly pointed straight at him with a smile. "That's a lead. And a lot of them lead nowhere, but I would rather have a lead that leads nowhere than no lead at all. My dad used to call these leads a break for freedom."

The priest laughed and now seemed almost as excited about the project as Molly. With her approval, he joined her as she hurried to her car. Enlisting a priest's help on Thursdays seemed to work out much better than on Sundays or Saturdays.

Molly and the priest set off for the high school. The headmaster there was a faithful member of Reverend Stevens's church and eager to help, particularly when Molly informed him that his little high school would get a mention when she presented her work to her client.

The former deacon, Walsingham, had grown up in Oxfordshire and, although initially trained as a nurse, pursued further studies that culminated in a PhD in theology with a focus in English history. Supported by a small stipend from the local high school, she had taught a course to the junior high schoolers.

"Our library has a few short booklets she wrote for her students to study by. Nothing profound, from my brief look at them, but maybe you'll find what you're looking for there."

Four thin paperbacks were nestled at the end of a long bookshelf near the middle of the small, 1970s-era school library. The headmaster and priest chatted while Molly sat near a gaggle of giggling high school girls to speed-read and take pics with her phone.

The course the deacon had taught concerned basic history of the Anglican church, of course starting with the role of Henry VIII in separating the Church of England from the Roman Catholic Church and the subsequent Elizabethan religious settlement. The class seemed more like an intensive Sunday School course, including divine texts and biblical interpretations by Anglican theologians such as Richard Hooker and Thomas Cranmer.

Finally, in the third booklet, the deacon discussed the building and rebuilding of the parish church of St. Peter at Cornwall. Originally a Norman church, it had been decorated with Gothic windows, which she had seen. As Father Stevens had mentioned, the church was rebuilt in 1830 and 1882, the later rebuilding seeing the addition of the existing west window.

But what happened to the archives? she wondered. While much of them were certainly still in the basement, they had to be incomplete. Molly had found no mention of the birth of the Victoria for whom she was hunting.

Deacon Walsingham drifted away from her discussion of church reconstruction to more mundane features of Anglican theology as interpreted within Oxfordshire, following this train of winding thought well into the fourth booklet. While Molly generally enjoyed reading obtuse texts for important information, she grew tired, every so often smiling weakly at the priest and the headmaster as they paused their chitchat to check her progress.

In a footnote near the third quarter of the fourth book, Walsingham wrote that an earlier deacon of the church, a man named O'Malley, had relocated a portion of the archives during the 1882 construction project "for safekeeping." Molly excitedly asked herself, *Why this portion? Was it located near the work on the west window?* No mention. *Where did it go?*

A second footnote followed just below. Although Walsingham seemed like a very straightforward, rigid historian and follower of church doctrine, here she waxed apocryphal. Deacon O'Malley had hidden the selected archives guided by the shadow of the church's spire at 8:38 a.m. on September 8, "as reckoned by the dial of Ahaz." Molly's smartphone practically leaped out of her pocket. In the Old Testament, the dial of Ahaz was mentioned in Isaiah 38:8 and in Second Kings. It was a sundial.

4

$\mathbf{W}$OW, THE ANGLICANS *liked to play games!* Molly took notes, hurriedly skimmed the rest of the booklet, and almost slammed it shut, to the evident distaste of the old librarian at the desk.

Molly grinned at Father Stevens as she stood. "This Deacon Walsingham—did people you know say they liked her? Doesn't sound like the life of the Sunday church party."

"She was a valued member of our school community," the headmaster insisted.

"Oh, I'm sure she was, and no doubt a master of her musty craft. But I think we have a lead. A weird one, but a lead."

Molly and Father Stevens returned to the church. She strolled around his small office, pondering the numerous relics displayed on his walls, coffee table, and bookcases. This place looked like a well-stocked New England antique shop. There were busts of church elders and military commanders, posters both large and small of theater productions from London and New York, commemorative ceramic plates, and a large assortment of children's dolls that appeared to be true antiques from the nineteenth century.

"Your collection is very full." She beamed at him.

"Yes, it's an old habit I inherited from my late uncle. Can't stop myself from buying things at flea markets and can't muster the courage to throw anything away!" He laughed as he poured Molly a cup of hot coffee.

"We had a room at the library back in college that looked like a larger version of this collection. I also remember a museum of sorts down near New Orleans that was filled with such curiosities from the bayou and jazz culture down there." She catalogued the relics in her mind. "Is there a general theme you're going after?"

"Nah, not really. Just a bunch of random stuff. Folks who sold it at their estate sales and flea markets must have deemed it garbage."

She touched one of the dolls. "No, they're not. Not at all. You seem drawn to both military and church figures."

"Well, no doubt I'm drawn to figures that could have been my own forefathers, I guess. Several of them served with the British Army, many in India."

"No doubt each of these relics has a story, something the artist was trying to convey. And each relic also carries the myriad stories of the people who held it before you did. Maybe one day someone will possess these and think about you!"

"Doubt it! Immortality is a seldom-captured quality. I'm sure I don't have it." Stevens sat back at his desk. "I like having you around the place, Ms. McMurphy. You're the first person who's shown any interest whatsoever in these oddities. But back to our little games—what have you found?"

"Oh, please, call me Molly. It's a bit odd, but it seems that this Deacon O'Malley relocated some of the archives during the second reconstruction in 1882. Not far. I think he buried them on the church property. Does the church still own the land it had back then?"

"It may have been a bit larger earlier, but plots in this village haven't changed much for a couple hundred years now."

"Well, presumably, or so Walsingham tells us, we need to be at the church when that sundial on the south porch points to 8:38 a.m. on September 8."

"That's four days from now!"

"Exactly. Lucky thing I didn't show up here a week from now, although I'm pretty sure there's some app that could have pointed the way through a simulation of the sun and the earth and the sundial." She fondled her phone. "Good. Nothing for me to do until then. I think I'm going to head back to London and see if I can figure out who Victoria's husband was. I need to find out her maiden name, or else whatever we find in that archive can't be explicitly matched to the person I'm looking for."

"But why hide the archives in such a way? Very strange," the minister said thoughtfully.

"I've seen many strange things in my work, Mr. Stevens, I assure you. Sometimes it's just people trying to have fun. It's kind of neat that through that booklet we're essentially talking with Deacon Walsingham. And on September 8, perhaps we'll share a laugh with Deacon O'Malley."

5

MOLLY ATE DINNER in a pub in Cornwall before heading down the road, back to London. She preferred to drive at night and preserve the daylight hours for work and play. The highway rode quicker at night, too, she often found—at least after rush hour.

So, Mr. Horace, who were you?

Dr. Samuels didn't know his ancestor's profession, and she imagined there were more than a few Horaces in England and London. She wasn't even sure Horace and Victoria were married in London. But with the heart of English archives there, that's where she would focus. She had four days to work on this before heading back to Cornwall for the eighth. *What a stroke of luck,* she thought with a smile that soon faded—because on the other hand, Molly was a bit suspicious about the timing of it all.

While most of her clients were quite straightforward, could Dr. Samuels have known that September 8 was an important date? *Could he have sent me on this mission specifically to meet that date at the church?* Strange things had happened before during her research voyages. The past and the present often had hidden agendas.

She cleared her mind and focused on the road for an hour or so, staring at the monotonous highway lines, but soon found her mind returning to the mystery at hand.

Marylebone. Dr. Samuel's grandfather had told him a story about Marylebone. Not a common locale name. There probably wasn't anything to it, but when she was essentially searching in the dark for a black rubber coin, Molly had to follow any idea that came her way.

At a rest stop, she sat on the hood of the rental car and pulled out her phone. After a quick check of email, she searched the term "Marylebone."

It was a relatively affluent section of central London within the City of Westminster, a neighborhood based around the parish church of St. Marylebone. Random associations came up on a quick search: Marylebone Village, Regent's Park, Baker Street, Marylebone Cricket Club, Lisson Grove, Harley Street . . . *Harley Street is in Marylebone.* Molly knew Harley Street well. Since the nineteenth century it had been known for having a large number of private medical and surgical specialists and currently boasted both clinics and hospitals.

Could Dr. Samuel's grandfather have been telling a story about someone in his past, perhaps his father or grandfather? Could he have been referring to someone on Harley Street? An incredible long shot, but if she found nothing with Harley Street, she could search the rest of Marylebone.

Molly had called ahead to reserve her room at her usual hotel on Fleet Street near Ludgate Circus, and she lugged her small rolling suitcase up to the elevators. Sleep was the goal now.

※ ※ ※

The Royal College of Physicians had a museum in Regent's Park, also located within Marylebone. She attacked that first after a late morning.

"Hi, I'm Molly McMurphy, a researcher from the States," she greeted the young Asian woman behind the front desk. "I'm trying to find if you have records of a particular physician or surgeon here in London, from the early twentieth century, probably."

"Glad to help, miss." The woman leaned across the desk to shake Molly's hand. "We can search our online directory and list of manuscripts here, if you'd like. The hard copies have been stored away and aren't usually accessible." She sounded like she had learned English pronunciation directly from Henry Higgins.

"Okay, we'll start there. I may eventually have to apply for permission to see the originals, but let's hit that if we need."

"Good." The woman sat back down at her computer. "This digital record is pretty thorough. We seldom find anything in the archive that isn't on here. Who are you looking for?"

"I hope he's in there. I'm looking for a Dr. Horace."

The archivist tapped at her keyboard and after a moment declared, "Nothing."

"Shoot."

"Was he a surgeon, perhaps?"

"I have no idea. I'm not sure if this person was even in London at any time."

"Well, if he was a surgeon"—the woman tapped at her keyboard again—"he'd be entered as Mr. Horace."

Molly laughed as she remembered that male British surgeons were called "mister" instead of "doctor." In the early eighteenth century, physicians were the only ones who possessed an actual university medical degree. Surgeons didn't have any such qualification—although starting with the founding of the Royal College of Surgeons of London in 1800, they did take an examination and put MRCS after their name.[1] But the tradition held, and to this day surgeons were referred to as "mister."

"Yeah, try that!"

"Here, Mr. Stanley Horace. Mmm. A general surgeon whose practice on Harley Street was active from 1887 to 1906."

Molly was so happy that she hugged the archivist.

"I can't thank you enough for your help."

Molly was a frequent user of the English General Register Office online archives, which held birth, marriage, and death certificates and other documentation dating to 1837. She'd once had to visit their physical site in Southport, London.

Back in the hotel, she logged onto the site. The internet was indeed a wonder. A search that would have taken her a thirty-minute drive to Southport (depending on traffic) and perhaps a two-day search of the physical records now took her nimble fingers ten minutes or so on the keyboard.

Mr. Stanley Horace had been married in 1891 to Ms. Victoria Lambert. That was the name. *Perfect.*

Now three days to kill. Molly always enjoyed London, despite the congestion of the place, and luckily had packed some light, fun clothes to walk the city in the late summer. Following the guidance of a childhood English friend, she had remained a fan of Arsenal from a distance and managed to grab a ticket to a game. Otherwise, she spent long afternoons in the parks reading, never short on reading materials packed onto her tablet.

6

SEPTEMBER 7 ARRIVED, and it was time for the drive back to Cornwall. Father Stevens was anxiously awaiting her and even offered her a room. A widower, he kept a neat, if spartan, home.

"Early evening, Ms. McMurphy? We have to be up for our 8:30 appointment, eh?" The older man seemed eager to help and even more eager for company. "I've never been on such a little adventure, and it's all taking place around my own little church!"

"I must say this research trip is a bit more interesting than I'm used to. Mostly it's just hunting through archives like the neat files you have down in the church basement, turning up names, making connections in other documents, pretty standard stuff. But here we're dealing with a sundial and hidden archives and cryptic messages from a set of former deacons of a small English church. A bit more excitement than I bargained for."

She took another sip of the fine single-malt beverage he had offered her, and they laughed and planned for the next day.

A sundial's projected time varied from official time during the course of the year due to the elliptical orbit of the earth around the sun and the tilt of the earth's axis. But whoever set out this guidance by the sundial in 1882 was observing the position of the sunlight's reflection off the sundial's gnomon and style on the same date. So like would be compared to like. The solar time, on the other hand, did have to be corrected for the longitude at which the sundial was located. Cornwall was west of Greenwich, so the sundial in Cornwall would show an earlier time. With a difference in longitude of -1.61º, a sundial would see a difference of four minutes per degree. So the sundial in Cornwall would see 8:38 at about 8:32.

Regardless, they just needed to be ready. Molly couldn't sleep and woke Father Stevens at 7:30 to head to the church. As they strolled down the street, Molly smiled up at the blue sky—she would have hated to wait a year for another sunny morning. Her thoughts the night before had been aggressive, veering toward hauling out the shovel and digging a deep moat around the church if this were a cloudy day.

The shadow cast by the low church spire was not long, and they would find their point fairly close to the church building. Molly stood by the sundial, careful not to block the sun with her tall frame, and Father Stevens stood on the grass along the western side of the church property. Just a few minutes.

Molly shouted, "Time!" and Father Stevens rushed to plant a chopstick from his kitchen into the ground where the point of the shadow hit the ground. Molly bounded over and hugged him, beaming a smile and laughing. "I'm sure the deacons were rooting for a cloudy day."

"But we got 'em! Let me go grab the shovel. This lawn needs to be resodded soon anyway."

Although Stevens offered, Molly grabbed the shovel out of his hands and got to work. Her days playing field hockey at school had cultivated her skill with the overhead lift, and she made short work of the digging.

The shovel clanged against a metal plate. She carefully dug wider and wider, revealing a box, and she and Stevens managed to haul it out of the ground. It was a bit rusty but otherwise intact. How strange that the deacon had made the effort to put this out here back in the 1880s, considering that the rest of the archives had been preserved quite nicely back in the basement.

In fact, when they opened the box, it looked like these documents repositioned for "safekeeping" hadn't borne the brunt of time as well as the larger set of books in the main archive. If they had discovered this box in another 100 years, who knows what they would have found. Deacon O'Malley hadn't sealed them well.

The two small books were readable, though, and Molly didn't stop to eat or drink but went straight to work. They both contained similar rows of names and dates. Father Stevens brought her a cup of coffee from the kitchen upstairs, and she casually sipped the brew while combing the records.

Victoria Lambert's father wasn't English. He was German. Also, Victoria was actually twenty-four when she married Mr. Stanley Horace in 1891. A girl named Victoria Lamprecht had been born to Elizabeth Church and Oskar Lamprecht in 1867. The name was a recognized German-English translation, the location was appropriate, and the birth year was close enough. No other Victoria was found in the rest of these additional archives.

The great thing about research was that it was never really done. Every discovery posed a new question and a new goal. Even a published paper or book.

Who were Oskar Lamprecht and Elizabeth Church? Molly spent the rest of the day and the next morning re-scrutinizing the main and hidden archives to see if either of these individuals were born in Cornwall. They weren't. And any records of prior businesses or institutions in the village had probably been destroyed in a fire near the main square in the 1950s, Father Stevens glumly told her.

"Folks working to create a census of larger Oxfordshire tell me that there's a huge gap in records of the people who lived and worked in this village during much of the nineteenth and early twentieth centuries. All we have left are their grave sites."

Molly pointed a finger gun at him and shouted, "That's it! That's where we go next. Where's the cemetery?"

"It's not in Cornwall. It's in the main center of Chipping Norton, a short drive from here."

"Then warm up the engine, my friend." Molly didn't finish her coffee, instead marching out of his little office to the stairs. Stevens rushed to keep up with her.

"Some folks from around here could have been buried in Oxford, but we'll check over at Chipping Norton first and see what we find," he added.

The two jumped into the minister's car, and he sped toward the turnpike and drove past a couple of exits. The cemetery was closed for new burials but open for visitors, and finding no directory at the main office (*You would think that's the only thing a cemetery office needs to have*, Molly thought), Molly marched her way up and down the rows of old tombstones with Stevens skulking behind her and making quick chitchat with the attendant, who was also a parishioner of his congregation.

Molly took photos of a few interesting tombstone inscriptions, some dating as early as the late seventeenth century.

Then she stopped.

Near the middle of the cemetery plot sat two adjacent stones with fairly legible inscriptions: Elizabeth Lambert and Oscar Lambert. Oskar had anglicized his name by the time he died in 1879 at the age of forty-eight. His wife had lived another sixteen years, dying in 1895, although her birth date was impossible to decipher. No one had left flags or other commemoration at their grave sites; if any relatives remained in the area, they were not the kind to pay respects to distant ancestors on a regular basis.

Near the bottom of Oscar's tombstone, a metal badge fixed into the stone gave the already minimally inscribed and serious facade an ominous quality.

She pointed at it after taking a few pictures. "Is this a shield or motto from these parts?"

Father Stevens bent over to take a closer look.

"Never seen that—no idea. Some of these people were in all sorts of societies. Masons, that sort of thing. But I've never seen that around."

Or Glory, she pondered. She took comprehensive pictures of the tombstones and the surrounding area, along with a marked map from the main office, in case Dr. Samuels wanted to come visit himself, and then headed back to the church.

It was getting close to dinnertime, and Father Stevens invited Molly to join him for a hamburger and beer at the pub she had already frequented a few times. The food was good, and the place was small and grungy, just as Molly preferred.

While Father Stevens ordered food for them, Molly was already at work on her laptop.

That "Or Glory" motto below the skull and crossbones apparently formed the insignia and badge of the Seventeenth Lancers, a British cavalry regiment known as the Duke of Cambridge's Own. The

Seventeenth was raised in 1759 as a regiment of Light Dragoons by Colonel John Hale of the Forty-Seventh Foot after he brought news to the king of General James Wolfe's victory at Quebec, as well as of Wolfe's death. In mourning for his commander, Hale chose the death's-head badge with the motto "Or Glory." The Seventeenth first served abroad during the American War of Independence, when this regiment became the first cavalry sent to the colonies. The Seventeenth later saw action in the West Indies from 1795 to 1797 against the French, and again in India in the early nineteenth century.

The most famous engagement of the Seventeenth Lancers, however, came in 1854 in the Crimea against Russia—as part of the charge of the light brigade later immortalized by Alfred, Lord Tennyson in his narrative poem of 1854. Of the 147 Seventeenth Lancers who made the charge, only 38 were able to answer roll call after the battle.[2] *Was Oscar Lambert one of them?* Molly wondered.

If Oskar Lamprecht had indeed been with the Seventeenth Lancers in Crimea, and if he had continued with the unit after the war, he may have also seen action during the Indian mutiny of 1857, although he presumably returned to England before his daughter, Victoria, was born in 1867.

Molly told the excited Father Stevens about the badge and the connection with Lamprecht while the two of them devoured large burgers and drank a couple of beers each. He had never heard of the Lancers and wasn't aware if they'd had any special presence in Cornwall. He was intent on Molly also pursuing the family of Elizabeth Church in the days to come.

Molly sent an email to Dr. Samuels to give him a short summary of what was happening, figuring she would continue the pursuit until she arrived at a dead end. Discovering where a German named Lamprecht had been born would be a challenge, but she prepped herself for a long slog through Samuels's ancestry.

Molly planned on an early morning, perhaps going through the church archives again. Relaxed by her victory, however, she let herself sleep in the next day.

When she awoke, she trudged up to Stevens's office, which she had made her mini-headquarters. After a short chat, he headed downstairs to prepare some coffee. She unpacked her laptop and casually stared again at the assorted relics around her. A poster on the wall caught her eye—more specifically, the words on it did: THE 17TH LANCERS.

Molly feverishly typed into the Google search box. The Seventeenth Lancer's Waltz had been produced in 1905 to celebrate the regiment; and an original poster of the 1905 release was on Father Stevens's wall!

Molly's long legs bumped into the minister's desk as she staggered to the wall and grabbed the framed picture off its hook, holding it close, amazed at the coincidence.

When she returned the picture to the wall hanger, she felt a hard object on the back of the frame. She flipped the picture frame, and her jaw dropped when she found a black stone disk taped tightly there.

The carvings appeared to be heraldic symbols, likely family crests and shields, surrounding ill-defined characterizations of a horse's head and a futuristic outline of what seemed like a frog—or maybe it was prehistoric; early figures sometimes looked similar to stuff in modern art museums. The etched figures encircling the imagery, however, were the strangest part: arrows pointing every way, but if read along the circumferential course, they pointed up and down.

This artifact was far more interesting than the casual collectibles comprising the rest of Father Stevens's collection, and she put down the frame to take several close photographs before putting the poster and disk back on the wall.

Where did he get this? Could its placement behind the Seventeenth Lancers Waltz poster mean this is related to Oskar in some way? Was this Oskar Lamprecht's stone disk? She had to find where Stevens had gotten this.

Molly shouted down to the first floor and heard no answer. "Mr.

Stevens, I need you! I have a question." She grabbed her backpack and rushed down the stairs.

The cupboard was empty. The coffee pot was still hot, and a single, still-steaming cup had been poured. She walked into the main church hallway and knocked at the bathroom doors in the back. She shuffled down into the basement. Everything was calm.

She found the south door open, but Stevens wasn't outside on the patio. Molly hurried around the building and once again explored all the rooms inside, shouting his name; he was nowhere. His car was parked neatly in his church parking spot, locked. She ran down the street to his house and pounded on the doors. No answer. Molly used the church phone to call the local police. The constable responded that there must be a rational reason for Father Stevens's sudden departure. They wouldn't conduct a search until more time had passed.

With the church doors open and no one coming by, Molly buried herself again in the church archives, finding no other mention of either Elizabeth Church or Oskar/Oscar Lamprecht/Lambert.

On Sunday, when the Anglican congregation arrived, she introduced herself to the parishioners and told them she hadn't seen Father Stevens in several days. After a few more days of frustration—his house doors remained locked, and none of his neighbors had seen him—she made sure the local police would continue their search before she headed back to London to explore the archives there as well as make a quick trip to the National Archives at Kew.

She scoured online archives from the continent and India as well as her own homemade digitized records but again found nothing. Either this family came from somewhere far off or nowhere. *Similar to my own*, she thought sadly.

7

Back in the United States, she spent a few weeks in Washington, DC, tying up loose ends related to her project on the Hubble engineer and writing up her report for Dr. Samuels. She included high-resolution photos of the stone disc that apparently was connected with his ancestor and asked if he had any ideas regarding where she could continue the search for Oscar Lambert and Elizabeth Church. He had none.

Surprisingly, on the phone he did not seem interested in her continued pursuit and did not wish to meet and discuss her findings in person, a request that most of her clients made clear from the beginning of her work. He instead assured her that he was content with her efforts and needed nothing more from her.

❊ ❊ ❊

Molly's next eight months were spent on steady, slow work. A legal client hired her to help formulate an historical account of the pre-Revolution laws of Braintree, Massachusetts; a professor of sociology at Auburn had her conduct research for his book on gender dynamics in late nineteenth-century Alabama; and the Dutch government hired her to expand on her previous work related to a seventeenth-century architect of the Prinsengracht canal in Amsterdam.

In late June of the following year, when the work on Dr. Samuel's ancestors seemed like a distant memory, she was contacted by a new client, who arranged a meeting at a coffee shop back in New Haven.

This peculiar fellow said he had bad memories of the Yale library and preferred to avoid the place. She didn't ask for details.

A woman met her at the local college bookstore/lunch spot.

"Good afternoon." Molly shook her hand. "Are you here with Mr. Barnsworthy, the gentleman who called me?"

"Oh, no, sorry about the confusion, Ms. McMurphy. Mr. Barnsworthy is not available to meet with you in person, unfortunately. I'm Sasha Daniels, his agent. Nice to meet you." She waved over a waitress. "Would you like some coffee? Breakfast? Please, join me and we can chat."

Sasha Daniels indeed seemed like someone's agent: tall and slender in a business pantsuit, middle aged, and with a tight hair bun and glasses that demanded respect for her wisdom and circumspection.

Molly thanked her and ordered a coffee. "I understand from my very brief discussion with Mr. Barnsworthy that he's interested in the US Army's Twenty-Fourth Infantry Division. What particularly is he looking for? A summary of their work, particularly during Korea, could easily be found in a published history of the Eighth Army. He wasn't very clear."

Ms. Daniels laughed—Molly was relieved to find that she knew how—and buttered her toast. "Mr. Barnsworthy is often brusque, even with me. Over the years, I've learned to put two and two together to deduce what he's looking for. He's interested in a specific firsthand account of that division's activities during the war, which he believes are held by the Pentagon in their archives."

"So, the idea is just go there, find this account, write up a summary for him? That's it?"

"Yes. Nothing fancy! I hope this isn't too simple a project for someone of your experience and abilities, Ms. McMurphy. Mr. Barnsworthy, as I'm sure you expect, is willing to provide you any resources and compensation requested, of course. You may even stay at his apartment in Washington if you'd like. He won't be there, of course."

"Oh, I don't think that will be necessary, but thank you. Does Mr. Barnsworthy perhaps have other projects he may later require my assistance with as well?"

"Not that I know of."

"Well, Ms. Daniels, I have several other active projects on my schedule right now, and if you know of no pressing need by your client for me to pursue this right now, could I get back to you in several weeks regarding whether I have time to pursue this?"

"There's no pressing need at the moment, although I must forewarn you, Ms. McMurphy, my client is a man who changes his mind quickly and without notice. At any moment, he may call me and ask me to demand that you drop everything and pursue his project immediately."

"Excuse me? Demand?"

"I misspoke. I meant he may request that you pursue this sooner rather than later. He has not done so, as of now."

"Well, I have not accepted his offer as of now either. So please don't tell Mr. Barnsworthy that I have. I am currently working on several other projects and will get back to you."

"I understand. You work very hard, which is a testament to your keen abilities, Ms. McMurphy. Thank you very much for meeting with me," Ms. Daniels said, laying down her corporate credit card for the bill.

"And thank you for coffee, Ms. Daniels. Have a nice day, and if our paths cross again, I look forward to speaking with you."

As Molly scampered across the street against the traffic light, she shook her head. She was used to clients sending representatives to speak with her; governments did so all the time. But a project to merely find and summarize a manuscript in a known location seemed more like an assignment for a college student (or even a precocious high school student).

She was sure this mysterious client would pay her well, but unless she knew he would be a good contact for her in future projects or himself give her several projects, she didn't want to turn away other clients who also were paying her very well to fulfill assignments that required more skill and source hunting.

So, Molly resumed her ongoing projects in Amsterdam, in Braintree, and exploring both primary and secondary sources online and in libraries that dealt with gender issues in the South during the late nineteenth century. These projects were not by any means exciting, but they were at least challenging. She also spent more time with the Rosicrucians, hoping to one day compile that scattered work of years into a book. She worked on documents reflecting the working relationship between Thomas Vaughn and his wife, Rebecca Vaughn, in the development of his ideas of natural philosophy.

With her hired projects completed, however, and not feeling overly inspired by the NFL preseason games in August, eventually she called Sasha Daniels.

8

They met at the same coffee shop, and this time Ms. Daniels gave Molly the name of the person who was purported to have written the document on the Twenty-Fourth Infantry Division. A simple task was better than no task, Molly figured. Anyway, it was always nice to get back to Washington; she enjoyed the museums and walking the Mall.

A quick online search gave her a barebones background. The Twenty-Fourth Infantry Division was formed during WWII, seeing action in the Pacific theater at New Guinea and the Philippine Islands, and then took part in the postwar occupation of Japan. Due to the unit's early involvement in the Korean War, the Twenty-Fourth saw heavy frontline action against both the North Koreans and Chinese before being withdrawn to the reserve force following heavy casualties. In Korea, they were under Lieutenant General Walton H. Walker as part of the Eighth Army, which was decisively defeated by the Chinese at the Battle of Ch'ongch'on River. After the war, the Twenty-Fourth served patrol duties in Korea.

Molly had to use Pentagon resources at least once a year, so she had good friends at the archives. They went for a fun dinner in Dupont Circle and the next day easily found the book she was looking for, held in a large box that contained all Korean War–era documents related to the division.

The author, Corporal Randolph Humphries, had been an auto mechanic, but he must have spent his downtime taking notes that were later compiled into a neat, rather well-written and casually detailed account of the role the division played from the beginning of the war in 1950 until they were pulled back into the reserve force. Then he was reassigned to the 187th Infantry Regiment of the 101st Airborne Division, at which point he stopped writing. She looked a little further and found that he had died of a respiratory infection in 1951. *Too bad*, she thought. *This fellow could have been a good historian if he had made it back.*

Most of his account, she realized, had later been retold in various forms by many historians of the war. The Eighth Army's role—in particular, losing to the Chinese forces invading from the north—had been an important turning point. She took pictures and notes but was not sure what this added to published knowledge about this division, this army, or this war.

Always searching for an angle that would make her work more fruitful, however, Molly studied every subordinate phrase, every cited source or described person, and every footnote. *This car mechanic sure enjoyed his footnotes*, she thought with a chuckle.

One footnote struck her interest. Humphries referred briefly to a diary kept by one of the officers in the division, a Captain Robert Ogilvie. He said this diary related "important information about further activities of our division" in the war. He did not describe further. Apparently, the diary wasn't a private one, but he didn't say what he had read in it, although he implied that he had indeed seen it.

Molly turned her attention to Captain Ogilvie. He was listed in a registry of the Twenty-Fourth Infantry, without any particulars of his role. She searched through a few boxes of artifacts from the Twenty-Fourth, as well as a larger set of documents holding more general relics from the Eighth Army, but found neither his diary nor reference to it in other sources. A quick Google search also yielded no findings. This diary, if it still existed, hadn't been published or listed among digitized manuscript repositories.

Here an online ancestry site came in handy. A Robert Ogilvie of the right age had been born in 1918 near Cedar Rapids, Iowa.

Following the war, he had married Margaret Thompson in 1953, had two sons, and died in 1975. His wife also died young, in 1979. His eldest son had died, but his younger son lived in German Village, Ohio.

This town had made their phone book available online, and a few hours into her search, she was making a call to Robert Ogilvie's son, Todd.

The Ogilvie family knew of his service in Korea but didn't have much in the way of details. They also had never heard of Corporal Humphries. As for a diary, Todd Ogilvie's wife, Julia, remembered only that there was an old box of her father-in-law's various possessions in their attic. She thought it looked like old clothes.

This seemed like a dead end, and Molly gathered her things and climbed into her car for the drive back to New Haven, ready to write up a summary of her findings for Mr. Barnsworthy.

A call came from Ohio the next morning. Julia Ogilvie had found Robert's box in the attic, and beneath some old pants and ties were financial documents, as well as a small, handwritten notebook. She and her husband couldn't definitively identify the handwriting, but a date written on the first few pages was from July 1951.

9

WHILE STILL ON THE PHONE with the kind and helpful Ogilvies, Molly booked a flight from Hartford to the Port Columbus airport, near German Village. Todd and Julia said they would be glad to have her come take a look.

Molly had discovered a talent for getting people interested in the projects she was working on. This had worked excellently with Father Stevens and certainly did now with Todd Ogilvie, who knew little about his father's role in the war but was curious. As for Father Stevens, wherever the poor man was now, the authorities hadn't located him. She had called Cornwall to check a couple of times.

Molly rented a car and drove out to the Ogilvie address. Todd Ogilvie was a short, overweight, and friendly middle-aged fellow. He had lived his whole life in German Village, spending only a short few years at a junior college in Cincinnati. Having worked in construction most of his life, he was now in the process of retiring.

"I'm quite excited to meet you, Ms. McMurphy. I'm surprised anyone's heard of my father, let alone has any interest in him."

The elder Ogilvie had been a teacher in Columbus, rising to the level of superintendent of schools. Otherwise, as his son put it, he never did much. No sports, no arts, no real interests beyond work, as far as he knew. He spoke about his father as if Robert were a distant relative, or even a stranger. They must not have been close. Or the specifics had faded with time.

"I am interested in what's in that little book, if you can decipher the handwriting. Looks like chicken scratch to me. How did you find him in the first place?"

Molly gave him and his wife the rundown of her project, avoiding giving away her client's name. They hadn't even known he was in the Eighth Army, and Molly gave them a summary of that unit's role in the war. They seemed intrigued. Julia Ogilvie expressed regret that they had never pressed Robert to speak about the war, though apparently he hadn't spoken about his past much in general.

After sharing a coffee, they marched Molly up to the attic.

The random assortment of odds and ends had apparently been thrown together from Robert's belongings just after he died of a heart attack at age fifty-seven. With his family standing behind her, Molly pushed aside his financial papers after a quick glance for any handwritten or typed notes.

The notebook was small, indeed written in chicken scratch. She took the book downstairs where there was more light and planted herself at the Ogilvies' dining room table to read and capture photos. Deciphering the handwriting was the challenge here, and she painstakingly transcribed the entire text onto her computer as she read.

Although not as talented a writer as Corporal Humphries, Captain Ogilvie was far better connected. His appreciation of the larger diplomatic and military-strategic context in which the US Army and the Eighth Army were fighting was almost at the level of a State Department observer or later historian.

During the war, Ogilvie reported being in frequent contact with his cousin from back in Ohio, whom he never mentioned by name but who had been an agent of the OSS during WWII and then continued with the CIA after its formation in 1947. Molly asked the Ogilvies about this cousin, but they said Robert had never mentioned a cousin. In his writings, however, the two seemed close, almost like brothers.

Robert Ogilvie's cousin had described a group of individuals, both within and outside his agency, who were committed to supporting the local war effort in Korea while strenuously ensuring, through whatever means, that it did not expand into a world war through the entry of either China or Russia. They were concerned that the Truman administration was committed to defending South Korea even at risk of a larger war.[3] Ogilvie's cousin told him about a contact he had among this group of individuals, a person he referred to only as Nathan.

In closed meetings, this cousin insinuated, administration officials as high as Truman himself were persuaded to forcefully limit the conflict. The disconnect between the administration and MacArthur, the supreme allied commander in Korea, arose because the general was determined to defeat the enemy, wherever those battles needed to be waged.[4]

When the United Nations adopted a resolution calling for assistance to the South Koreans, Chiang Kai-shek's nationalist Chinese forces on Formosa pledged 33,000 KMT troops to assist in the effort. Ogilvie's cousin described his phone ringing for hours from various members of this group, apparently in Washington, who feared that Mao's forces would enter the war if the Chinese nationalists involved themselves. A few hours later, the Joint Chiefs determined that the nationalist forces were not sufficiently equipped or trained for such conflict.[5]

This cousin implied—though did not definitively state—that Averell Harriman, Truman's national security advisor during the war, was "closely allied with their interests," referring to this nameless group of individuals. Later, he claimed that Harriman was in fact "one of their number." In 1950, Harriman had traveled to Tokyo to meet with MacArthur to instruct him that Formosa should not become a base of operations against mainland China.[6] MacArthur disagreed, and Harriman subsequently supported Truman in firing the general.[7]

This cousin of Ogilvie was obviously privy to many of the high-level communications between the Truman administration, the

Pentagon, and General MacArthur. The difficulty, he felt, was that the administration was not exactly straightforward in their directions to the general. They never gave him clear parameters of how far he was supposed to go. He was told to conduct required military operations to either push the North Koreans beyond the thirty-eighth parallel or destroy their forces. To what limit? If he saw no threat from Peking or Moscow, could he proceed beyond the thirty-eighth parallel and occupy North Korea?[8]

Zhoe Enlai, the Chinese premier and foreign minister, declared that China would not tolerate such a violation of the thirty-eighth parallel, indicating that Chinese troops would intervene.[9] Ogilvie did not mention Truman's own visit to meet with MacArthur personally that year.

As the Eighth Army pushed north, Ogilvie's cousin repeatedly wired him for information on their positions. If only Molly knew the identity and position of this cousin. *I might be reading a firsthand account of military espionage in action*, she thought excitedly. In the fall of 1950, MacArthur reported that his positions seemed to be known to the Communist forces. Ogilvie acknowledged his possible role in this set of events.

To corroborate this account, Molly searched her textbooks on her iPad. MacArthur had written that "there was some leak in intelligence. . . . [Walton] Walker [the commander of the Eighth Army] continually complained to me that his operations were known to the enemy in advance through sources in Washington."[10]

If she could find further corroborating evidence for his account, this diary by Ogilvie might provide the basis for a significant historical book. Now, this was exciting. Molly was so glad she hadn't rebuffed Barnsworthy.

In 1950, the first secretary of the British Embassy to the US was H. A. R. "Kim" Philby. The second secretary was Guy Burgess. The head of England's American department was Donald MacLean. As members of the Cambridge Five, along with Anthony Blunt and John

Cairncross, in 1963 they were discovered to be double agents and defected to the Soviet Union. Ogilvie's cousin referred to the first three as being in contact with Nathan.

Molly had to sit back and breathe deeply.

This was why she had pursued a career in research. This kind of find did not come every day. This group of individuals had passed on information of the Eighth Army's positions to support the Communist forces in opposing them and therefore prevent an advance by UN forces into China. And prevent World War III. Unfortunately, she had no supporting evidence, and she knew neither the identity of Ogilvie's cousin nor who this Nathan was.

Robert Ogilvie then seemed to relax into a more mundane diary entry. He wrote about individuals in his unit, their mess hall, difficulties with jeep mechanics (he never mentioned Humphries, however). After a couple of pages, he just stopped in the middle of an entry, in the middle of a sentence, even, and Molly shuffled the pages.

Four blank pages, and then he began writing again. He must not have been able to write up to the end of the war, because his new entry was dated 1971. She continued to transcribe his chicken scratches, which now seemed slightly more legible, as if he had taken at least a correspondence penmanship class in the meantime.

Robert Ogilvie met his cousin in Ohio in 1971. For someone he described so closely, Molly found it remarkable that he never mentioned the man by name. Back in Ohio, as Ogilvie exclaimed, "things got even more interesting!"

They drove to Columbus in the winter of 1971 to meet with Nathan. Robert then wrote for half a page about the Italian restaurant where Nathan entertained them in Columbus; he seemed to be a man who enjoyed his food. Molly glanced at his portly son, who also seemed fond of culinary pursuits. Sadly, Robert never described Nathan in any way—never gave a last name or described his appearance.

As they drove from the restaurant, Nathan informed the two cousins that he had recently returned from Prague. Ogilvie's cousin inquired if his work had been successful. Nathan nodded and explained to Robert that he and his colleagues, members of an institute that was often in communication with the group of individuals he had helped during the Korean War, had, with that group's strenuous backing, obtained "the father of lead-206 and vessels at the northern end of the Cotentin peninsula." Nathan then went on to talk of soccer matches, to Molly's regret. The diary soon ended. Robert Ogilvie died in 1975.

Ogilvie's small handwriting translated into thirty-four typed pages on Molly's laptop. Chicken scratches could be economical of paper use. *But what did Nathan mean? And why was he telling these two so much?*

Lead-206 . . . Physics and chemistry had never been Molly's strengths.

Lead-206, she found, was the end product of the uranium series of nuclear decay, in which uranium-238 decayed through eighteen members, all of which eventually decayed to lead-206. The Middle English word for lead was "*plumbe*," Latin "*plumbum*." Operation Plumbat was a covert, 1968 Israeli operation to obtain yellowcake—processed uranium ore—from a Belgian mining company by orchestrating a sale to a front company in Genoa and then transferring the yellowcake drums to another ship while at sea. "Plumbat" also referred to the labeling of the drums. In Middle English, both "plumb" and "bat" were terms for deception.[11] Apparently, the northern end of the Cotentin peninsula had a city called Cherbourg from which, in the winter of 1969, an Israeli military operation rescued five boats that had been paid for by the Israeli government but not delivered due to the French arms embargo of 1969.

With his mysterious words, Nathan had been describing how this same group from the Korean War also later assisted the Israeli government through himself and his colleagues, who were members of an institute—Ogilvie had specifically mentioned that word: "institute." The only connection she could think of was to the

HaMossad leModi'in uleTafkidim Meyuhadim, Hebrew for "Institute for Intelligence and Special Operations—Mossad."

Why was he telling these guys all this? And why was Ogilvie so casually writing this in a diary he was just leaving around? Is this real? Is this a novel he planned on writing? It would be a good one. Perhaps Robert could have gotten Corporal Humphries, had he lived, to ghost-write it for him.

Molly had difficulty believing the candor of the writing here. People who knew these kinds of things didn't speak and write so much. Molly had read a good deal about diplomatic and intelligence services, and one common theme in the research that went into those books was that the story came together from many fragmented sources. There weren't people like Nathan and Robert Ogilvie and his cousin just writing to each other and eating cannoli at Italian restaurants and talking about these things.

Molly closed the small book and interrogated the Ogilvies. They knew nothing. She told them a very cursory summary of what Robert had written. They asked a few questions, and Julia even commented that the whole thing sounded like a movie. They had questions for Molly, for which she had no answers. Molly asked if Robert had written short stories or had any other creative writing interests. They of course didn't know.

If they wanted to decipher the awful handwriting, the Ogilvies were welcome to read what Robert had written, but they seemed satisfied with her summary. There was no way to make it sound ordinary, and they were more interested in the man's daily life during the war. Molly informed them that if Robert Ogilvie had indeed shared information that eventually passed to confirmed agents of the Soviet government, as he implied in his diary, this was espionage, and it was illegal. Todd and Julia listened quietly.

But Molly insisted there was no way to corroborate this statement with just this diary. No one knew who his cousin or this person who called himself Nathan was. If they really existed, they were likely dead. Molly planned to go back to the Pentagon archives and see if—there or elsewhere in Washington—she could find evidence of someone who mentioned Robert Ogilvie, someone who could have been his cousin. She promised that she would share this information with the Ogilvie couple.

The other question in the back of Molly's mind was how much of this Mr. Barnsworthy knew or needed to know. A recurrent difficulty in Molly's work was how far to go and how much she needed to share. Her job was often to answer very specific questions. But research findings often led to more questions, which led to more research and findings. Some of her clients pushed her to go the distance; many, like Dr. Samuels, did not care. The instructions from Sasha Daniels had been clear: she was to find and summarize the diary of Corporal Randolph Humphries. That was all. She'd already gone above and beyond, perhaps unnecessarily.

She had the entire record of the Ogilvie diary, and if Barnsworthy sent Sasha Daniels to "demand" Ogilvie's diary summary as well, she would have to provide it. But if he didn't, this extra trip to Ohio would be for Molly's own research and on Molly's own dime.

10

THE OGILVIES were such a pleasant couple that Molly happily accepted their invitation for dinner and a movie night. The two had never had children and lived a quiet life together in their small house. Todd had even constructed many of their furniture pieces himself and was glad to show Molly his garage/workroom.

"See here, Ms. McMurphy, here I made my own custom workbench, complete with shelves and drawers and containers just like I like them."

Molly stroked the finely molded wood. "It's beautiful . . . and remember, please call me Molly! You're like me. I sometimes forget when people tell me that. What kinds of projects have you been up to out here?"

"Mostly furniture, but last year I made a small sailboat for the son of one of my work partners. He spray-painted those little pictures over in the corner, see?" She glanced quickly at the "artwork," which looked like old, tie-dyed T-shirts on the wall.

"Nice." They walked back into the house. "You go to any of the games in Cleveland, or do you like Cincinnati perhaps?"

"Browns fan, born and bred!" He smiled as he pulled a handkerchief with the team logo out of his pocket and proudly held it up.

"I'm so sorry, my friend," she laughed.

"How about you?"

"Bears. Always."

"Eh, they ain't so hot these days either . . ."

"But every season and offseason is dedicated to doing better and doing great things. The Browns, on the other hand, seem consistently dedicated to mediocrity."

Julia punched Molly lightly in the shoulder as she joined the conversation. "At least they are consistent. We always know what to expect. It's fun rooting for a team that loses. We're very loyal people!"

Julia ordered pizza, and Todd handed Molly a beer from the fridge. After all her trips, a quiet evening eating pizza and watching stupid comedies with the Ogilvies was welcome relief. The Pentagon archives could wait an evening.

After a nice breakfast the next morning, complete with bacon from a local farm, Molly packed her bags and headed out to her rental car in the driveway, chatting with Julia.

She turned the ignition and got only a clicking sound. Molly pounded on the steering wheel in frustration. None of the dome lights had been left on—she almost never turned those on anyway—but somehow the battery must have died. Maybe it was old to begin with.

She jumped out of the car with a dejected look and casually kicked the front tire, thinking about what to do.

"When's your flight?" Todd asked after trying to start the car himself. "I could drive you over there quickly."

"Couple hours, but I hate to leave this rent-a-car in your driveway."

"Oh, we don't mind, Molly. We can take care of it." Julia smiled. "This wasn't your fault, but I must say, you should let the rental manager hear about this. This was a big company?"

"Yeah, I always use Hertz. I've never had a problem."

"Here, let me bring my car out of the garage. Maybe we can jump it. But really, I don't mind driving you, Molly."

A loud smack came from inside the house. Then a door slammed.

"What's that? Who's in there?" Molly darted her eyes at the startled Ogilvies as if they were hiding someone or had a (large) pet she hadn't been introduced to.

Todd raced toward the front door as Julia began to cry. "He'll grab his gun. It's right near the front door." But a shot thundered from inside the house, and Todd Ogilvie was thrown backward down the front steps, blood oozing over his shirt.

A man holding a shotgun and dressed in black with a skull cap emerged from the front door and stared down at the dead man. "Looking for this?" He aimed the gun at Julia and Molly, and a *BOOM* erupted as they dove to the ground behind the car.

"Crap! Shit!" Molly gasped as they scuttled into the bushes and ran for the road. Julia was screaming and had to be half dragged as the man slowly crossed the front yard, shooting blindly into the bushes. He drew a semiautomatic pistol from his side pocket and continued to fire. Molly pulled Julia toward a thicket of low trees to their right. A man across the street, who was walking out to his car, sprinted back into his house as Molly yelled to him to find cover.

The man in black maintained his slow, methodical pace, like a killer in a horror movie. "Mrs. Ogilvie, step out of the trees. I will not hurt you. I will simply shoot you dead. I want the other one."

Molly and Julia kept to the road. A police car rolled by, and Molly jumped into the street, diving instinctively to the ground as the man in black fired. The police officer abruptly turned on his siren and reversed onto their road. When Molly scrambled back from the street, she found Julia in the bushes—face down, dead. Tears streaming down her face, Molly rushed further into the trees as the policeman started firing back; the man in black had apparently refused to halt.

Molly dashed into a neighboring backyard and across the grass, hearing the policeman cry out, shouting into his radio for backup. She spotted the man in black steadfastly marching into the yard after her. Instead of running, she jumped into bushes and started retracing her tracks, back toward the road. Her only chance was that police car. She was sure the whole neighborhood was dialing 911, but the sirens she heard were in the distance.

As the man in black calmly called for her to come out and surrender, Molly looked swiftly over her shoulder to make sure the man was still in the yard, then bolted out into the road and jumped into the police car. Luckily, the policeman had not taken his keys, and she slammed on the gas while bullets peppered the car. Screeching down the road to the nearest turn, she sharply sped off on the perpendicular road. Sirens converged at the Ogilvie home, but two patrol cars quickly fell in behind her.

While her law-abiding instincts demanded she pull over for the cop cars chasing her, the image of that man in the black suit and skull cap forced her to press the gas pedal further, speeding up a highway on-ramp without thought. A state trooper joined in the chase. Tears streamed down Molly's pale white cheeks. Her mother's voice came from a more sensible part of her mind, telling her she had gotten herself into a mess and she was making things worse.

She fumbled around the police car dashboard for the emergency lights and gradually pulled over onto the shoulder, the flashing cop lights surrounding her. The policemen, some looking almost as scared as she was in her rearview mirror, erupted from their cars with guns drawn and aimed. She sat in the seat and just raised her hands. Slowly, she reached down and opened the car doors, the police shouting at her to keep her hands where they could see them as she exited the car.

One of the officers immediately slammed her against the police car hood and handcuffed her. Molly was sobbing by now, shaking her head at the policemen surrounding her. One with a kinder voice instructed her to walk toward one of their waiting squad cars. He gently pushed her head down as she bent her tall frame into the back seat.

Molly didn't say anything after they instructed her that she would be questioned once they arrived at the station. She heard them radio ahead that they had recovered "one of the suspects."

What happened? The whole thing was a blur in her shocked memory. *Was it a robbery? Did someone come into the house and realize they were home?* But that was nonsense. He had been intent on killing, and she was sure she remembered him saying he "wanted the other one." He wanted Molly. *What's going on?* She started to cry again and dropped her chin to her chest.

At the station, they quickly pulled Molly into a secure holding room. A few minutes later, a detective in a suit grabbed her by the shoulder and led her, still handcuffed, into an interrogation room. Molly sat alone for at least a half hour, just staring at the wall, thinking, crying, not saying anything. Unlike the TV shows, this room had no mirror. Just cold, white walls. A camera was perched in a corner of the ceiling.

The same detective who had put her into the interrogation room entered and sat in the chair across from her. "Please state your full name."

"Molly Megan McMurphy, sir."

"Yes, that matches the ID we found in your backpack in the rental car. What were you doing at the home of the two victims? What was your role in all this?"

Molly sat silently for a second, telling herself it was time to calmly tell her story; it was her only chance. She told him about her background and job, her research of the diary—without any of the juicier details—and the help the Ogilvies had given her, that she was a guest in their home, and that they were attacked after she found her rental car battery dead in the morning.

"So do you know the man with the gun?"

"Of course not! That's like asking someone who got mugged if they know the mugger. He was a stranger who just attacked us!"

"Sometimes they do. I need to ask."

"I'm sorry, sir. You're doing your job. The best place to get the answers to your questions is to ask that man in black."

"He's dead. SWAT took him out two streets down, just a bit after you headed off to lead our men on a bit of a chase. Not sure where that fits in, and that's the part that bothers me, I'll be honest with you, Ms. McMurphy."

Molly started to cry again. She couldn't help herself. The detective didn't offer to remove her handcuffs or give her a tissue.

"I was scared! Can't you see that? Here I am, doing my work, a guest of such a nice couple, and we get attacked, and this bastard, whoever he was, just kills these two in front of me. And he was clear the one he wanted was me! I'm a researcher—the nerd you knew in school! I don't do anything that involves this kind of thing!"

"Why was he after you then? You must have some connection. You can see why I'm still asking questions. This doesn't make sense."

"Why? Why?! You're asking me why?" Molly's customarily calm voice was now high pitched, livid. "If I knew why, don't you think I'd tell you? I have no idea why."

"Who knew you were making this trip?"

Molly stopped and thought. She could think of no one. She hadn't communicated her plans to Mr. Barnsworthy. She hadn't even discussed much of the Humphries diary with the staff at the Pentagon. She tried to think if she'd ever mentioned Ogilvie. Well, she had looked him up at the Pentagon, and then online, finding his son in Ohio. But as far as she remembered, that was all work she had done on her own. The staffers in Washington were her friends and happy to help, but she knew what she was doing and went about her investigations on her own. She was pretty sure she hadn't discussed it much, but maybe . . . She couldn't remember definitively, and she told the detective that. He was taking notes on a pad.

Of course, the more she reasoned, the more she realized she had learned a lot that someone might have a problem with her knowing. *But who knew about a tiny diary sitting up in some attic in Ohio for* x *number of years?* It was so esoteric, without corroborating evidence, and therefore not even useful to her—other than for curiosity's sake.

But the gunman had been intent on capturing her, or killing her. The Ogilvies were just standing in the way, as far as he was concerned.

While she was glad he was dead, she wished he were alive to answer questions. She told the detective that. He didn't say anything, simply stood and strode out the door. Another man entered and removed the handcuffs, to her relief, but told her to stay still. She was being watched and could not leave the room.

Again, she sat alone. This time it seemed more like an hour had passed. She called out to the video camera that she needed to use the ladies' room, and a female police officer soon arrived to escort her, then put her back in her chair. Again, she sat. The detective came in once again to quickly inquire if they could speak to anyone who knew of her trip to Ohio, as if she would suddenly have a different answer.

She waited again. It seemed like it had been hours since she'd entered this room. The entire experience was painful and frightening.

The detective returned and offered to grab her a cup of coffee, which she declined.

"Ms. McMurphy, I've just received a call from Washington. Someone from the FBI office over in Cleveland is coming to speak with you. Now, I can tell you this: I've been through many cases that have gone to court, and if you know anything else, it is in your best interest to tell me. We can get you a lawyer, of course. You're obviously entitled to that."

"So, you still think I was part of this?"

"I don't know." He looked down at his notepad again. "I don't know." He grabbed his pen and jotted a few more notes. "But if the FBI knows you're here and wants to come speak with you, they know something you might know and are not telling me."

"Really, I'm perplexed by them coming here too. I've never encountered federal law enforcement. I'm a researcher; that's it. Please, believe me."

"I wish I could, Ms. McMurphy. But this is all too strange." His phone rang, and he answered, listening quietly. "Funny. Now another team from the FBI is coming. For all your denials, you seem to have some federal friends."

Molly shook her head, at least able to hold back her tears. "I have no idea what is going on." He sat silently and stared at her. "Could I please have that coffee you offered?" He curtly smiled and rose. "Thank you, sir."

When he returned with her coffee, she waited and sipped it for a few minutes.

A man in a gray suit entered the room and sat after flashing his FBI badge. He was a tall, handsome, older man, in a finely tailored gray suit, his gray hair neatly combed back. He folded his large, strong hands in front of him. They looked like age wouldn't have stopped them from crushing walnuts.

"Good day, Ms. McMurphy. In a couple moments, once this local precinct gives the final word, I will be taking you into our custody."

Molly opened her mouth to speak, but he waved her to stay silent.

"We will speak in a moment—not here," he said quietly. She frowned at the older gentleman, perplexed. *He must be a senior FBI agent*, she figured. If this were a movie, Gary Cooper would play this guy. Tall, broad shoulders, strong jaw.

The detective walked in and nodded to the FBI man, who rose, took out a pair of handcuffs, and quickly cuffed her with her arms in front. "Follow me, please, miss."

He walked toward the front with a purpose, nodded crisply and wordlessly to a man who appeared to be the local precinct chief, and led her down the steps to a waiting black Town Car. He put her in the back seat and climbed into the front, calmly turning the car in the driveway and heading onto the main road, and then the highway. He didn't say a word, and Molly kept quiet. This man didn't seem like he wanted to talk.

As they approached a rest area, the FBI man pulled the car in and parked. He quickly walked around to her side of the car and opened the door, bent down with a key, and unlocked the handcuffs, throwing them on the back seat. He offered her his hand. "Please."

Although not sure what was happening, Molly placed her thin fingers in the man's large palm, and he moved her into the front seat of the car. He climbed into the driver's seat and got back on the highway.

"Sir, they said another FBI team was coming for me as well. Are we going to them now? Where are we going, please?" She waited a moment as she watched him glance coolly in all three of his mirrors.

The man leaned back and smiled, turning slightly to wink at her. "It's a pleasure to meet you, Molly." He paused as he moved into the left lane. "Please, call me Nathan."

Molly stared out her passenger window. Then back at the man. Then out her window. "Where are we going? Did you know about my trip?"

"Come now, Molly. Let's get acquainted first before all these cumbersome little details. I know you've had a rough day, to say the least. Must make your usual research seem quite hum-drum, eh? Would you like to stop and grab a coffee? A demitasse, perhaps?"

Molly finally made the connection.

"Nathan? So, Ogilvie's diary? . . . You're real."

Nathan tilted his head back and laughed. "Surprised, pleased, or dismayed, Molly?" He grinned as he patted the steering wheel, gently undulating across lanes through the midday traffic. "Or all three at once? Yes, I'm right here."

"*Are* you from the FBI?"

"I won't be constrained to one country."

Molly narrowed her eyes at his vague answer. "Ogilvie mentioned an institute. I assumed Mossad."

He smiled. "Mossad keeps things so secret, Molly, that you could be one of their agents and not even know it." He laughed again. "You can think what you like. I won't stop you from thinking."

Now Molly took her turn saying nothing for a few minutes. "I don't understand. What have I got myself into?"

Nathan nodded and looked serious. "I wish we could just chat, Molly, but I sense you're a bit frazzled by today."

Molly's voice instantly became shrill. "Frazzled? Of course I'm frazzled! Someone just tried to kill me! And he killed those lovely people."

"Yes, I was sorry to hear about the Ogilvies. Collateral damage is unfortunately part of the picture in these things, a lot of the time."

"So you were involved with this?" she demanded.

"Me? Oh, no. I'm here to help you, not to kill you. I'm whisking you away from all those sorts of people."

"What people? Who cares about my research?"

"The research itself is not the problem. It's the findings of the research that . . . Well, later."

"What do you mean? You're not FBI? Was the real FBI coming for me back there?"

"I can't imagine why they would be. Can you?" He took an exit off the highway. "Here, let's stop at this little park, and we can talk."

Nathan offered her his hand to help her out of the car. He certainly played the part of an old-fashioned gentleman. He led her to a bench beside a large, man-made pond, complete with water fountain in the center.

"This pond"—he smiled—"reminds me of a very small version of Lake Geneva. Used to enjoy a beer by that lake." Molly sat silently. "On a clear day, you can even take in the sights of the Mont Blanc from there."

It was difficult for Molly to sit with someone so relaxed, although she noticed he occasionally glanced behind them and into the trees. When he looked at her, though, his smile was comforting.

"Please, Molly, let us formally shake hands, at least."

She slowly extended her hand across the bench and felt his strong grip.

"You seem to know me. So you must know how confused I am and—"

"What's happening? Yes, a question, for sure."

"Who were these people Ogilvie's diary spoke about? In Washington? Obviously someone trying to influence the war?"

"Unfortunately, I can't tell you much yet."

"Why?"

"I can't tell you that either." He winked at her again. "Let me just say this." He suddenly pointed into one of the trees. "Look, Molly! That beautiful bird!" She darted her eyes into the trees, initially frightened, worried that he was pointing to another attacker. "You know, it almost looks like that bird—we see them back in Europe . . . a bird that likes hemp." The bird flew off, and Nathan watched it.

"You were saying?"

"Oh, sorry, got distracted there. I have a lovely garden at home—makes me attuned to nature. Gardens are wonderful."

"Yes, but—"

"Again, sorry," he laughed. "I was going to say, I think of them as the psychohistorians of the Second Foundation. Let me just put it that way."

"I don't understand."

"You've read a lot, Molly, but you need to read more!" He composed himself and recited calmly: "'It is at the period of coalescence, when the Second Empire that is to be is in the grip of rival personalities who will threaten to pull it apart if the fight is too even, or clamp it into rigidity, if the fight is too uneven. . . . This third probability consists of a possible compromise between two or more of the conflicting personalities being considered. This, I showed, would first freeze the Second Empire into an unprofitable mold, and then, eventually, inflict more damage through civil wars than would have taken place had a compromise never been made in the first place. Fortunately, that could be prevented, too. And this was my contribution.' Good ol' Asimov."

Molly struggled to find some clarity amid the nonsense. "So, they seek to create a balance of personalities."

"Or an unbalance. It depends on the time and the place and the situation."

"And why are you—"

"Again, there is so much I cannot say, Molly."

"But who was Robert Ogilvie's cousin?"

"I certainly can't tell you that. I can't even tell you if he or she is indeed past or present."

"Will it always be like that, or can I find him?"

"There is great strength in being no one. Great strength in not even existing. You understand, Molly?"

She didn't understand and was getting annoyed at the lack of a clear answer. "If I go back to Washington and look for documents about him—"

"You will find nothing. And you should find nothing. Just do your normal work, Molly, understand? Go about your daily life and have a good life. Go see your friend Samantha. Eat pizza. Enjoy!"

Her stomach dropped. "How do you know about Samantha?"

He just smiled at her. They sat for several long minutes, staring at the water and a family of ducks.

"One thing, Molly, about my work: I once served as a special advisor to the British Fifth Northumberland Fusiliers. My old companion there, Ormond Sackler, had a wise friend who once read of Winwood Reade. If you are curious, and only if you really are, go to their headquarters and follow their anniversary."

She shook her head and pondered his words.

"I will take you to the airport now." He reached into his pocket and pulled out an airline ticket. "Your backpack with your laptop will be there. Go to Delta check-in station number seven and ask for

Richard Brown. There will be a sandwich for you in the front pocket. You like roast beef?"

Molly stared dumbly at Nathan. He winked at her again. There was so much more to be said, and yet so little. "Nathan," she whispered, trying to hold back more tears now.

"Yes, Molly?"

"Thank you."

11

RICHARD BROWN nodded with a wide smile as he handed Molly her backpack at the Delta counter and pointed her toward security, wishing her a safe flight. Sure enough, neatly wrapped in the front pocket was a large sandwich, which she held with trembling fingers as she ate near the gate, waiting for her connecting flight to New Haven.

The events of the past day lingered thick in her mind. What she'd thought was surely a fictional story from the Ogilvie diary had become frighteningly concrete with the attack and even more so after her intriguing albeit frustrating interview with Nathan. He said so little and so much at the same time. That was the hard part.

She downloaded Isaac Asimov's Foundation Trilogy while in the airport and scanned quickly through it on her tablet. Nathan likened this group from Washington or wherever to the psychohistorians of the novels, who under the direction of Hari Seldon's research attempted to direct events surrounding their empire. Nathan suggested, per the diary, that the real-world group had also provided guidance to the Israeli government in their covert work to obtain nuclear materials.

This can't be, her historian background insisted. These were separate, disparate events. At different times and places. *But what did my research uncover?* First she had found the curious stone disk of Oskar Lamprecht and then the far more curious diary of Robert Ogilvie. *Does the disk mean anything? Is the diary's story real? Are they both part of something bigger?*

Nathan had seemed serious when he told her to just go about her normal work. Like he was instructing her to walk away. And part of her certainly wanted to. *But then why did he add the part about the Fifth Northumberland Fusiliers headquarters? Does he want me to stop or continue?* He certainly did not hire her for another research job; that was clear. His message was more of a statement, with a direction.

Nathan had mentioned an Ormond Sackler. A quick Google search informed her that in the early, rough plot outlines of his stories, Sir Arthur Conan Doyle had named Sherlock Holmes's sidekick Ormond Sackler before he finally settled on the name John Watson. John Watson had been a captain in the Fifth Northumberland Fusiliers.[12]

Enough. Get it out of your mind, Molly, she ordered.

Molly returned to New Haven to putter around, accomplishing the daily tasks of life. She walked over to the hospital and visited with Samantha, sat long hours reading about the Rosicrucians in the library, and paid her bills with the money soon forthcoming from Mr. Barnsworthy. She met with two new potential clients, both of whom came to her terribly excited about jobs that were neither interesting nor fun. She turned down both and went about her relaxed life, even taking in a stimulating weekend of shows and dinners in New York with several of her old college mentors, who now considered her a friend.

And yet Nathan's words haunted her. They occupied her mind on the commuter train back and forth from New York; jumped into her thoughts while she read the Rosicrucian texts and Isaac Asimov's Foundation Trilogy; pervaded her imagination as she reread the Tolkien trilogy.

She had to go. She had to visit the headquarters of the Fifth Northumberland Fusiliers. Although there was no money involved, this hazy "research project" was all she could think of, and she couldn't rest until she tried to explore wherever Nathan was directing her.

12

MOLLY LOOKED UP the name Nathan had given her and learned that Sir Arthur Conan Doyle mentioned Winwood Reade in the story *Sign of Four*: "'Winwood Reade is good upon the subject,' said Holmes. 'He remarks that, while the individual man is an insoluble puzzle, in the aggregate he becomes a mathematical certainty. You can, for example, never foretell what any one man will do, but you can say with precision what an average number will be up to. Individuals vary, but percentages remain constant. So says the statistician.'"

A British historian, explorer, and philosopher, Reade's two best-known works were *The Martyrdom of Man* and *The Outcast*. John Fleming, a Princeton professor of English and comparative literature, wrote that while Reade professed a disbelief in immortality, he did not profess to "know." He was not actually an atheist. He believed in a Creator but not in mankind's revealed religion—not in standard Christianity. His Creator existed at a higher level.

In Fleming's book review of *Martyrdom of Man,* he stated that *Martyrdom* was often called a "universal history," a history of the whole of civilization from its earliest times. Human history was a centuries-old fight against ignorance in the form of superstition and religion. War was an imprisonment of men's bodies, while religion was an imprisonment of the mind.[13]

Interesting information, to be sure, but Molly wasn't quite sure how to use it. She moved on to the subject of the Fifth Northumberland Fusiliers.

Formed in 1674 as the Fifth Regiment of Foot, Fifth

Northumberland Fusiliers became a fusilier regiment in May 1836 and was redesignated as the Fifth Northumberland Fusiliers Regiment of Foot. The regiment was increased to two battalions in 1857 and saw active service in the Indian Rebellion and the Second Anglo-Afghan War.

In the 1870s, they moved into Fenham Barracks in Newcastle-upon-Tyne. Following the Childers Reforms, the barracks became the depot of both the Royal Northumberland Fusiliers and Durham Light Infantry in 1884. From what Molly could find, Fenham Barracks were their only headquarters—and her destination.

Another flight to London. A longer drive, this time to Newcastle-upon-Tyne. Gaining access to the military barracks at Fenham was a rather long, bureaucratic nightmare, requiring a day and a half of paperwork, numerous phone calls, and researcher references from the US. Molly was accustomed to these handicaps to her work, but she couldn't help thinking, *Wouldn't it be nice if Nathan showed up to help and I could casually smile my way past the security officers this time?*

Although Nathan had not suggested a deadline for her trip, she found herself sitting in her small hotel room with a sense of urgency. She figured the lockers at the base were the most reasonable place to start—a bunch of steel boxes that could hold anything.

Finally, on the morning of her third day, the British Army guards nodded her into the barracks headquarters, where she was told the barracks rules by a sergeant and led to a basement room filled with rows and rows of lockers. These were where the soldiers stored their personal belongings, and the sergeant watched her closely as she searched for the locker she claimed her research had directed her to.

She racked her brain for clues. The anniversary of the Fifth Northumberland Fusiliers was St. George's Day, which marked the day of his death in 303 AD: April 23. *This may figure in accessing the lock*, she thought as she studied the lockers while the sergeant paced grimly behind her. *But which locker?* These each bore the name of the soldier to whom they belonged. She walked the long rows. No locker with the name George. *Sackler?* None. *Watson?*

There were two with the name Watson; she would try them both.

The locks were designed with three four-digit dials. She entered *4/23/303* as *0004-0023-0303*. Wouldn't open. She tried the same on the second Watson locker. Nothing. She stared at her phone, pretending to look something up as she thought hard.

April 23, 303 AD, was the date of St. George's death on the Gregorian calendar, which had been introduced by Pope Gregory XIII in 1582. At the time of St. George's death, however, they were following the Julian Calendar, which had taken effect in 45 AD. Now she consulted Professor Google—April 23, 303 AD, translated to May 6, 303 AD.

She dialed *0005-0006-0303* on the first locker.

It opened.

The locker contained two large, leather-bound books. The covers were in good condition, but as she pulled them out and carried them to a nearby table, she could see the pages were well worn.

She gasped as she opened the cover of the first book. It was an 1872 edition of Reade's *Martyrdom of Man*. Molly quickly realized it was the first edition. A handwritten inscription in the top right corner of the title page read, BESTOWED ON MYSELF ON 26 JANUARY 1887 AT PHOENIX LODGE 257, SOUTHSEA. She fondled the pages, looking for an inscribed name of the book's owner, but found none, neither in the first book nor the second: the 1861 edition of Reade's *Veil of Isis*, a book he had written about the Druids.

Following a hunch, she Googled the date and discovered that Doyle, a mystic and spiritualist, had been initiated as a Freemason on 26 January 1887 at the Mason's Lodge 257 in Southsea.

She glanced quickly through the pages. This owner had carefully underlined various entire paragraphs and passages in both books. His notations were cryptic, however. He wrote only in zeros and ones. Up and down the margins of many pages, zeros and ones over and over, in meticulous handwriting. No words. Binary code.

Molly had promised she would take nothing from the barracks, and she dutifully and methodically used her phone to convert each page, with close shots of the binary sequences, into pdf files, hundreds of them. The sergeant sat and rested while she worked but said nothing.

She returned the books to the locker and reset the lock. The phone in her hip pocket felt heavy as she headed back toward the elevators.

She said nothing of what she had found to the soldiers upstairs, and they did not ask. Nor did they look interested. She thanked them and went to her waiting rental car, her mind almost blank as she skipped dinner altogether and drove back to London.

13

*W*HAT DID I JUST SEE? Molly was sure those books had belonged to Sir Arthur Conan Doyle, although she would double-check his handwriting elsewhere. Passages from the book had been carefully underlined, but the apparent binary code in the margins was the ultimate mystery. Nathan had sent her to these books. This meant something.

She felt so curious and so empty. In all her years of research—after having read Ogilvie's diary, stumbling upon Lamprecht's disk, and now staring at these ones and zeros—she had never simultaneously felt this curious and bewildered.

Molly rested and slept during the flight back across the Atlantic. Her other investigative journeys always left her thinking of people, of events, of new directions for her research. That thinking step was crucial to her work, dating back to her high school projects. The action, the actual work of research, was only a small part of the process. The thinking and planning were essential. But she had nothing right now. She had uncovered only mysteries, and she wasn't even sure they were real.

Molly grabbed a late Korean dinner in Queens before driving up to her farmhouse near Stamford. Even the low-grade bustle of New Haven was too much for her. She needed some real quiet.

She had bought this farmhouse about two years earlier and left it just the way it was the day she bought it. Built in the 1890s, it looked like it had never been modernized past 1920. The extensive farmlands around it had been sold off over the years, with one man's farm becoming a suburban/rural neighborhood for about twelve families. Still, each home was a good distance apart, and the land parcel was of decent size, perfect for a casual walk in the spring or fall.

After a shower and a hot toddy in front of some stand-up comedian on YouTube, Molly headed up to bed, trying not to think at all about her findings or how she would discover new avenues. She felt uncomfortably passive.

In the morning, she drove up to the Yale library to clear her mind, eager to read about the Rosicrucians. Somehow those zany mystics had become rest and relaxation in the face of the far more enigmatic group she was on the road to discovering. Thomas Vaughn, in his enchanted endeavors in spiritual alchemy, appeared a man similarly in search of the unknown, strange, occult. He never seemed to fully understand his chemical work. Molly McMurphy now felt the same way.

She spent a lazy day in a long reading and note-taking session on Vaughn's wife, answering several work-related emails regarding new requests, and sorting out her bank and credit card statements. Robert Ogilvie and Nathan and Sir Arthur Conan Doyle drifted further and further away amid the hum-drum university scene around her.

One of her proposed projects was close to home: researching some of the players and coaches on the Stamford Bombers and Pioneers, minor league baseball teams in the '40s. There was something majestic about these players working and training and playing so hard for a team and a league that no one outside of maybe a thousand people would ever care about (only 80,000 people were reported to have attended games in the entire Colonial League, which lasted only three years, from 1947 to 1950). It was inspiring to believe that fulfillment existed in doing the best you could at what you did, regardless of who remembered you or your work.

The project was rejuvenating, and she enjoyed interviewing former coaches and players. Molly visited old ball fields and read newspaper accounts in the public library.

During a weekend at home reading and writing on the porch, she noticed a worsening leak in her kitchen sink. It had always been a slow drip, but over a couple of days it grew worse, to the point she noticed a difference in her monthly water bill. Molly told friends and colleagues she often did her own repairs, but that typically meant groping the leaking pipe, looking it up online, thinking about how she would fix it, and dialing the number for the repairman she usually contacted with such problems.

"Old house out on Murray Road, right? I can't do tomorrow. How about I come take a look Tuesday afternoon?"

"Sounds good, Larry. Hopefully it's a quick fix. See you then."

Indeed, she wished she could fix these things herself, but quick fixes never seemed to happen in an old house. Luckily, Larry was steady and reliable. He never created extra work, and he was calm and diligent.

She came home early on Tuesday and met Larry on her front porch. He took a look at the sink and ordered the required parts over his cell phone. Something about a gasket, she heard, but she understood little.

When he returned two days later, he arrived with a young man in tow.

"Molly, this is Maurice. He's a student plumber at the community college over in Bridgeport. He'll be helping me out today."

Molly went to shake the young man's hand, but he replied with an uninterested grunt and trudged into her kitchen. While Larry liked to chat while he worked, his novice was a silent worker. Plumbing certainly didn't seem to be his calling: he did the work with nary a moment of enjoyment on his face. Molly could never work like that. *You do the best work at what you love*, she thought.

Molly paid Larry in cash, and he whistled as he strolled out to his truck with Maurice. "Let me know if anything doesn't work right,

Molly! You take care!" His old white pickup sauntered down the thin road like a vision in a Steinbeck novel.

With that inspiration, Molly grabbed the *Grapes of Wrath* off her shelf and headed to her sunroom/office. She still had a good deal of data on minor league baseball players to sort through, but it was time for a break.

14

A SLOW WEEK went by. Molly finished her report on the Stamford Bombers/Pioneers and started on a new project for the law library up in New Haven. Back at the farmhouse, Molly organized scattered mementos.

Then, one evening, as she reached under the kitchen sink for a new sponge, she felt a wood panel shift, and a heavy envelope plunked to the floor.

She was always finding oddities in this old house, but the envelope looked new. Nothing was written on the front, but when she flipped it over, she was startled to see her name scribbled along the envelope crease. Below was typed, FOR YOUR EYES.

Molly sat at her small kitchen table, at first mystified, but she quickly remembered the plumbers at work. It must have been the unfriendly Maurice. With a knife, she sliced the envelope open. A note and old key slid out onto the table.

> Visit the Austrian National Library.
> The key is your entryway,
> from the basement below the Papyrus collection.
> Al-jebr e al mokabala

This was typed in small letters, no signature.

With random notes and keys now showing up in her house, the whole scenario seemed more scary than real. Molly rested back in her chair and sighed, closing her eyes. Everything she'd been through—even the parts that seemed now like a dream, such as meeting

Nathan—were following a pattern, or at least a direction. Something, someone was directing her to these clues. She was offered neither pay nor any way to conclude her work, as if she were merely being invited to satisfy her own curiosity. Yet the effects of her search had been devastating; therefore, the events in the Ogilvie diary had to be real. Perhaps the attack at the Ogilvie home was directed at her discovery. *Who sent that man? And where do the cryptic numbers and arrows inscribed on old stone disks and the binary code scribbled in margins come into it? What does it all mean?*

Molly slowly rose and poured herself a hefty shot of a single-malt beverage. Then she stared out the kitchen window, wondering why the note had been placed in her house, wondering whether she was being followed or watched. And not least of all wondering, *Where is the new clue leading me?*

One thing Molly had learned was that when new challenges and opportunities came up, she needed to think carefully about what she was doing to avoid mistakes, but then just jump right in. Life should be lived.

She sat in front of her laptop and looked up the Austrian National Library. The library was the largest in Austria, located in Vienna's Hofburg Palace. Originally the Imperial Library of the Middle Ages, the collection was put together by Duke Albert III (who lived from 1349 to 1395), an Austrian devotee of literature, history, and art who commissioned translations of Latin works into German and created a workshop for illustrating manuscripts. In 1722, Holy Roman Emperor Charles VI began constructing a permanent library in the Hofburg Palace, which was later reorganized by the Holy Roman Empire and eventually renamed the Austrian National Library in 1920 by the Republic of Austria under the German Reich.

She translated the non-English statement at the bottom of the message. *Al jebr e al mokabala*: Arabic, meaning "restoration and reduction." The Arabic words themselves drew up many Google results, the most curious being from an old mathematics book by

Augustus de Morgan, a nineteenth-century British mathematician. He used this phrase in his 1849 book *Trigonometry and Double Algebra*.[14]

She booked a flight for the next weekend, just one way. As she had come to find on these strange trips to she-knew-not-where, the timetable was always open ended. She grinned and sipped her Glenlivet. It was time to jump right in.

15

THE SATURDAY FLIGHT left in the evening, with a stop in Oslo. Molly took the time to dig further into de Morgan's background. Born in India in 1806, Augustus introduced the term "mathematical induction." His father, Lieutenant Colonel John de Morgan, served in the East India Company, and Molly took particular note of this since it suggested important connections for Augustus within the British colonial enterprise. Schooled at Trinity College, Cambridge, he served as mathematician at University College London and focused his work on algebra and logic.

She had a bit of a wait at the Austrian National Library, now a hot destination for tourists the world over. The Hofburg had been built in the thirteenth century and undergone various changes and additions over the years. It currently served as the main residence and workplace of the Austrian president. The library itself was a marvel of baroque architecture, lined by gorgeous, wooden bookcases, with special exhibits of maps and documents in the large aisles. The tourists loitered, snapping pictures. Molly searched for the papyrus collection.

One of the docents directed her into the room, where she marveled for a moment at scrolls mounted behind fiberglass and ancient statues and masks. The extensive and growing collection was situated in the Neue Burg wing of the library and arose from a gift by Archduke Rainer to Emperor Franz Joseph I in 1899. The exhibition also contained stone objects from the fifteenth century BC to the sixteenth century AD.

Careful to maintain the look of a simple tourist, she darted her eyes back and forth to determine the positions of the guards and spotted an ostensible service door in the corner. She saw no sign indicating an alarm on the door and was relieved that none sounded when she finally darted through it on her sixth circumnavigation of the room. A set of plain metal service stairs led down, and she begged the research gods to make this the correct pathway to the basement she had been sent to. *It seems to me that if someone is this interested in me finding these clues, they should be on hand to guide me.* Then she thought, with a touch of trepidation, *Maybe they are.*

Molly descended as quietly as she could. She was pretty sure none of the guards had seen her enter but wasn't sure about surveillance cameras. The way out of the basement was a problem to address later.

A series of zigzagging corridors led off in all directions from the bottom of the stairs. She held the old key tightly, suspecting—based on the evident age of the key—that the door it opened wouldn't be one of the more modern-looking utility closets she passed, although she did try the key in every door she could.

At the end of a hallway, which appeared to narrow in width as she proceeded, its ceiling almost too low for Molly's tall frame, there was an old wooden door, but the key did not fit. She pushed anyway, and without even the slip of a latch, it opened into a second, smaller corridor leading to the right. This was less well lit. At the end she beheld an even older door.

The key fit and turned. She opened the door but paused before entering. The room was pitch black, leaving her scared to close the narrow door behind her. She swept her arms out in front of her and to the sides, and found a wall to her left and a gnarled metal light switch.

An incredible number of lights came on when she flicked it up, and she quickly closed the door behind her. The hanging electric lights were blinding and appeared to be of an early twentieth-century style.

The light revealed trees, grass, train tracks, water, and stones in a wash of color. A huge diorama spread before her, fanciful and startling. She touched one of the trees—fabric, but constructed to look remarkably real. There was a path for her to follow to the right and then forward. Train tracks headed off to the left, and she started to follow them. The room was filled with a model train set, amazing in detail and care, the train cars almost as tall as Molly. The most amazing part of this was that it was not listed in the museum tour book, instead isolated in the basement like an old, forgotten treasure.

She followed along the train tracks, and then on patches of walking trail lined with stone. A tree log was perched on her left in the position of a seat, and she sat down. Further to her left was a wall painted as the night sky, with stars and moon. And at its topmost extent, a bright orb—looking more like the sun than the moon—produced a ray of electric light focused onto a painted pool of glimmering water.

The sun shining in a night sky. Where is that? She closed her eyes tightly. She had read that. *Augustus de Morgan—Al-jebr e al mokabala, restoration and reduction. Al-jebr, algebra.*

Molly recalled that in *Alice's Adventures in Wonderland*, Alice fell down a rabbit hole and ate a cake that shrank her to just three inches tall. A caterpillar came in, smoking a hookah (a further Arabic reference), and showed Alice a mushroom that if eaten in the proper proportions could restore her height. One side of the mushroom grew parts of her, while one side shrank parts of her. Restoration and reduction. Augustus de Morgan might have had connections with and an influence on another nineteenth-century British mathematician and logician, Charles Dodgson, who wrote under the name Lewis Carroll.

The Walrus and the Carpenter, she suddenly realized. A narrative poem in the fourth chapter of *Through the Looking Glass*, it was recited to Alice by Tweedeldum and Tweedeldee. Molly found the text quickly on her phone.

The sun was shining on the sea,
Shining with all his might:
He did his very best to make

The billows smooth and bright—
And this was odd, because it was
The middle of the night.

And to the right of the diorama scene, the moon, isolated in the corner, bore a woman's face rather than a man's, staring in clear disapproval at the sun.

The moon was shining sulkily,
Because she thought the sun
Had got no business to be there
After the day was done—
"It's very rude of him," she said,
"To come and spoil the fun!"

Molly stared back and forth between the poem and the scene. She crossed over stones and painted water toward the moon and touched it. A panel in the wall slid to the left, revealing a small piece of paper within. On it were written numbers, both Roman and Arabic numerals: IV, II, 6,7. IV, II, 10,11, 13, 14.

She copied the numbers onto her phone and put the paper back in the slot. Now she looked back to the "pool of water." The sunbeam was clearly focused on it, and she walked to it, poking at its surface. A piece of the water scene flipped over, and an additional set of numbers and words were written here: GIBBON WROTE OF GREAT COLLAPSE. DETAILED ROLE OF OUR MAN AT THESE PAGES. Below were listed the numbers I, II, I, 2, 6. III, II, 2, 5.

Molly copied the numbers and quickly looked back at the poem. She didn't know how much time she had.

The sea was wet as wet could be,
The sands were dry as dry.
You could not see a cloud, because

No cloud was in the sky:
No birds were flying over head—
There were no birds to fly.

She touched everywhere along the sea scene, the sand, the sky, and found nothing. Further to her right walked cartoonish figures representing the poem's protagonists, tears painted on their cheeks and pouring from their eyes.

The Walrus and the Carpenter
Were walking close at hand;
They wept like anything to see
Such quantities of sand:
"If this were only cleared away,"
They said, "it would be grand!"

A pile of tiny stones lay at their feet—a rendering of sand, she assumed. She grabbed at a piece of sand, and a block of stones shifted aside, with a new paper beneath: V, II, 1, 2, 5. VI, I, 2. VI, III, 6.

"If seven maids with seven mops
  Swept it for half a year,
  Do you suppose," the Walrus said,
"That they could get it clear?"
"I doubt it," said the Carpenter,
  And shed a bitter tear.

Molly smirked as she darted her eyes back and forth between the poem and the intricately woven scenes before her—seven maids with seven mops, walking from ahead of her toward the pile of sand. She touched their frocks and mops, initially finding nothing. But one of the maids had a hat that came off, disclosing the paper lying on her beautiful hair: VI, III, 8, 14. VI, IV, 1.

Another cartoonish walrus, kneeling beside four small oysters.

> "O Oysters, come and walk with us!"
>   The Walrus did beseech.
> "A pleasant walk, a pleasant talk,
>   Along the briny beach:
>   We cannot do with more than four,
>   To give a hand to each."

She grasped all over the oysters and the Walrus, to her dismay finding nothing. However, one of the oysters sat separately, off to the right on one of the stones, with a long beard and a winking eye.

> The eldest Oyster looked at him.
> But never a word he said:
> The eldest Oyster winked his eye,
> And shook his heavy head—
> Meaning to say he did not choose
> To leave the oyster-bed.

She grabbed at this elderly oyster, and it opened like a music box: VI, IV, 1. X, III, 16. X, IV, 2. As she pulled the paper out from the oyster box, a set of gears started winding to her right, evidently sparked by opening the oyster, and a small train of four little oysters marched/rolled out to a quiet music jingle.

> But four young oysters hurried up,
>   All eager for the treat:
>
> Their coats were brushed, their faces washed,
>   Their shoes were clean and neat—
>   And this was odd, because, you know,
>   They hadn't any feet.

One of the oysters, the second from the front, was holding up a piece of paper with its small puppet hand, and Molly grabbed it as the oysters trotted past her: XII, I, 5, 6, 7. XII, II, 10. XIII, II, 5.

> Four other Oysters followed them,
> And yet another four;
> And thick and fast they came at last,
> And more, and more, and more—
> All hopping through the frothy waves,
> And scrambling to the shore.

Sure enough, someone had been reading this pithy poem closely. The gears continued turning, and more and more oysters marched out. One was wearing a piece of paper folded into a paper hat on its head, and Molly was lucky to spot it in time to grab it: XIII, III, 3, 4. XIII, III, 6,7 . XIV, III, 6.

After three more oysters had passed on the carousel, a wall to the left rotated around an central pillar, and the Walrus and Carpenter again appeared, sitting on a rock. The train of oysters surrounded them.

> The Walrus and the Carpenter
> Walked on a mile or so,
> And then they rested on a rock
> Conveniently low:
> And all the little Oysters stood
> And waited in a row.

Molly grabbed at the main characters and then the rocks they were sitting on. One slid to the side. XV, VI, 3, 4, 7.

"The time has come," the Walrus said,
"To talk of many things:
Of shoes—and ships—and sealing-wax—
Of cabbages—and kings—
And why the sea is boiling hot—
And whether pigs have wings."

As the rock slid, she heard a new latch from above click, and a large number of these described objects, including cabbages, descended on strings from the ceiling. The wings on one of the pigs, she saw in the back, was made of a folded piece of paper. II, XVI, III, 2. XVI, VII, 2. XVII, I, 9.

"But wait a bit," the Oysters cried,
"Before we have our chat;
For some of us are out of breath,
And all of us are fat!"
"No hurry!" said the Carpenter.
They thanked him much for that.

Molly glanced at this portion of the poem and rapidly searched for a picturesque figuration of this stanza but saw nothing. However, next to the Walrus, on the opposite side from the Carpenter, a wooden model of a bread loaf, pepper grinder, and vinegar bottle rose from the ground.

"A loaf of bread," the Walrus said,
"Is what we chiefly need:
Pepper and vinegar besides
Are very good indeed—
Now if you're ready Oysters dear,

We can begin to feed."

Under the loaf of bread: XVII, V, 1, 2. XVIII, I, 2, 5.

>"But not on us!" the Oysters cried,
> Turning a little blue,
>"After such kindness, that would be
> A dismal thing to do!"
>"The night is fine," the Walrus said
>"Do you admire the view?"

Again, nothing changed for this stanza.

>"It was so kind of you to come!
>And you are very nice!"
>The Carpenter said nothing but
>"Cut us another slice:
>I wish you were not quite so deaf—
>I've had to ask you twice!"

From the back of the loaf, Molly pulled away a wooden slice, like a small door that came off the contraption, and inside were the numbers XVIII, I, 6, 7. XIX, I, 1. XX, I, 1, 2.

>"It seems a shame," the Walrus said,
>"To play them such a trick,
> After we've brought them out so far,
> And made them trot so quick!"
> The Carpenter said nothing but
>"The butter's spread too thick!"

The only object Molly saw in the scene to investigate was a stick of butter sitting on the ground near the bread, but although she pulled hard at it, it did not give.

The Walrus began to move its arms like a stiff, awkward robot from Disney World, and it pulled a handkerchief to its eyes.

> "I weep for you," the Walrus said.
> "I deeply sympathize."
> With sobs and tears he sorted out
> Those of the largest size,
> Holding his pocket handkerchief
> Before his streaming eyes.

Growing impatient, Molly grabbed the cloth handkerchief out of his hand and found the numbers XX, I, 4. XX, III, 3. XX, I, 4. XX, III, 3. XXI, IV, 2. She smiled as she peered again at her phone to see the poem was almost over. There were only so many Walruses and oysters she could take.

> "O Oysters," said the Carpenter.
> "You've had a pleasant run!
> Shall we be trotting home again?"
> But answer came there none—
> And that was scarcely odd, because
> They'd eaten every one.

Molly jumped backward as a large platform in the floor slid away and the oysters fell into a dark cavity below the diorama, the Walrus and Carpenter still sitting there, the Walrus wiping tears from his eyes. The Carpenter's arm began rotating and raising forward, the palm supinating as it rose. Molly approached to look into his palm, which was tattooed with words: HIS WINE COOLER IS GUARDED BY OUR MAN WHO REGRETTED HIS MORTALITY. She snapped a photo of the words and stepped back to wait for more clues in the scene. But all was still and silent. There were no more secrets to be revealed.

Molly walked back along a gravel path, only stopping to let the long train set (thirty cars, she counted) roll by into a tunnel, and made it to the door. Cautious, she listened at the door before pulling it open, then flicked the switch on the wall. The lights on the diorama shut off with a loud click, and she exited back into the dim hallway.

She thought of the only number clue that had been accompanied by words: "Gibbon wrote of great collapse. Detailed role of our man at these pages." She knew that English historian Edward Gibbon had written *The History of the Decline and Fall of the Roman Empire*, a six-volume tome, in the late eighteenth century. Perhaps the numbers she had gathered referred to pages in this monumental work.

Molly's sense of direction was not great but was at least adequate, and within a few minutes she was back at the stairwell. Glancing at the clock on her phone as she reached the door leading back out into the papyrus room, she was glad she had started her day early. It was almost 3:40 p.m., and the library would be closing in about an hour.

With no window in the steel door, she would be lucky to exit without being seen, but she knew of no other way out.

Fortunately, the room was empty. Molly rapidly walked out to the main library vaults, where tourists were still ambulating along the glass display cases. Behind her, she noted a sign indicating the papyrus collection was closed for cleaning.

Curious if this library's edition of Gibbon's work itself held any further clues, she made her way to the circulation desk and asked where it could be found. The librarian made a search of their online catalogue and informed Molly that the library's edition was currently not on-site. He had only suggestions as to where it could be—either on loan or taken out by one of the members. Regardless, Molly took a map and, in the forty-five minutes she had before closing time, circled the shelves where the volumes had once been but found nothing.

16

She spent the evening in Vienna and found an available flight out the next afternoon, with three connections. Between the flights and layovers, she had long hours to cross-reference the numbers from the hidden diorama papers with the book volumes, paragraphs, and line numbers from the Gibbon history. She also pondered the suggested de Morgan–Dodgson/Carroll connection.

De Morgan described algebra as a "science of symbols." The conservative Dodgson thought of symbolic algebra as an absurdity, which he playfully lambasted along with much of the more adventuresome mathematics of his day in his Alice stories. De Morgan signified a move away from universal arithmetic, in which symbols had a real corresponding number or denoted a physical entity, to a purely symbolic algebra analogous to dimensions greater than the fourth, in which there need be no physical entity, where negative and irrational conclusions were possible.

In Gibbon's history, "our man" must have referred to several men and women, since the events described on the indicated pages spanned hundreds of years. Molly tried to develop a cohesive picture of the role of these persons and forces. She realized that much of her summary could only be speculation, but relying on what little she had gleaned from Ogilvie's diary as well as Nathan's quote from Second Foundation, she thought she could surmise this group's role as indicated in these specific passages from Gibbon. That was, of course, assuming such a group could be a continuous and consistent influence over so many centuries, which she continued to doubt.

She focused on analyzing the lines specified on the scraps of paper, starting with the first she had found.

"The various modes of worship, which prevailed in the Roman world, were all considered by the people as equally true, by the philosopher as equally false, and by the magistrate as equally useful. And thus toleration produced not only mutual indulgence, but even religious concord," she read.

Perhaps manipulating religious views was central to their efforts. The "magistrates" subscribed to the view of the philosophers—it was all false—with the caveat that religion could be used to manipulate. They chose pontiffs from among the senators. They encouraged public religious festivals in order to "humanize the manners of the people." They harnessed the powers of divination as an instrument of policy. They encouraged religious tenets in governing daily life. They allowed local religions to flourish unhindered, since they realized each religion was most conducive to the particular group and climate that created it. This, in part, was why the Roman conquerors destroyed statues and buildings yet often allowed local religions to continue. Paganism thus persisted until the waves of Christianity overwhelmed them.

The passages suggested some complicity in the overthrow/assassination of tyrants such as Caesar, Caligula, Nero, and Domitian: "They attacked the person of the tyrant, without aiming their blow at the authority of the emperor." Resulting discord among the people, however, could not be avoided by the group.

The next number clue brought Molly to Commodus (who lived from AD 161 to 192), a vicious tyrant hated by everyone. "His ferocious spirit was irritated by the consciousness of that hatred, by the envy of every kind of merit, by the just apprehension of danger, and by the habit of slaughter, which he contracted in his daily amusements. . . . He had shed with impunity the noblest blood of Rome: he perished as soon as he was dreaded by his own domestics."

Marcia, his favorite concubine; Eclectus, his chamberlain; and Laetus, his Praetorian praefect, conspired (possibly with help?) to kill him in his bedchamber. Commodus was replaced with Pertinax (AD 126 to 193), a praefect of the city, an old senator who had risen from low birth to a rank of esteem.

Pertinax sought to heal the wounds of Commodus's tyranny. He recalled exiled victims, released political prisoners, and restored their honors and fortunes. He gave official burials to executed victims, and "in the inquisition of these legal assassins, Pertinax proceeded with a steady temper, which gave every thing to justice, and nothing to popular prejudice and resentment." He remitted taxes that had been levied indiscriminately by Commodus. This unnamed group meanwhile maintained some sense of stability and fair dealings within the government and the Roman financial system, at least during the relatively short periods of time where either cooperating leaders were in place or the presumed group could create the leaders themselves.

The passages that followed did not give Molly a clear sense of where influence was coming from and in which direction it was focused. There were too many varied figures and interests, and she wondered if there were other hidden or lost documents that would have made this all clear. The Praetorian Guard, in particular, was a force with unclear and changing roles and interests. As an elite group of the Imperial army, serving as both bodyguards and intelligence resource for emperors over centuries, the guard could be seen harboring individuals potentially useful for group influence. The Guard seemed to also have its own selfish aims; for instance, it was dissatisfied by the fall of Commodus and the rise of Pertinax, fearing the strictness and discipline Pertinax insisted on bringing to the government.

Was this group for order or disorder? Maybe for both at different times? Molly wondered. There were times that conflict drove world events, population movements, and technological developments, and was in a terrifying way an instrument of progress. As Nathan observed of Asimov's Second Empire, conflicting forces could "pull it apart if the fight is too even, or clamp it into rigidity, if the fight is too uneven."

The Guard seized one of the senators and intended to bestow the Imperial purple on him. But the senator threw himself at the feet of Pertinax. A young and ambitious consul from an ancient family, Sosius Falco (prominent in the 190s), sought to seize the throne himself but was crushed when Pertinax returned to Rome. Eighty-six days after the death of Commodus, 200 to 300 soldiers marched on the Imperial palace, joining a conspiracy among the palace guards and some of the palace servants to overthrow the emperor. Pertinax was beheaded and his head paraded to the Praetorian camp.

The subsequent emperor, Septimius Severus (AD 145 to 211), was a mystic, a devotee of magic, divination, interpretation of dreams and omens, and astrology. He had lost his first wife and in his search for a second sought only fortune. Julia Domna (c.170 to 217), a lady of Emesa in Syria, was just such a lady, of fine, royal birth. Although of advanced age, she was beautiful and had "a lively imagination, a firmness of mind, and strength of judgment, seldom bestowed on her sex."

These qualities never made a great impression on her husband, but she administered the empire during the reigns of her sons, Caracalla (c. 188 to 217) and Geta (c. 189 to 211), and kept the empire together "with a prudence that supported [Severus's] authority, with a moderation that sometimes corrected his wild extravagancies." She was a devotee of letters and philosophy, of art and of men of genius. Molly found the amusing caveat "If we may credit a scandal of ancient history, chastity was very far from being the most conspicuous virtue of the empress Julia."

Severus Alexander (c. 208 to 235) was raised to the throne in 222 by the Praetorian Guard after they murdered his cousin Elagabalus (c. 203 to 222). Since Alexander was only seventeen years old, the government was controlled by two women, his mother, Mamaea (c. 180 to 235), and his grandmother Maesa (c. 165 to c. 224). Mamaea chose sixteen of the "wisest and most virtuous senators" to be an Imperial council for the emperor, led by Ulpian (c. 170 to 223).

This council restored order to the government. They purged the city of foreign superstition and luxury and the government departments of family cronies. "Learning, and the love of justice, became the only recommendations for civil offices; valor, and the love of discipline, the only qualifications for military employments."

Molly felt drawn to these women of power and influence, Julia Domna, Mamaea, and Maesa. They were so clearly singled out in the selected passages, and Molly saw this as evidence that this group, if some such society could really have existed, was directed not only by men.

The Praetorian Guard loved Alexander, whom they had placed on the Imperial throne and saved from tyrants. But as his leadership under Mamaea was governed by reason and a sense of justice, they soon grew more dissatisfied with his virtues than with the vices of his predecessor. The praefect Ulpian (c. 170 to 228) was likewise a champion of the rights of the people and of the laws, and an enemy of the soldiers. An uprising among the soldiers and guards led to mutiny and civil war that raged in Rome for three days. The people left Ulpian to his fate, and he was murdered in 228 at the feet of Alexander, who tried in vain to defend him and obtain his pardon.

This was the weakness of government in the face of soldiers. Mutinies abounded all over the empire during the reign of Alexander, and he himself was sacrificed to the discontents of the army in 235. If Alexander's reasoned leadership, under Mamaea, was indeed a goal of this group, there seemed to be stronger forces of disorder rising to stop them.

Another of the number clues led her to a passage on Naulobatus (years unknown), a chieftain of the Heruli barbarians. He capitulated to the Romans and was brought, with a large group of his countrymen, into Rome, where he was made a consul, the first time such honors were bestowed upon a barbarian. Another passage mentioned that when the Goths invaded Athens, one of their chiefs stopped them from burning the libraries of the Greeks with the argument that if the Greeks remained addicted to books, they would have no time to apply themselves to arms. This might signal that the group had a desire to preserve learning, books, and art.

Molly moved on to read about Diocletian (c. 244 to 312), Roman emperor from 284 to 305. Just before 300, he banned alchemy and destroyed an Egyptian archive of alchemical texts. Gibbon was not clear on the purpose of this, but perhaps the mysterious group Molly was chasing through history was concerned with the impact on the economy, as one of the goals of the alchemists was to create new gold, which of course would devalue the currency.[15]

At least, this was all Molly could speculate from the limited passages.

The indicated Gibbon passages then focused on the peace treaty formulated between Persia and Rome under Diocletian. Gibbon stated that the "history of Rome presents very few transactions of a similar nature, most of her wars having either been terminated by absolute conquest or waged against barbarians ignorant of the use of letters." The treaty of 299 was made between Diocletian and the Persian king Nerseh (c. 228 to 302). This treaty, along with that of 363, helped to define the Roman–Persian border, at least its southern sector, until the end of the sixth decade, achieving the greatest concessions the Romans were to receive from the Persians.[16]

Diocletian and Maximian (c. 250 to 310) reduced the powers of the Praetorian Guard and the Senate, the latter by moving the emperors outside Rome. "As long as the emperors resided at Rome, that assembly might be oppressed, but it could scarcely be neglected." The previous emperors had issued laws that had to be ratified by the Senate. By living apart from Rome, the emperors now assumed the legislative as well as executive privileges, "instead of consulting the great council of the nation."

And so began the Senate's downfall. "The name of the senate was mentioned with honor till the last period of the empire; the vanity of its members was still flattered with honorary distinctions; but the assembly which had so long been the source and so long the instrument of power, was respectfully suffered to sink into oblivion." The Praetorian Guard was forever put down by Constantine (c. 272 to 337) in 312. Diocletian's later edicts against Christians were not among the indicated passages in the Gibbon text.

Although no specific historical names were indicated for individuals in the mysterious group of influencers, the selected passages suggested that they helped establish a hierarchy of the church magistrates, with presbyter, minister, and bishop, as well as creating the synods. "The catholic church soon assumed the form, and acquired the strength, of a great federative republic."

Molly moved on to the next clue and found "The impatient clamors of the multitude denounced the Christians as the enemies of gods and men, doomed them to the severest tortures, and . . . required . . . they should be instantly apprehended and cast to the lions." This passage may have referred to persecution following an edict by Emperor Decius (c. 201 to 251) in 250. The local magistrates and provincial governors gratified the rage of the people, "but the wisdom of the emperors protected the church from the danger of these tumultuous clamors and irregular accusations, which they justly censured as repugnant both to the firmness and to the equity of their administration. The edicts of Hadrian [reigned 117 to 138] and of Antoninus Pius [reigned 138 to 161] expressly declared that the voice of the multitude should never be admitted as legal evidence to convict or to punish those unfortunate persons who had embraced the enthusiasm of the Christians."

While Constantius Chlorus (c. 250 to 306) could not overall reject Diocletian's and Maximian's edicts against the Christians, he himself held no animosity to the Christians and tried to protect them. "He loved their persons, esteemed their fidelity, and entertained not any dislike to their religious principles."

An interesting term popped up as Molly continued her reading. Apparently "eunuchs" governed over Constantius Chlorus since he was a "feeble prince . . .

> destitute of personal merit, either in peace or war; as he feared his generals, and distrusted his ministers; the triumph of his arms served only to establish the reign of the eunuchs over the Roman world. Those unhappy beings, the ancient production of Oriental jealousy and despotism, were introduced into Greece and Rome by the contagion of Asiatic luxury. . . . [R]educed to an humble station by the prudence of Constantine, they multiplied in the palaces of his degenerate sons, and insensibly acquired the knowledge, and at length the direction, of the secret councils of Constantius. . . . But the eunuchs were skilled in the arts of flattery and intrigue; and they alternately governed the mind of Constantius by his fears, his indolence, and his vanity.
>
> The most distinguished of these eunuchs was Eusebius (died 361), "who ruled the monarch and the palace with such absolute sway."

The Gibbon passages seemed to highlight both the overall influence of the eunuchs in general and of Eusebius in particular. Whether this group created the practice or merely used it, the eunuchs would certainly have been a tool as powerful among the monarchs as religion was among the people.

Molly moved on to the next indicated passage: "The learned Eusebius has ascribed the faith of Constantine [known as Constantine the Great, c. 272 to 337] to the miraculous sign which was displayed in the heavens whilst he meditated and prepared the Italian expedition." But Constantine's conversion was a slow process, and it was only upon his death that he was baptized. By then, "war and commerce had spread the knowledge of the gospel beyond the confines of the Roman provinces."

"The nocturnal vision" Eusebius referred to "appeared to the fancy of Constantine, as he slept within the walls of Byzantium. The tutelary genius of the city, a venerable matron sinking under the weight of years and infirmities, was suddenly transformed into a blooming maid, whom his own hands adorned with all the symbols of Imperial greatness. The monarch awoke, interpreted the auspicious omen, and obeyed, without hesitation, the will of Heaven."

Although it sounded more like a scene out of a movie, the passages focusing on this dream of Constantine's led Molly to imagine a plot to create this vision, by means of drugs and actors, in order to influence Constantine to found Constantinople. Molly's imagination was starting to get the best of her, no doubt aided by the bourbon she was sipping in a Paris airport bar.

She went on to learn that barbarians were gradually enrolled into the Roman armies, bringing the empire together but also forecasting its ruin—for "the most daring of the Scythians, of the Goths, and of the Germans, who delighted in war, and who found it more profitable to defend than to ravage the provinces, were enrolled, not only in the auxiliaries of their respective nations, but in the legions themselves." Constantine even bestowed the consulship on barbarians. *Could this have signaled recognition by a group of statesmen that the empire would have to fall eventually, and were they, over time, guiding that fall?* Molly pondered.

Molly accepted the notion that Gibbon was indeed referring to a long-standing role of "our man" in the course and history of the Roman Empire. She had to; she had no definite indication to the contrary, other than rational common sense. She also appreciated that this couldn't be the complete story. There must have been memories and documents lost or still hidden, maybe ones that Gibbon had seen or heard of, that explained many of his references in more detail. But the suggestion of his passages was that this group, whatever it called itself at the time or since, was a group of persons attempting, clearly not always successfully, to direct government and societal events on a large, long-term scale.

The forces of disharmony so natural to mankind, however, were always at work, and that was why this group could make strides in one direction and then rather quickly run into contrary forces, whether they be the Praetorian Guard or fiendish rulers, that redirected the path of the empire in another. That was no doubt why such an effort had to be directed over generations. Society was much larger and more powerful than this group or any group of persons, but they seemed to use and bolster the instruments developed within that society, such as religion, money, and the eunuchs, to exert their influence.

Molly felt much more tired when the plane touched down at JFK than she had felt on her customary research jobs. What she was finding was both magnificently exciting and scary. Walking through the terminal toward the airport shuttle, she endeavored to clear her mind. And stopped to eat a donut. The immensity of what she was being led to find deserved a quiet moment with the "pillow-sweet cloud" that was a glazed donut, as a wonderful friend of hers liked to call it.

17

As she exited the terminal by baggage claim, Molly heard sirens and saw the lights of police on the departure concourse above her and stopped with the usual onlooker's eagerness to gawk at the mayhem. An older man near her on the shuttle line told her he saw on his Twitter news feed that some armed hostiles had attempted to enter the terminal, one of the baggage claim personnel had discovered their weapons, and a SWAT team was on scene. Molly had probably just missed them as she plodded downstairs for her donut. She tried to shrug off the coincidence. These events were way too common these days.

Molly boarded the shuttle without incident but could see on her phone that the authorities were currently putting the airport on lockdown. She leaned back in her seat and sighed, determined not to allow paranoia to convince her that every violent incident had something to do with her research.

She dozed off periodically on the traffic-hampered ride up to Connecticut. The message about the wine cooler from the Carpenter's palm sat meekly in the back of her mind, but she had not forgotten. That was the next challenge.

Molly woke up here and there and chatted with the shuttle driver. He had driven airline crews, tourists from all over the world, and many, many tired businessmen who had glibly shared with him stories—whether true or more likely fanciful—of their romps around the globe. He was a short, chubby sort who seemed eager to share, and Molly enjoyed his conversation.

She was dismayed when she finally climbed up to her little

farmhouse to see that she had left a couple of lights on. While willing to spend freely and have fun on her many trips, Molly liked to save up at home and for a short, silly moment regretted the pennies she would pay for the extra volts. *Funny how we have pet peeves that make little rational sense but are all the more persistent for the absurdity.* She turned on the TV to whatever sitcom was on and sat her tired body down.

With her tall frame, Molly always found tight airline seats painful, particularly on her legs, and she lounged back and tried to drain her thoughts of Imperial Roman conquerors, many of whom lived their lives thinking they were invincible and were now only remembered by the few scholarly masters, their "permanent" grave sites becoming illegible relics. She remembered what Xueqin Cao wrote in his *Dream of Red Mansions*:

> From old till now the statesmen where are they?
> Waste lie their graves, a heap of grass, extinct. . . .
> Sordid rooms and vacant courts,
> Replete in years gone by with beds where statesmen lay;
> Parched grass and withered banian trees,
> Where once were halls for song and dance!

18

IN THE MORNING, Molly drove over to the local post office to pick up her held mail and glumly sat at the kitchen table to sort out the bills from the useless paper-wasting advertisements. Luckily, the latter were more numerous. One letter, however, gave her pause. It was a personal-looking envelope from the local CBS TV affiliate, with the name of one of their producers on the top right; she recognized the name, as he was one of the people who had hired her for the baseball job.

The local news station wanted to interview her, on air, about her minor league baseball research project. *Mmmm, this could be fun.* Getting her face and name out there was never a negative for a girl who needed referrals. How to spark excitement about the Colonial League was a stiffer challenge. It was such a short-lived league, and none of the players became MLB stars, but the personal anecdotes were at least charming.

That afternoon, she put in a call to the producer and set up her TV spot early the next week. It would be a fun, short retreat from her now omnipresent "research."

After spending a few days combing through her notes and written summaries on the baseball research, she had refamiliarized herself with the names and dates. She spent a few long showers reciting witticisms for the TV audience, which always sounded so fantastic under the dripping water but too rapid and unwelcome when shared with real people.

Molly headed to the TV studio on the designated Tuesday afternoon. The guard at the front desk walked her onto the newsroom control floor, and she took a seat in the glass-enclosed conference room a few hours before the feature. Reporters liked to get a full sense of the interview beforehand. A young clerk or intern with uncombed, tousled hair and a plaid shirt that was slightly too tight and corduroy pants that were slightly too long rushed in holding a small laptop. Molly remembered similar days back at school.

"Hi, uh, Ms. McMurphy," he blurted as he dropped the laptop on the table. "I'm Roger Parkson. I'm now . . ." He fumbled with a cabinet along the wall, which opened to a coffee machine. Hardly looking Molly in the face, he asked, "Would you like?"

Molly grinned as she stood to help him with the machine. He didn't seem to know where the on switch was. "Thank you, yes, please. And you were saying, you are?"

"I'm the intern working with Daisy Montgomery. She'll be interviewing you. She's a cultural affairs reporter. Well, she's more like an anchor now, except when she's out doing—"

"Yes, I know who she is." Molly smiled as she poured him a cup before her own. "You guys are on TV every night, remember? And you emblazon her name over the bottom of the screen so often I think you've burned it into my plasma screen." Molly laughed as she sat back down at the table. Roger took his coffee and finally made eye contact.

He had bushy hair, an uneven beard, and thick eyebrows, but a pleasant if somewhat clueless expression and a friendly smile.

"Uh, sorry, I'm not usually the one who interviews the guests. Sarah's out today. My job is to basically go over what you'll be talking about, and then I'll report to Mrs. Montgomery before your on-air interview."

"Sounds reasonable; go for it."

He finally seemed to calm down. "So, what's the idea of your project?"

Molly tried to pass the beer test—describing a project briefly to someone, as if just chatting over a beer. She had a professor once try to teach her the skill of summary. Roger took notes on his laptop as

Molly went over the basic history of the Colonial League and the Bridgeport teams and a few of the notable players.

"Did you get to look into Mario Cuomo's statement in the Ken Burns documentary *Baseball* that he played for the Bridgeport Bees in 1949, when he got to bat against Whitey Ford? I've read that was bogus."[17]

Molly clapped and laughed. "Spot on, Roger! You're a baseball fan. I can tell."

"Yeah, a bit. More a fan of the history." He gave her his broadest smile yet. "I'm still rooting for the '27 Yankees, basically."

"You're right! Cuomo did state that he played for the Bees in 1949, and when I first watched that great film by Burns, I totally believed all of it. I only found this all out during this project, Roger. It's amazing what you're told and retold only to find it's garbage when you actually do the data mining. Cuomo never played for the Bridgeport Bees!"

"Some players back then played under other names, though." He patted the table like he had made a conquest. "In 1921, Lou Gehrig played for the Hartford Senators of the Eastern League as Lefty Gehrig."

"And as Lou Lewis."[18] This guy loved pointless trivia as much as Molly did. As a kid, she used to shout at the screen when *Jeopardy* was on. "Nobody's found any evidence that Cuomo played under another name like that. The Pittsburgh Pirates signed him in 1949 to 1950, and he later signed with the Pirates' farm team in Brunswick, Georgia, also called Pirates. That's where he got beaned in the head."

"Probably made him qualified for politics."

Things seemed to be wrapping up, and Molly drummed her fingers on the table. "So, now that we've escaped the confines of the Colonial League, am I ready for my interview?"

Roger stood and shook her hand. "It's not you I'm worried about being prepared, Ms. McMurphy. It's Mrs. Montgomery I need to rapidly teach now." He grinned as he headed toward the door.

"Roger?"

He turned around

"Call me Molly."

She sat and read from her iPad for about a half hour until a second intern, this one quiet and determined and more aware of his surroundings, led her to the set. Molly relaxed as a makeup artist attempted to enhance her reddish, slightly freckled cheeks, applied eyeliner around her grayish eyes, and added a redder lipstick on top of what she had already put on at home. Molly had only been to a spa once, with her friend Samantha and their other roommate from school. At the time she'd thought it a royal waste of time, but now she saw how some might find it relaxing and invigorating. *Maybe,* she thought, *I should broaden my horizons to the less scholarly pursuits. Nathan should come back and buy me a weekend trip!*

They had her walk onto the set at the appointed time, and she firmly shook Daisy Montgomery's hand. Montgomery had no doubt just had the full-press makeup experience herself and played the plasticized facial expressions perfectly.

"You see, Daisy, the Colonial League was Class B minor leagues. That means they were four levels below the majors. So, to get from there to a team like the Red Sox or Yankees was no doubt a stiff challenge, and that's why these players and managers were constantly courting the major league scouts, which was one of the more fun parts of my research. They did everything to charm them. The Colonial only lasted from 1947 to 1950 and was one of many minor leagues that existed during the baseball boom after World War II. They sometimes played against the major league teams in New York and New England back then, exhibition games and such, and so while the Colonial League players seldom if ever got to the majors, they at least played against them and knew them."

Daisy Montgomery brought up the Mario Cuomo story as well.

After the program, Molly got to chat a few minutes with Montgomery and the other anchor, who was curious about her research consulting. They suggested the TV station could use some of her services. Molly was happy to find that the visit might be productive for her business. They had all her contact info, and she gave them her usual shtick about her eagerness to provide research assistance and guidance. She could rattle it off in her sleep at this point.

Molly went to the bathroom to rinse her face of all the cosmetic wonders and headed out to her car. The sun was staying warmer later in the day as the heat of summer took hold, and she ducked under trees to avoid the sun. Emerging between parked cars in the small lot, she heard a screech of wheels as a red, two-door Ford jolted to a stop just to her left. Molly jumped right and forward, barely missing the bumper.

"Oh, Ms. McMurphy!" Roger Parkson jumped out of the car, shock on his face. "I'm sorry! I totally didn't see you coming from behind that car!" He rushed toward her and grabbed her backpack off the ground. "I really . . . I feel so—"

"Roger! Good thing my old knees can still jump! And good thing you've got good reflexes," she joked as she grabbed the bag from him. "I'm okay. I should have looked before popping out. I'm sorry." She tried to gain control of her breathing, and the young man sympathetically patted her on the back. "No damage. We'll live!"

"Please, Ms. McMurphy . . ."

"Again, Roger, please call me Molly."

"Can I—"

"No, no, I'm good. You go on. It was good to interview with you. Hope your internship goes well." She readjusted her bag. "Take care, and good luck, Roger."

"Your interview on-air looked great. Good luck too."

He lowered his head and slunk back behind the wheel, clearly embarrassed. Molly made it back to her car without further incident and drove home after picking up Italian takeout for dinner.

19

She spent the next few days poring over the Gibbon passages again and further detailing her summary of those findings. Meanwhile, she finished up her report on the Colonial League teams and submitted it to the two local baseball historians who had hired her. She then spent three productive days back at the school library, reading more on the Rosicrucians while investigating references to wine coolers.

One afternoon, she met with a potential client in the library courtyard. This older gentleman was looking for help researching colleges for his grandson. She sweetly told him that she didn't engage in such projects but knew a few college counselors who might be able to help him. Perhaps she had to make her small online advertisements clearer. *Always room for improvement.*

After an afternoon spent with the Rosicrucians in the large reading room, she was gathering her things to head out and drive back to Stamford in the early evening when a familiar voice came from behind her.

"Ms. McMurphy! Funny to run into you here. Have you been sitting here long?" It was Roger Parkson, carrying a backpack of his own and with his hair more carefully combed this time. "I was in the periodical room down the hall!"

"Oh, Roger. How are you?"

"Fine, thanks. Basic schoolwork day, you know. You come here often?"

She gave up on asking him to call her Molly and shook his hand. The two walked together toward the circulation desk, where she waited while he checked out a couple books. "What are you studying?"

"Tribal rituals of Western Africa. I'm an anthro grad student. I have a great professor of African art and music. I've learned a lot."

"Interesting! A bit different focus than your work at the TV station, I bet."

"Eh, that's just a part-time gig—some pizza money. You know." Now he chuckled and gave her a smile.

"So funny running into you. I didn't know you were a student here. Not bad. Hey, I'm sure you have other stuff going on, you students do always, but, well . . ."

"You wanna grab a pizza?" he asked. She was a bit surprised he had the confidence to ask. The quieter, nicer guys seldom did, she found. That was the story of her dating life.

"Yes. I'd love to, Roger." She made one last effort. "And call me Molly, remember? Or only one slice for you tonight."

He grinned. "Of course, Molly. Thanks."

They chatted as they strolled up to the main set of restaurants near campus and grabbed a table at a popular Italian dive the college types frequented. Roger, it turned out, had been an undergrad in the college right next to where Molly had lived, so they knew many of the same spots and professors.

"Does the TV station recruit much at the university? I never saw them when I was here, but that was at least a couple years ago."

"Yup, that's how I found them. One of the profs who's a fellow at my undergrad college has worked with them, and he put me in touch. When did you graduate?"

"Just three years ago, although when you're out in the real world full-time, it seems like eons since school days. What's Daisy Montgomery really like?"

"She—"

"C'mon, be honest." Molly filled his beer glass from the pitcher, smiling broadly. "She seems like she could be . . ."

"Demanding?" He chuckled. "Yup, you got the right vibe quickly, Molly. She's been big at the station for years and likes things done exactly as she wants them. Not flexible."

Molly took a long sip from her glass. "I could tell. I've worked with that sort. They can no longer imagine anyone would do anything differently than they do. Painful, that's what I call them!"

Roger laughed as he grabbed another slice for himself and put another on Molly's plate for her. "She's a bit of a trip. And not always nice about it."

"She saves that big, pretty smile for when she's on air, I bet."

"You share yours more freely, Molly."

She leaned back and smiled weakly, saying nothing.

"So, how exactly does this research consulting gig work? You basically just research a topic? How general are the questions? Seems like it could be sort of open ended. That's what I struggle with in a lot of my seminar papers."

"It can be, and that's why I have to grill my clients to narrow and focus their search, and on what answers they want to find."

"So, the clients direct you mostly?"

"Mostly. They direct the questions, I direct the process to find the answers."

"And who are these people? Are you able to tell me what you're researching now?"

"Nothing too exciting right now. The baseball project you know about is the most fun of them. I'm working at looking into laws that were put in place up in Braintree, Massachusetts, from before the Revolution. Helping some folks over in Holland look at an architect who constructed one of those big Amsterdam canals."

"Who are these people who hire you? Any students just paying you to polish off a term paper for their lazy asses?"

Molly sat back in her cushioned seat, slurping down another draft of beer. "No! That's one of my rules!"

"I know a couple guys around here who would pay you handsomely to help 'em out, but who are the big guys?"

"Like a doctor, Roger, I never share any of their names and such, unless they tell me to for some reason."

"Just one little name, for a friend?"

"Nope." Molly grinned widely at him. "You know, Roger, I haven't had such a nice chat with a guy since about sophomore year. I'm glad we ran into each other after our little scrape in the parking lot."

"Ha! Almost forgot that. Sorry again. I'm a dope behind the wheel."

"You just gotta always be thinking that the other guy's going to do something stupid, like me walking out there without looking!"

They each paid their half of the bill, and Roger held the door for her. When they were at her car, shaking hands turned into a half hug.

"Well, we got our numbers, so stay in touch, Roger."

"Definitely. Give me a call whenever you're back in the city."

"I will. I'm going out to visit my parents in Cincinnati next week, but I'll be back at work after that."

On the drive to her farmhouse, Molly decided she'd give Roger a call when she got back. She would run the whole thing past Samantha the next day over the phone, as she always did with these things—Samantha had a better person radar than Molly, who tended to be exquisitely negative about lots of people—but Molly had a good feeling about this one. Although she was wrong about these things more often than she was right . . .

The next day, Samantha was her typical self, encouraging her, as she so often did these days, to explore and then drifting off in conversation to muse about her own pursuits of the heart.

20

MOLLY REMAINED CAUTIOUS and went on with her work (this time mostly gathering her records for tax purposes)—and waited for Roger to give her a call. Although her curiosity continued to focus more and more on her secret group of world conspirators, standard jobs, no matter how boring, would need to pay the bills in the meantime. She completed her projects for the Alabama historian and the Dutch government, gave a long talk to an audience of lawyers up in Boston regarding her research into the legal history of Braintree, Massachusetts, and followed up her work on the Colonial League with a shorter project on high school baseball and football in central Connecticut.

Roger finally called after a week and invited her to lunch at the grad school, where she enjoyed chatting with him and his friends. A couple of days later, she called and invited him to join her and Samantha for a lunch out on Long Island Sound. Her friend was similarly impressed with Roger's candor and calm demeanor.

"You know, many of my jobs seem silly or boring at first but turn into something interesting, or even great," Molly commented after they received their appetizers.

"Roger, you'll always find Molly excited about even the smallest things," Samantha chimed in, leaning back on an outdoor couch overlooking the water, drinking an IPA from a local microbrew featured at this popular lunch spot.

"Yeah, I think what I'd like is to hire Molly's enthusiasm itself for a day. It would get me through this painful year of seminars and papers! Gets old after a while."

"I drank my way through senior year." Samantha grinned. "Bong 'n keggers was the solution."

"I can't believe you look at a course book like that and can't find something to excite you, Roger. Take a look at it in a few years, after you've been out in the doldrums of the real world, and you'll regret you didn't attack your classes harder now and think of all sorts of classes you wish you could take."

"Again, crazy enthusiasm." Roger smirked at Samantha and munched away at his nachos. "Hard to believe."

"The greatest gift someone could give me"—Molly beamed at them, straightening out her skirt, which Samantha insisted she wear for the group date—"would be to give me another year of college. Now."

"They do have online alumni college courses."

"But to actually be there, in the room. What's more exciting than a discussion in a seminar?"

"You would think." Roger burped quietly into his beer and looked at the two girls with an embarrassed grimace as he grabbed his napkin. Molly and Samantha laughed.

"Can't handle the beer, Roger?" Molly punched his shoulder.

"That's me. Sit here with two girls and just burp away. Not an expert with the ladies. I'm sure you could tell at the TV station, Molly. Samantha, she must have been laughing all over after she left that day."

"After you almost hit her with your car?"

"You told her?" Roger looked shocked.

"Roger, I wasn't laughing at you. I promise." Molly clinked her glass with Roger's, patting him on the back. "Don't ever let your history slow you down, Roger. Not an expert with the ladies? That isn't an indictment."

"Yup, impress her, Roger!" Samantha stretched her back and grinned at him, calling over the waiter to order another pitcher to share.

"Maybe one day, after I make the big bucks, I can buy Molly that year of college. And then laugh at her."

"Big bucks?" Molly inquired. "What're you doing next year? I never asked. You're not continuing on a PhD track? You're not continuing that internship, right?"

"Nope, I'm out of there in two months, actually. I need to devote my time to my master's thesis."

"So, what're you doing?"

"I ain't doing a fancy research gig—I can tell you that much. I accepted a starting-level post with McKinsey, down in New York."

"The e-banking/consulting route." Samantha nodded. Molly knew she had thought of going that route herself, before changing her mind at the last minute to go to nursing school back in Oregon, closer to home. "A bunch of our classmates did that."

"All of my friends from college are doing that," he continued. "Even the guys who thought of med school or grad school and one of my grad school profs is switching that way. The money they talk about is just hard to pass up."

"What's the thesis on? Last chance to expand your mind before McKinsey closes it shut!" Molly laughed.

"Nah, they'll have a lot for me to think about. And they'll pay me to do the thinking rather than charging me for it." He poured beer for himself and the ladies. "I'll be writing about some of the recent contributions of mandible contouring to early human evolution research."

"Physical anthro . . . Did you focus on that? I remember going back and forth with social anthro and physical," Samantha said.

"Yeah, I did too, but ended up focusing more on the physical side—more interesting classes for me. I was also thinking of doing bio, so it fit well for me."

"Where did you grow up, Roger?"

Roger seemed happy to go along with Samantha's treating this lunch a bit like an interview. "Out near Sacramento, Cali. New Haven has been a nice change."

"Different atmosphere, no doubt."

"Very different, but I've liked it. It's been a fun five years."

"And you decided to stay out here, in New York?"

"At least for now. Never know where that job or another job takes me, of course."

"You wouldn't want to go back to the anthro track?"

"Probably not. It's been fun for school, and when I started the grad program, I thought I'd find interesting avenues for work, but now I don't see it as real work to do for years and years."

"Not just because of money, I hope," Molly said, shaking her head. She knew she was incredibly lucky to have found a way to do what she loved while making good money, but she was always dismayed when students put off their dreams for the sake of cash.

"No, contrary to all your uppity jibes, we ain't doing it just for the money." He shook his head back at her.

"We're sure you're not, Roger. We don't mean anything," Samantha assured him as their meals finally arrived. "Nursing has been a good run for me. I get to work with a lot of interesting people, both good and bad." She smiled. "Of course, you'll be doing interesting stuff, I'm sure. And speaking of not doing interesting things, what sorts of projects are you working on, Molly? Maybe you can make Roger your intern!"

Molly laughed and dug into her burger without delay. For some reason, it seemed they had been last on the waiter's list. "I finished up another project on Connecticut baseball and football. A bit along the lines you heard about in the TV interview."

"That was cool stuff," Samantha said.

"Yeah, and Roger is a baseball history geek. Fits to have him talking to me, right?" Molly nudged him, and he patted her thigh playfully. "I also finished off a project looking at a canal architect, for the Dutch government. And gave a talk up in Boston on old laws in Braintree, back in the eighteenth century."

"Those must have been brutal." Samantha rolled her eyes.

"The laws? Yeah, they were strict back then. Mostly just not understanding that different people do things differently sometimes."

"I meant the whole research thing." Samantha looked at her wryly.

Molly smirked, first at Samantha and then at Roger. "Roger, Samantha thinks whatever I do is boring and painful."

"Just because it is—that's all."

The conversation came full circle back to her defending why she loved her job. "When you really get into it, all these projects are exciting."

"Because you're being paid to do them," Roger insisted.

"That helps, no doubt. But a lot of them do become exciting. Like, take the project I just got hired for. You both know Mozart's Requiem, right?"

"Heard it on a date down in New York once." Samantha took a long draw from her beer and dug into her salad again. "Concert was better than the date."

"I'm sure the music at least was. I've heard it. You can pat me on the back for that, Molly! I'm cultured!"

She slung an arm around him in a half hug. "I'm proud of you, Roger. Of course you're cultured. You even know about Lefty Gehrig. Well, did you know that Mozart died while writing the Requiem?"

"Yeah, that was in that movie *Amadeus*!"

"Yup, and the guy who finished it was Franz Xavier Sussmayr. He was a conductor and composer in Vienna. Someone hired me to look into his 'Der Retter in Gefahr,' a politically themed song he wrote. Earlier than the Requiem. But they want me to look into that, where it came from and such."

"So, who are these people who hire you? Who's interested in this

Sussman, or whatever." Roger winked at Samantha, as if goading her on to criticize Molly's work some more.

"Again, I can't tell you, Roger."

"It's like protected health info to her."

Samantha grinned at him. "Roger, she's given me that line so many times. I'm used to it."

"They assume their privacy, so I respect it," Molly sighed. "Who knows what they're using my research for? They're entitled to keep it secret. If you made some financial inquiries to a broker or something, would you want him or her to shout it around?"

"C'mon, we're just curious who goes after this stuff. Who's so lazy they have to hire a consulting researcher. Never heard of such a thing," Roger murmured, to Samantha's obvious approval.

"It's not that they're lazy. They're just busy doing other things. And they have the resources to hire someone like me to do the work. This research work takes time, and careful planning."

"And traveling. Roger, she always tells me about these exotic places she's been. She goes all over."

"Exactly, and all that travel takes time and money. And time itself is money for these people. It's worth it to them to pay me to do it. Who knows where this Sussmayr work will take me, or how long it'll take me? And it'll be interesting, I'm sure."

"Well, you keep us updated on what you find. And if it's worth your price," Roger quipped. "When are you going to start on it? Or do you ever just take a break while they're paying you? Like to help me with my mandible project?"

"No, no, no." Molly stole one of Roger's french fries while he was looking at Samantha. "No student help and definitely no mandible contouring or evolution research or whatnot. That stuff is fantastic on the Discovery Channel, but I ain't no lab animal."

"You going anywhere for this one?"

"Probably Austria. Sources seem to be sending me there. I'll send you two a postcard. One card for both of you. I'll text you a selfie."

Indeed, Molly was heading back to Vienna. The plane tickets had been bought two days earlier for later that same week.

She sent Roger a quick email before she left to wish him luck on his school projects and said she'd call when she got back. Molly was out of the country before he had time to call her again.

21

Sussmayr's political cantata "Der Retter in Gefahr" was completed in 1796, four years after he finished Mozart's Requiem, although it only had its first performance a little over 200 years later in 2012, with Terrence Stoneberg conducting the choir and orchestra of the Providence Presbyterian Church in a new edition by Mark Nabholz.

One of the violinists who had worked with Stoneberg on that performance had hired Molly to explore the details of and early inspiration for this piece. He wanted to know about influences on Sussmayr during his time as a student and cantor at a Benedictine monastery in Kremsmünster from 1779 to 1787. He also later had served as a violinist in the orchestra in Kremsmünster.

Her client had arranged for an assistant to take her from the airport in Vienna directly to Kremsmünster. The student was short and painfully thin, with dark hair cropped extremely short, a tight white shirt buttoned up to the top, straight black pants, and pointy black leather shoes. He looked like a '20s college student. Or a Goebbels wannabe.

"Thanks for meeting me," Molly greeted him. "Am I scheduled to meet with Mr. Krinsky today or tomorrow? Do you know?"

"Mr. Krinsky unfortunately had an appointment out of town and could not meet with you himself, Ms. McMurphy. I'm Helmut, one of his students, and I have access to the sources he spoke with you about and can show you—either tonight or tomorrow, whichever is best for you."

"I see. So, his intention was for me to utilize these sources alone to arrive at a summary for him? This needs to be translated, I imagine? Do you have a profess—"

"I'll review the documents with you and translate. This does not need to be an official translation."

"Has this set of manuscripts been previously officially translated? If so, I could use that, and would prefer to use that. If not, archival sources recommend we obtain an official vers—"

"No need. I insist, Ms. McMurphy. And Mr. Krinsky insists as well. There is no time for a translator. This document stays with us."

Molly was trying to be cordial and cooperative, but she had long insisted on the appropriate treatment of documents, manuscripts, and archives, whether that meant appropriate physical care for old documents or appropriate interpretation/translation of sources. That was part of her professional responsibility. She sat silently in her seat, watching the stale highway go by.

"And how long is this set of documents or manuscripts? Are they original?"

"I can't describe them in the car, Ms. McMurphy. Please, we will be there in about two hours. I'll show you then."

"Translators at the university can be—"

"Ms. McMurphy, please. Mr. Krinsky gave me specific directions."

"I understand." Frustrated, she shook her head. "Thank you, Helmut."

The car remained silent for the remainder of the drive, Helmut not even looking at her as they sat for twenty minutes in standstill traffic. *For a musician, this fellow has little heart*, Molly thought. She wished she had studied her Duolingo German lessons better.

They arrived at the monastery, or at least the library that now stood in its place. It was modern and simple but neat, with rows and rows of liturgical texts—either from this monastery or from places of a similar period. The furniture, also period, struck Molly as more interesting than the religious texts.

Helmut took her to a dorm-style room adjacent to the library where she could leave her things and then walked her past the short series of stacks into a standard-looking cafeteria, well lit by soulless fluorescent bulbs.

"Ms. McMurphy, we can eat here. Please, order anything."

The cafeteria was otherwise deserted except for the two older women stirring soups and stews behind the food counters. Molly looked at Helmut, and he gestured to the deserted food line without a smile or even a nod.

As the women served her a plate of a delicious-looking beef stew complete with crispy toasted bread and a soda, Helmut took a hot cup of tea and sat at a nearby table, away from the windows.

Molly ate her stew, and Helmut drank his tea in pure silence. He watched her eat but said nothing. Molly couldn't take this any longer, no matter how much they were paying her. Ten minutes had felt like an hour.

"You're a tough guy, Helmut." She gave him her prettiest, wide smile. "You drove all the way here and you're not hungry? The stew is really good, by the way. I highly recommend."

He looked down at his cup.

"How's the tea at this place? I love a good cup of tea. Twinnings, you know. English breakfast always gets me going!"

He met her encouraging gaze without expression.

"And Earl Gray . . . soooo mellow," she purred as she stuffed a few more spoonfuls of stew into her mouth. "And Darjeeling!" She waited for him to say nothing. "Darjeeling! Get the party started!"

She finished her stew, went up to the counter, had a second helping, came back, smiled at him but said nothing, and ate her stew. Molly then took her can of Coke in hand and put her foot up on the next chair to relax, sipping away at her sweet caffeination.

"Would you like to see the documents this evening or tomorrow?"

"Your call, Helmut. I'm flexible." She looked around the vacant cafeteria. "Feels like the bong 'n keg is about to begin around here. It may interfere with our"—she made air quotes—"translation. Or whatever you want to call it."

"I think now is a good time. It is 10:30 p.m."

"Cool." She stood and picked up her tray, which Helmut immediately grabbed from her and took to the disposal himself. "Thanks, buddy." Molly giggled quietly as she followed him out of the room.

She followed his prim white shirt down the short hallway back into the library. He knew exactly where the documents were and led her to the end of the furthest bookcase in the back of the library, grabbing an old folder from behind a book and opening it for her. She was startled to see it wasn't protected in any way. She gasped as he touched the corners of the old pages without gloves. There were twelve total, bearing rather large, handwritten German text.

He leafed through the pages, closed the folder, and led her back up front to a study table.

"So, this has just been sitting on that bookshelf between those books?" Molly marveled at the precious document. "Not air controlled or anything? For how long?"

It must have been preserved in some way, she was sure, since the paper looked fairly good for its age. She wished she could do analysis to at least confirm its age, if such a project really hadn't been undertaken before. Helmut seemed to know little or nothing about it, a student filling out a task.

He took out a notepad. "Should I begin the translation?"

"Might as well. We seem to have no other, you say. Maybe what you translate can lead us to another translation. You know the language, at least." She drummed her fingers on the table and for a scant second believed (or imagined?) that Helmut actually gave a faint smile of agreement. *Evidence of life?* she thought facetiously.

She did not read over his shoulder as he worked. For some reason, he insisted on handwriting his translation instead of typing it on Molly's laptop, but that would work. Molly sat back and relaxed. Nothing to do but surf the web.

His translation didn't seem bad. The document had been compiled by one of Sussmayr's students (who didn't mention where he was located) who worked on the "Der Retter in Gefahr" piece in 1794, two years before it was officially released by Sussmayr. He seemed to be a scribe for the composer, including detailed explanations of the movements of the piece, complete with quoted music stanzas, which—she managed to find in one of the more modern books in the library—were a close approximation of what Sussmayr finally published in 1796.

A good deal of time was spent discussing the orchestration requirements, seemingly in preparation for putting together a performance of the work. She was sure musicologists would love this account of a piece in its early stages of creation. The document didn't say much about Sussmayr himself and did not at all mention Sussmayr's time or role at the monastery, but it did relate, toward the middle of the text, that on some of the choral ensemble points, Sussmayr had himself written a short document that could be found "beneath his lectern."

Molly took close photos of the original document, suggested to Helmut that the library consult a manuscripts expert to better preserve this musical text, and took pictures of his translation to copy later. Helmut again insisted the document could not be taken to a real translator, and she was disturbed at his disinterest in bringing it to a professional archivist—but then again, he seemed pathologically uninterested in anything.

"Now, what's this lectern?" She stood in his way as he tried to slink out of the library after pointing her toward her room. "Have you seen something like that?"

"I've never seen any lectern. And other than two chairs in the foyer, all the pieces here are not original to the monastery." At her insistence, he did look in the catalogue of the library possessions and found no lectern. Neither did Molly on a short walk through the museum. A bunch of period pieces, but nothing that could remotely be called a lectern, if that was indeed the correct translation of the word this student had used.

In the morning, Helmut dutifully drove her back to Vienna, and after a casual evening, she hopped on an early-morning flight back to New York. Sitting back in her window seat, she was taken aback to see that the gentleman sitting next to her on the aisle and two sitting behind her were dressed in dark suits and looked like football linemen. Big necks with small brains. If anyone wanted to make trouble on this flight, they'd avoid this set of rows.

The man on her row nodded and smiled, but she saw him and the guys behind her neither speak a word nor read nor listen to music for the entire seven-hour flight back to JFK. *Must be dedicated business travelers*, she figured. *Flying is like standing in a silent elevator to them.* One helped take her bag down from the overhead compartment when she landed and ended up riding in the same CT limousine on the way back up to Stamford.

22

MOLLY GOT HOME in time for a late-afternoon nap. She nestled in her bed under a fleece cover, a satisfied smile on her face at knowing this nap would keep her up all night reading and watching TV. People always regretted those naps, but she was never sure why. If only it were cloudy and raining outside—that was the peace she needed after a rather dull trip to Vienna.

The next day, she got up and, over a cup of Irish breakfast tea, began copying Helmut's rather regimented handwritten notes into a Word document. She figured the document would be of more interest to musicologists than historians of Sussmayr or his contemporaries. If it had regarded a more well-known work by a more celebrated composer like Brahms or Mozart or Sibelius, this document would have been worth thousands, at least. The student who had written it never included his name, so he was unfortunately an anonymous contributor to the panoply of human intellectual endeavors.

The number of these anonymous contributors to human discourse, Molly was sure, far outnumbered those who were later even remotely known. And the recent, enormous intellectual internet traffic and mania of self-publishing, powered by improvements in literacy, had far expanded that number. Still, it was a pleasure to be part of that dialogue of ages.

Molly took a few days to start on another project while writing up her summary for the Sussmayr work, spending long afternoons back in the library and visiting her college club. She strolled over to the hospital to meet Samantha for lunch one day.

Molly had offered to write Roger a letter of recommendation for the club, but he only seemed slightly interested. One evening, though, he called her up and after a long chat invited her to join him for an evening at one of the Connecticut casinos, where she'd only been once, years ago.

❊ ❊ ❊

The walk up to the grand entrance showed the casino had been relandscaped likely four or five times since Molly had been there back in school.

"This place is pretty in nice weather." Molly stopped and grabbed a few shots of the large forest around them with her phone. "You come often? I remember every weekend back in school there were a few cars full of kids heading out here."

"I've only been twice. Mostly just sat at the bar. I can do the slots a bit, but the cards are too complicated—and you'll see some of the tables are really pricey!"

"Fun place to hang out, though." She held the door for him, and Roger slouched into the large entrance hall. "The whole place is probably safer if you're without any real income. I could lose a whole project's fee in one evening at this place!" Molly grabbed Roger's arm to point at high-stakes poker tables in a smaller room adjoining the main casino floor. "Full house! I just wanna walk in there and yell that—freak 'em out!"

They walked around for a few minutes, scoping out the layout. There were a few restaurants on the main hallway, and Molly insisted they try this location's version of the pizza place she loved back in New Haven. "Let's see if they've really duplicated the brick ovens in here. They even started serving salads in New Haven."

"A sign of the times," Roger muttered, putting his arm around Molly's back. He gave her a light kiss on the cheek as he guided her into the busy pizza spot. The line was long, but the place was big, and they were seated within a few minutes.

"So, how was Vienna? I've never been."

"Oh, you should go! It's a lot of fun, beautiful too. Great museums, and you can see where the composers like Beethoven were."

"You should have asked me to go with you!"

She smiled and grabbed his hand across the table. "I get too absorbed by my work on those trips. You'd hate me if you went. Maybe we can go sometime and do absolutely nothing over there."

"That would be cool." He waved over a waiter and ordered a pitcher of beer and then pointed at Molly. "And the young lady will be having . . . ?"

"Pepperoni?" she suggested. Roger grinned and patted his belly. "Yeah, medium pepperoni, all mozz, light on the tomato sauce."

"Well done."

Roger waved the waiter off.

"No salad for the lady?" He smiled sarcastically at Molly.

"Nope. I'm a purist."

"Your slimness argues you eat more salads than pizza, my dear!"

"Oh, I'm good at hiding it. When I eat salad, I eat salad. When I eat pizza, I eat pizza."

"Your job must have you running around a lot too. What kind of stuff do you wear on these trips?"

"Eh, depends. Just research at a library can be pretty casual. If I have to meet with someone, I try to look presentable, you know. Not like a businesswoman, of course, just like a smart researcher. I wear glasses sometimes."

"I've never seen you with glasses! Contacts?"

"Yeah, since I was a kid. So, you seen any new movies?"

Roger hiccupped after downing half his beer glass. He frazzled his already frazzled hair a bit and undid the top button of this shirt. "Molly, to be honest, I'm much more interested in what you were doing in Vienna. I've never known anyone who seemed to find such a satisfying career after school. You totally seem like you're doing what you want to do."

Molly sat back and stared at him with a slight smile. "Really, like anything, it has its ups and downs. There are some days and projects that drive me nuts! But c'mon, I'm not quizzing you on your thesis, am I? So how about—"

"Really, I'm just curious what you've been working on. Any clues on who you're talking to?"

"Roger, you know I can't say that." She kicked his leg under the table. "I haven't done much lately. Just got a new job to examine an heirloom clock out in Wyoming. They just want to find out where it was made and who made it and its history."

"Why do they care?"

"It's a family thing. You'd come to find that lots of people care about a lot of small things if you talked to the people I talk to."

"Any big travel plans for that? That seems like the most exciting thing about your work, going to all these places."

"Sure, it is exciting. I have no idea where this project will take me. Probably some libraries or museums in Wyoming to start out, and then, who knows."

"And how about that composer? Did you find his big symphony?"

"Nope, nothing that exciting. It was a document one of his students wrote about one of his pieces, with a lot of details about the piece. The music lines, the orchestration, the mood of different parts. Very technical. But kind of cool to see an original document like that, from back then, written by a student who knew the composer writing it."

"Did you find who the student was?"

"Sadly, the poor guy didn't sign his name, at least on the pages that survived. Kind of sucks for him. Otherwise he'd be mentioned in—"

"In your report. I'm sure he'd be dancing in his grave knowing you were mentioning him in some arcane report!"

"Well," she laughed and grabbed more beer as the pizza arrived, "he could have been mentioned in a book somewhere, in a history of Sussmayr."

"That's the composer?"

"Yeah. He wasn't very well known. Apparently, Sussmayr left some further notes on the piece that are 'under his lectern,' per the student's notes. Or at least what I was able to get translated."

Roger quickly served a slice to Molly and took two for himself. The pizza did seem authentic, Molly was happy to find. She thought that it could never be duplicated, but she bet some of the chefs from the New Haven mothership had been sent out here to start this new location.

"So, where's this lectern? Did you see that? Sounds almost like Sherlock Holmes, running around from one clue to the next."

"Never found the lectern. Not at all sure where it could be, but I wish I could. The project itself is done without it, I'm pretty sure, but I always am curious to take these projects beyond the focused questions my clients have. You're right; the work sometimes makes me feel like Sherlock Holmes. But you've done research for your papers, right? It's kind of more of the same thing. One idea or clue leads to the next. One thing you find mentioned in one book or chapter leads you to look at another book or manuscript. That's why many of the research projects are potentially never-ending!"

"Luckily my papers have an ending."

Molly grabbed his hand and held it tightly, pulling him away from his pizza. "Hopefully, my dear boy, you're ending those papers at the right place with a good conclusion. You sometimes are so scatterbrained. I'd be curious to read what one of your papers sounds like! Do they look like they were written by someone who doesn't own a comb?"

He quickly stroked at the front of his hair, flattening it down. "Or a pair of jeans that fits? C'mon, I do get dressed up nicely sometimes. You remember that French restaurant we went to?"

She smiled and laughed at him. "You outdid yourself that night. Good job, congratulations. Morgan Stanley will teach you. Probably a suit every day?"

Roger groaned and helped himself to more pizza and beer. "McKinsey. Only downside of the place."

"Only?"

"Yeah! It'll be awesome. You'll see. My brother works for them out in Cali and loves it."

"You never told me you had a brother! Older, younger?"

"Older. Kind of a jerk, but he stays in touch, at least. You?"

"Only child, so I'm very spoiled."

"And probably expect the same from a boyfriend."

Molly smiled at her plate for a moment. "Is that how you want me to think of you, Roger?" she finally asked, looking up curiously.

"I'd be honored . . . Ms. McMurphy! I remember you telling me over and over to call you Molly!"

"I remember hoping you would, finally, but was not then sure you were smart enough to take the hint!"

"Oh, one thing!" He slapped his palm on his forehead. "I just thought of something. That lectern! You know, Molly, if you're going to dignify me by calling me boyfriend—"

"And you'll condescend to call me likewise." She smirked.

"Boyfriend? No, I'm not going to call you that." They held hands again across the table. "If I'm going to be boyfriend, I think I've gotta help you with your work somehow, whatever I can do. I do that stupid internship with Daisy Montgomery and all those slobs at the TV station. I could be like your intern!"

"I don't think you'd like that, my friend." She tapped her long fingers on the plastic tablecloth. "And I'm sure you have enough to focus on with your own school projects."

"Okay, got it. Just keep me in the loop with what you're up to, Molly. If you're going to Vienna or Prague or Beijing, I at least want a postcard."

"I ain't taking you on those trips. You know that, Roger."

"It's not you, I assure you, my dear. I'm just so fascinated by Sanzmutter."

"Sussmayr." Molly grinned back at him widely. "He's a forgotten composer who finished Mozart's Requiem; you can at least call him by his real name!"

After stopping at an ice cream shop on the main casino floor, they took in the sights among the slots and at a musical acrobatics show before driving back to New Haven. Her road was completely dark as Roger pulled up to her little farmhouse.

"Ah, good, all that casino hiking got me good and tired. Care to come in and join me for a hot toddy before heading home, Rog?"

"I'd love to, but I've gotta be up early tomorrow. Next time, dear." He leaned over and gave Molly a hug and kiss. "Sleep well, Molly. Always a fun time with you."

"You too, Rog. Talk soon, okay?"

23

Molly dragged her tired body up into her house, shut the door, quickly freed herself from her tights and skirt and blouse, and sat on the couch in a loose T-shirt and sweatpants, a hot drink heating up on the burner. This was her favorite part of the day, and she just sat back and stared at the ceiling. Without looking, she turned on the stereo by remote and played her CD of Dvořák's piano quintets.

In the morning, as she sipped her coffee before heading off on a few errands and then back to the library, Molly sauntered through her house, half expecting to find new hidden treasures—or even better, notes!—awaiting her. Not too long ago, she would have been terrified at the thought of anyone being in her house or watching her. But now, she almost relished the idea of a new clue, a new avenue for discovery, even though she knew not what she was discovering.

After a few days working on her favorite Rosicrucians and talking to potential clients who had little or nothing of interest to offer her, she met up with Roger at the grad school dining hall.

"Molly, I was thinking the other day about that German composer you were talking about."

"Austrian," Molly corrected with a smile.

"You know what I mean. There's this music prof. I asked one of my friends about him. Perhaps he could have some info for you. I hear he's into Brahms and stuff."

"'Brahms and stuff'?" she scoffed, then shrugged. "You're right: doesn't hurt to ask."

"Exactly, so I invited him over here for dinner tonight."

"Oh. Wow. You are becoming my little assistant, Rog!"

The professor failed to arrive until the two were enjoying their dessert, Molly eating ice cream and Roger crunching through a dry bowl of cereal.

Professor Munroe was a short, portly older man in tight suspenders.

"Sorry I'm so late. I was just dawdling in my office. So, Ms. McMurphy, Roger here tells me you're a consulting researcher." He chuckled. "Guess that's what we are around here, but you're getting paid to do it!"

Molly shared some academia quips with the older gentleman, who seemed nice, albeit eccentric. Perfect for a music professor. She then gave him a rundown of her Sussmayr research and question.

"I'm sure you know the Sussmayr quandary is one of the oldest in music history. Did he finish the Requiem? All we really can be sure of is that someone did, and most think he's likely the one. In 1825, a fellow named Weber challenged the authenticity of the work, which Mozart's wife, Constance Nissen—she remarried after Mozart died—argued was really Mozart's work since she relied on the continued payments of Count Walsegg-Stuppach, who had commissioned the piece.

"She also had the trouble of convincing people that Mozart had indeed begun and written most of the piece. Constance had become annoyed with Sussmayr—for some reason I can't find in my reading—and had thus asked other composers, like Joseph Eybler, Franz Jacob Freystadtler, Abbe Maximillian Stadler, to finish the work,"[19] she summarized, then shared what she'd learned from the booklet written by Sussmayr's student.

"Each has his advocates, no doubt. I agree that Sussmayr did it but wouldn't be surprised if someone proves me wrong."

"Did you ever hear of this lectern?"

"I've never heard it mentioned. But I do know that our rare-book library here recently acquired a letter that—they say, I haven't seen it myself—Sussmayr wrote to Breitkopf in 1800: the music publishing house, Breitkopf and Hartel."

"That's here on campus?"

"It should be here. Try the rare-books or manuscripts areas. You have access?"

Roger now looked excited, and Molly grinned at him, knowing what was on his mind. "Okay, Roger, here in New Haven, you can come with me on this mission."

Roger smacked the table. "I knew I'd get involved." He smiled and stood to shake Professor Munroe's hand. Molly likewise stood and thanked the man, taking his info in case she had further questions.

The original Sussmayr letter had indeed recently been purchased by the university but was still in the preservation and processing stage. Several weeks went by before Molly had a chance to explore it. She had never been first on the list of scheduled researchers to see a new document at the library.

※ ※ ※

When Molly strode into the library for her appointment, she was presented with the document in the rare-book section's sleek, pristine reading room. The document was printed and had handwritten notes in the margins. Addressed to the Breitkopf editors, it was signed by Sussmayr. She whispered to Roger in the quiet reading room as she typed into the translator app on her phone.

The basic text of the letter was simple, asserting Sussmayr's authorship of the completion portions of the Requiem. The surviving autographed manuscript of the piece showed a finished Introit in Mozart's hand, with drafts of the Kyrie and the Dies Irae sequence up to the start of the Lacrimosa, as well as the Offertory. Molly knew that Sussmayr had later claimed the Sanctus and Agnus Dei as his own.

The more interesting part of the letter before her, as Molly often found to be the case, was the handwritten notes, which she presumed were written by one of the editors at Breitkopf, perhaps Hartel, but which had no surviving signature or initials.

The margin writer had not written in contained, coherent sentences.

"It almost sounds like he was taking quick notes while someone was talking to him," Roger muttered as he stared at the translated words he was documenting on Molly's laptop. "He does say at the top—"

"That this is what Sussmayr told him." Molly nodded. "Perhaps it was Sussmayr in the room speaking to him as he jotted down these notes."

"Like Sussmayr sent him the letter, but then showed up in his office—"

"Or wherever."

"—to talk about it."

Sussmayr seemed to be claiming that he had stored scraps of notes dictated to him by Mozart on his deathbed in a "tribüne," which translated to "rostrum." A synonym for "rostrum" was "lectern." This tribüne was at Kremsmünster. The monastery where Sussmayr had worked, where Molly had visited with Helmut, was in Kremsmünster.

Molly grabbed Roger's shoulder, staring at him. "That's where I was in Austria. Kremsmünster. The monastery there is gone now. There's a library on that site."

"But maybe they have stuff from the monastery still there?"

"We looked," she said. "That Kraut dude who showed me the place said there wasn't much left that's original."

"Darn." Roger sat back in his chair and shrugged.

"I have to go back there."

"Now?"

"There's something there, Roger. Something I didn't see. Something that guy didn't show me. But he's the only one I spoke to there. He told me everything he knew, which wasn't much." *Or,* she thought, *he told me everything he wanted me to think he knew.*

24

MOLLY GAVE ROGER a hug and told him she'd be busy for a few days, but she'd text him. He begged her to take him to Austria, said he'd take time off from school, but she insisted that this was work time, not fun time. She was distracted and not that interested in talking, so he let her head home.

Back in Stamford, Molly rummaged around in her closet and packed the same set of clothes into the same roller suitcase she had used on all her prior trips. She was starting to feel like she lived out of that suitcase. She just came home and laundered the same clothes and put the same shirts and pants back into the bag and walked out the door again. Travel was a key part of her work, but this was getting out of control!

After a quick dinner, she sat in front of a TV sitcom and let her mind wander regarding how she would "attack" the monastery this second time.

The doorbell rang.

She cringed. She almost never had uninvited guests on this isolated road. Slowly approaching the door, she kept away from the windows.

"Who's there?" she demanded.

"Molly! It's me, Roger!"

"What's going on?" She still put her eye to the peephole to look out at him before opening the door. Too much stuff had happened to keep her trusting Midwestern attitude. It was indeed Roger, bearing a big smile. She quickly unlatched the door and opened it, almost too shocked to offer more than a stiff, perfunctory hug.

"Sorry, babe, didn't mean to scare you. Just wanted to see you before you headed out."

"Oh, really." She put her hands on his chest and gave a weak delayed smile. "You never do that. Took me by surprise. You know I'll be back in a few days. You can text me."

"I know. I know. But I want to go with you, Molly!" He gave out a whiny shriek. "Please, Molly. It would be so fun for us to work together. I'd help you! And then we could be together there in Vienna."

"I'm not going to Vienna, Roger."

"Yeah, whatever. Wherever Austria place you're going."

Now she laughed. "Roger, dear, you're at Yale. You can't call it 'wherever Austria place'!"

He laughed and lunged forward to give her a big kiss, holding her lips tightly to his with a palm behind her head, caressing her hair.

"Please, Molly, just let me. I have time—"

"Roger, Roger." She extricated herself from the kiss and embrace. "Really, Roger, I'd love to, but when I get to intense work, I can't be with you. I can't be with anyone." She headed back to the kitchen after closing and locking the door. "I'm just such an introvert when I work, Roger. You'd hate me if you saw—"

"I'll never hate you. Never."

"You spend a single day out there with me when I'm hunting a manuscript or lectern or whatever, and you'll hate me! You'll hate me good!"

Roger grasped her in his arms again, and this time she pushed him away more forcefully.

"Frankly, Roger, I'm not that into you just showing up like this out of the blue. First of all, you terrified me. Secondly, I told you over and over I don't want to bring you along on my work trips. I promise, we'll go somewhere just the two of us to relax, on a beach or something, one of these days."

"I haven't seen that happen yet!"

"We've been dating for four months. That's all. And you're acting—"

"I'm not acting. I'm telling you how I feel!"

"You're acting like we're attached at the hip. You're acting like I owe you something."

"I never asked you for anything. Just to take me along on your trip. You don't owe me anything."

"Yes, you're saying I owe you to . . . let you be my assistant or something."

"Your boyfriend!"

"Researchers don't need boyfriends while they're doing their research, Roger. You go to school. You know that."

"Really?" He laughed. "Are you too far out of college to remember the goofballs making out in the Sterling stacks?"

"So now I'm old? Boy, you're really getting a gold medal tonight, Roger." She chuckled without humor and waved her hand dismissively. She was trying to maintain a lighthearted front, but his insistence bothered her.

"That's bullshit, Molly."

Her smoldering irritation caught fire.

"Bullshit?!" Molly started pacing in front of the fireplace, contorting her face into a stern grimace. "Enough, Roger. Why don't you just go home before this gets any worse. I don't feel like fighting."

"You sound like you feel like fighting." He sat on her couch and pounded his fist into the sofa cushion. "You sound like you're dismissing me."

"I am dismissing you. I've told you, I work on my own. I'll go, find what I find, and come back. You know I'll come back, and I'll call you as soon as I do."

"But I want to be a part of your work, Molly."

"My work is my job, Roger. You have your schoolwork. There's a reason I don't have a partner in my consulting practice. I go solo, always have."

"Well, then, how about you try going with me?"

She searched hard for the right words. "Roger . . . I . . . This project is just too much."

"What project? I'm not sure what the hell you're actually working on."

Neither did she, but she didn't want to say that.

"Just a lot of variables, Roger, which I need to sort out myself."

"But if I know those variables, maybe I can help you sort them out."

Molly stamped her slippered foot on the hardwood floor. *What is wrong with him?* "No. No, you can't. I can't explain."

"Yes, you can!"

"No, goddammit, I can't!!" she finally screamed, pounding her foot into the wood, even kicking the stone fireplace, which sent instant pangs up her leg, worsening her rising anger. "Roger, you come over and think you can change my mind. You can't. I have no time for you right now."

"Those are breakup words, Molly."

"Oh really? Fine. If that's what you want, that's easy."

"No! That's not at all what I want! I was just repeating what you said!"

"No, you weren't. You were the first to say 'breakup.' Don't lie and deny it, you sonofabitch."

"Oh, now the names come out."

Molly stormed to the front door and savagely swung it open. "Out! Out! I'll consider calling you when I get back. Maybe."

"Maybe, bitch?"

"What the fuck did you just say?" Molly ran back at him with her arm raised to give him a slap, but he grabbed her forearm, holding her at arm's length as he swung around her and ran toward the door, stomping down the outside stairs.

"Fuck you, Roger. Fuck you!" Molly slammed the door powerfully.

25

MOLLY CALLED SAMANTHA the next day, told her friend the play-by-play details of the fight, and said she was 100 percent sure she never wanted to see the creep again. "Molly," Samantha laughed, "you haven't had a fight with a guy in a while, kiddo. This shit happens all the time, and then it's just makeup city."

Molly left a few emails unread and unanswered in her inbox and within two days was on a flight back to Vienna.

Other than Roger, she told no one. She rented a car and started directly on the two-hour drive to Kremsmünster. If Sussmayr had meant somewhere other than the monastery, she wasn't sure where to look. She had pored through books and webpages about the Austrian composer for any other mention of Kremsmünster but had found only his connection with that monastery.

Arriving at the front entrance to the library in the morning this time, she found it to be a much more cheerful place than on her previous visit with Helmut. "That guy must be a total ball of laughs on a date," she muttered to herself as she walked into the research office and found a much younger, much handsomer gentleman at the desk, eager to help her.

"Nice to find you including our library in your research, Ms. McMurphy. How did you find us?"

She explained that she was primarily interested in the role that Franz Xavier Sussmayr had played there.

"Sure, he had a long history as a musician and singer here. Many of our texts regard his role. You know about him and Mozart, I imagine."

She smiled. "Of course. But I was more interested in whether you have any of the original furniture or instruments from the monastery. In particular, I'm looking for a lectern that Sussmayr may have used."

The young man thought for a second and shook his head. "Most of the stuff you see here are period pieces, not original to the monastery, unfortunately. Except for a couple of chairs, I don't think anything else survived."

Molly drummed her fingers on his desk. "Was this area hit during the war?"

"I think so, but I've heard the monastery had fallen into disuse and poor repair earlier, in the 1800s. Things were probably sold off and such."

"Or just taken." She stared at him silently for a second. "Is there a basement or attic you could let me look through? I've come all the way from the States. Could I just take a look and satisfy myself I'm not missing anything before I head back?"

The young man contemplated her question, called his supervisor, and then accompanied Molly down into the basement. The attic was a tight crawl space for electrical and plumbing fixtures.

This much friendlier and more vocal German student was Martin, originally from Munich. He gave her a quick introduction as he walked her down a wide, L-shaped staircase into a well-lit, modern basement.

"This was all built well after the war." Martin gestured toward closed doors surrounding the large, rectangular basement space. "I'm not sure the year, but the entire library was not completed until the mid-eighties."

"I see," she murmured. "And these doors?"

"Just storage. Files and such—nothing historical."

He opened the doors one by one, allowing her to look into the small, medicinally white inner rooms, which were filled with file cabinets. She was satisfied she had seen nothing older than about twenty years, if that. Very utilitarian. She tapped her foot periodically on the tile floors, the anxious archeologist in her hunting for a hidden doorway, but there was absolutely nothing enigmatic about the place.

"So, how did you come to work here, Martin? Music background?"

"Music history. In fact, beyond some very rudimentary piano, I don't play an instrument myself. I just enjoy the history."

"Of what period?"

"Modern, Russian. Shostakovich, Stravinsky, Scriabin, Medtner, Glazunov."

"So Sussmayr's an old-timer to you!" She smiled.

He chuckled, "Yeah, I guess so. But music is music. At a place like this, you get to meet all sorts of music historians—researchers such as yourself."

"Well, I'm no music history researcher, but true. A bunch of us are traipsing around."

As they returned to the main floor, she gave him a short summary of her role as consulting researcher. This tall, thin young man sounded like he thought it a great line of work.

"Now, Martin"—she pointed to the roof—"as I'm sure you've found in all your music history work, leave no stone unturned in research. Can we crawl into the crawl space?"

He stared up at the ceiling. "I'm not even sure how we get in there. There's a locked door on the second floor that I've seen the electrical repair staff use, but . . ."

She gestured in the air as if she were holding a key, then pointed at the phone in his small office, wordlessly suggesting he call his supervisor again. After twenty minutes or so, the man came back down the hall to hand them a key. The supervisor said a few words in rapid German to Martin. Molly noticed a momentary, casual glance at the ceiling that through body language seemed to translate to "This is a pain-in-the-ass lady. Just show her her nonsense and get her out of here ASAP."

Martin nodded with a smile at Molly and walked her upstairs to the utility closet, where he opened a second metal door leading to a low-ceilinged attic via a narrow metal staircase.

Molly's hopes grew dimmer as she crouched behind Martin along the winding corridors filled with piping, electrical wires covering the walls. The heat from the pipes made the dark corridors humid and hot, and she fanned her light sweatshirt to get some air.

She heard Martin tapping at a metal object and came up behind him. He bent awkwardly under the low ceiling to look back at her, his right hand resting on a large, metal box. The puke-green object displayed what looked like an antiquated radiation safety warning on its top.

The lock pulled off easily, and the lid let out a loud creak as she opened it. Martin grabbed his phone out from his left thigh pocket and pointed its flashlight down in the dark box.

Wood. Old wood. Dented, chipped. But intact. Molly's jaw dropped, and Martin goggled back at her.

"Help me," she whispered, and he did not hesitate. It took them almost an hour to jostle the wooden cabinet down the narrow hallway to a larger foyer near the access stairway where they had light and space to tilt the wooden frame up onto its short legs.

With an angled wooden platform surrounded on its four corners by small eagles, the top of this piece looked ideal for displaying a book or books of sheet music. The cabinet below bore two large doors sparsely ornamented with sculpted roses, complete with thorns.

Molly realized immediately that she was staring at a very old object but did not hesitate to open the wooden doors.

She beheld torn sheets of scrap paper—many printed with musical scores, some with scattered notes, and some blank. On the back of these sheets, handwritten scribbles.

Tears came to Molly's eyes as she glanced over the German cursive. *This has to be it.*

Martin did not say a word, stepping back from the lectern and crouching to the ground, watching Molly as she spent long minutes closely photographing every single inch of every single scrap of paper. She had no time to translate these notes, nor did she want to in that building. She feared Helmut would know she had found more than she was supposed to find. Luckily, Martin seemed like an innocent onlooker.

He remained silent, merely joining her to transport the lectern back to its metal box. He had no suggestions or recommendations regarding what should be done with this clearly priceless item, but she hoped her quick eye contact with him implied that this was something he should never speak about—at least, not in relation to her. Like the booklet Helmut had translated, part of her felt all of this should be shared with the historian community.

They descended to the main floor wordlessly, and Molly was glad to see the supervisor had left. Martin directed her to the main door after grabbing his backpack and keys to lock the library as he left for the evening.

"Thank you, Martin," Molly whispered as they stood outside on the front steps. "Thank you. Thank you for your help." She smiled faintly, distractedly, and nodded.

He nodded back at her, looking almost awed.

26

MOLLY MADE GOOD USE of the online translator and her pdf app on her flight back to New York. She shrugged aside the offered soda and snacks as she studied each photo, magnifying and delineating the scribbled words and typing them.

Her flight and drive home were uneventful. She idly noticed a set of three silent men in suits sitting in front of her, behind her, and to the left across the aisle, similar to those she had noticed on her previous flight back from Vienna. They spoke not a word the entire flight to anyone, even the flight attendant, and she spoke only with her laptop.

These notes—*Clearly written by Sussmayr*, she thought, although without his name or initials written anywhere—included many musical quotations from Mozart, perhaps written on the musical staves as the famous composer dictated them to his friend from his deathbed.

Sussmayr also referred to their conversations regarding the potential for the binary number system, developed by G. W. von Leibniz, to characterize and store musical notations. In addition, Mozart had been told by another friend (the notes did not indicate who this was) that Leibniz had perceived a connection between his binary numbers system and *I Ching*, the Chinese divination text, with the potential for *I Ching* hexagrams to characterize both binary numbers and, in turn, an alphabet.

Leibniz's discovery of the binary number system was dated to 1679 and described in his "Explication de l'Arithmétique Binaire."

But Leibniz's embrace of numbers went beyond numbers alone. He believed that human thought and reasoning itself could be framed and codified in calculations. In his 1685 work, *The Art of Discovery*,

Leibniz wrote, "The only way to rectify our reasonings is to make them as tangible as those of the Mathematicians, so that we can find our error at a glance, and when there are disputes among persons, we can simply say: Let us calculate, without further ado, to see who is right." Symbols themselves, he felt, were a key to human understanding.

In turn, he defined a "real" character as directly representing an idea rather than a mere figuration of an idea. Symbols such as Egyptian hieroglyphics, chemical symbols, and Chinese characters he deemed to be not true real characters but rather such figurations of ideas. He suggested the development of a "universal characteristic," which would be based on an alphabet of human thought itself.

In his "Preface to the General Science" of 1677, he wrote: "It is obvious that if we could find characters or signs suited for expressing all our thoughts as clearly and as exactly as arithmetic expresses numbers or geometry expresses lines, we could do in all matters insofar as they are subject to reasoning all that we can do in arithmetic and geometry. For all investigations which depend on reasoning would be carried out by transposing these characters and by a species of calculus."

Interestingly in terms of the Sussmayr notes, Leibniz was a major European thinker who was deeply interested in Chinese civilization. He even considered whether the Chinese characters could themselves be a form of his universal characteristic and suggested that the Chinese were greatly advanced in philosophical mathematics.

The *I Ching* was a manual of divination of the Western Zhou period that was later adjusted through the Chinese Warring States and early Imperial periods into a cosmological text known as the "Ten Wings." The *I Ching* utilized cleromancy divination, by production of random numbers. The four numbers between six and nine were transformed to hexagrams made up of solid and broken lines, demonstrated by stalks of the yarrow plant, and were later arranged in an order known as the King Wen sequence, named after King Wen (1112 to 1050 BC), founder of the Zhou dynasty. The text of "changes," known as the *Zhou yi*, of the Zhou dynasty produced these transformations of the hexagrams. The *Zhou yi* text contained sixty-four hexagrams, each assigned a name, a short hexagram statement, and six line statements (the solid and broken lines).

Following his correspondence with Jesuit missionaries in China, Leibniz wrote the first commentary on the *I Ching* in 1703, positing that this system proved the universality of binary numbers as well as theism—since the broken lines (zero or nothingness) could not become solid lines (one or oneness) without God's intervention.[20]

By the time Molly found this information, her flight had landed at JFK. One of the silent, suited men nearby again lifted her suitcase down from the overhead compartment, and when she thanked him, he winked at her with a subdued smile. The men took their bags and followed behind her as she walked to the Connecticut Limousine counter, one of them joining her on the ride up to Stamford, sitting behind her, still not saying a single word. It almost seemed like a routine. *It's funny*, she mused as she glanced out the window at the I-95 traffic, *that this little nerdy consulting researcher has gotten used to this kind of thing.*

Walking into her house at around 10 p.m., she sent Roger a short text saying she was home and going right to bed.

27

MOLLY SLEPT WELL, woke up late, and sat at her kitchen table for an hour, sipping coffee and avoiding her email inbox as she relaxed in her inner thoughts. Binary code, *I Ching*, ones and zeros, numbers, solid and broken lines, yarrow sticks, sixty-four hexagrams. She was reminded of the arrows on the stone disk and the ones and zeroes in the margins of Doyle's copies of Winwood Reade's books.

She sat forward in her chair, alert.

This has to be a code. And it could all be related!

She didn't bother analyzing how her disparate research tasks had come to be connected. She was onto something.

The binary numbers could easily be figured into each hexagram, the first number the bottom line and the last number the uppermost, or sixth, line. Whether zero or one represented solid or broken lines she couldn't be sure, although she would start with zero being broken, the broken line indicating nothingness, as Leibniz had described it.

She took out her laptop and opened her expanded images of the stone disk, figuring to start with this shorter message. She painstakingly copied the up and down arrows onto a text document for easier left-to-right reference and started translating this, by each individual zero and one, into hexagrams—each sixth digit leading directly into the next hexagram:

100101 010100 101001 101001 001000 111111 100110
010001 111001 010111 100101 110010 110001 011111
010011 100100 111101 000111 011011 101010 010101
011011 011001 000001 000001 011001 101110 010101
011010 101100 010101 110001 101001 000001 110100

000011 100000 000011 000110 010011 010111 010111
100101 101001 110011 011111 010101 111010 111111
101001 000001 100101 010011 011010 111010 111000

In the King Wen sequence (there were other sequences later developed that she would consult next if need be), the hexagrams had an order, which she quickly accessed online. Sixty-four hexagrams. *Are they referring to the words or phrases that were defined in the divination texts for the hexagrams?* She tried this first and got a whole string of apparently random phrases, such as "Work for the Decayed," "Great Possession," "Peace," "Standstill," "Modesty" . . .

Are these words? Are these an alphabet? She tried to put herself into the mental role of whoever had developed this code, as if she were designing it herself. Clearly, hexagrams translating into an alphabet would be more useful. There was only so much one could do with sixty-four words.

This needed a sixty-four-letter alphabet. English had twenty-six letters. So not the English alphabet. Until 1835, English had the ampersand (&) as the twenty-seventh letter, after *Z*. Old English had thirty-two. If she included an additional six letters from older forms of English that had been discarded, there could be thirty-eight. Not even close. French? Twenty-six. No. Greek? Twenty-four. No. Phoenician had twenty-two letters (consonants only; vowels were implicit), Russian thirty-three, Albanian thirty-six. Arabic? Twenty-eight. And the Latin alphabet the Romans used? Twenty-three.

Sanskrit had different numbers of letters as listed in different texts: forty-three in the Siva Sutras; sixty-three or sixty-four in the *Paniniya Siksa*; forty-seven in the *Rik Pratisakhya*; fifty-two in the *Taittiriya Pratisakhya*; sixty-five in the *Vajasaneyi Pratisakhya*; and fifty-seven in the *Rik Tantra*.

Base64 was a group of binary-to-text encoding schemes to

represent binary data, which she would have considered had it not been developed in the twentieth century for specific MIME content transfer encoding. *Whoever developed this code was advanced,* she thought as she sipped her coffee, *but not that advanced!*

Braille had sixty-four characters based on groupings of six dots—analogous to the hexagrams. This was developed in 1829, so it could be a possibility. Genetic code had sixty-four triplets of nucleotides that made up the sixty-four codons. Too modern.

Molly sat on her couch and attempted to take a nap around midday but could not force herself to sleep, instead grabbing a large glass of water and sitting at the kitchen table again to attempt translating the six-figure binary "words" into hexagrams and, using the King Wen sequence, translating those hexagrams into Base64, Braille, and the *Paniniya Siksa* description of Sanskrit (then using Google to translate the Sanskrit into English).

She laughed out loud in her lonely kitchen as each translation produced total gibberish.

She supposed they could be using sixty-four hexagrams as a figuration of a thirty-two-letter alphabet, either repeating the thirty-two letters sequentially or starting from the top and bottom of the King Wen sequence and progressing toward the middle. She tried a thirty-two-letter version of Old English and Base32 computer code in various configurations of ordering the thirty-two letters against the sixty-four hexagrams. Nothing.

Lithuanian, Icelandic, and Polish—all thirty-two. Yes.

Including a break for a remarkably tasty delivery pizza, it took Molly until 3 p.m. the next day to translate the arrows into hexagrams and into these languages, each in a few different configurations of the thirty-two-letter alphabets and then using Google to provide a rudimentary translation into English.

Lithuanian? Gibberish. Polish? Even worse gibberish.

Icelandic?

Rússland verður ekki fá af Ottoman haust.
Í puppeteers draga strengi.

"Russia must not gain by the Ottoman fall.
The puppeteers pull the strings."

28

Molly created a table to compound the code:

#	hexagram	chinese character	Pinyin	translation	binary	icelandic	#	hexagram	chi	pinyin	translation	binary	icelandic
①	☰	乾	qián	force, the creative, strengthening, the king, god	111111	A a	⑪			tài	retreating peace & greatness	111000	I i
②	☷		kūn	field, the receptive, acquiescence, the flow	000000	Á á	⑫			pǐ	obstruction, standstill, stagnation, selfish powers	000111	Í í
③			zhūn	sprouting, difficulty at the beginning, gathering support, hoarding	100010	B b	⑬			tóng rén	concording people, fellowship w/ men, gathering men	101111	J j
④			méng	enveloping, youthful folly, the yielding of discovery	010001	D d	⑭			dà yǒu	great possessing, possession in a great degree, the great possessor	111101	K k
							⑮			qiān	humbling, modesty	001000	L l
⑤			xū	attending, waiting, nourished while awaiting	111010	Ð ð	⑯			yǔ	providing-for, enthusiasm, excess	001100	M m
							⑰			suí	following	100110	N n
⑥			sòng	arguing, conflict, lawsuit	010111	E e	⑱			gǔ	correcting, decay, work on what has been spoiled, branch	011001	O o
⑦			shī	leading, the army, the troops	010000	É é							
							⑲			lín	nearing, approach, the forest	110000	Ó ó
⑧			bǐ	grouping, holding together, alliance	000010	F f							
⑨			xiǎo chù	small accumulating, the taming power of the small, small harvest	111011	G g	⑳			guān	viewing, contemplation, view, looking up	000011	P p
⑩			lǚ	treading, conduct, continuing	110111	H h	㉑			shì hè	gnawing bite, biting through, biting and chewing	100101	R r

She sighed, arched her back over the chair, covered her eyes with her hands, and began to cry.

There it was. This was real. This blunt statement suggested that the group that had worked to prevent MacArthur from expanding the Korean conflict into a larger war with China had also sided with Britain and France in trying to prevent Russia's winning territories and power as the Ottoman Empire declined. She imagined what sort of documents and accounts could have characterized this group's "interference" in the Crimean conflict. Perhaps Oskar Lamprecht was one of their agents.

Still unable to sleep, she progressed into the night, attacking the coded comments in the margin of the Winwood Reade book.

From the "Preface to Martyrdom of Man":

Underlined Reade text: In the matter of religion I listen to no remonstrance; I acknowledge no decision save that of the divine monitor within me. . . . If therefore my religious opinions should be condemned, without a single exception, by every reader of the book, it will not make me regret having expressed them, and it will not prevent me from expressing them again. It is my earnest and sincere conviction that those opinions are not only true, but also that they tend to elevate and purify the mind. p. 3

Sir Arthur Conan Doyle's coded margin notes: Blind is religion itself, blindness it bestows upon man. The soul within man is his own, not governed by any higher divinity. The inner thoughts of man is divinity itself. No higher omnipotence, no higher creator or mover. It is the divinity of man that rules the world.

From "War":

Reade: "God made all men equal" is a fine sounding phrase, and has also done good service in its day, but it is not a scientific fact. On the contrary, there is nothing so certain as the natural inequality of men. Those who outlive hardships and sufferings which fall on all alike owe their existence to some superiority, not only of body but of mind. It will easily be conceived that among such superior-minded men there would be some who, stimulated by the memory of that which was past and by the fear of that which might return, would strain to the utmost their ingenuity to control and guide the fickle river which had hitherto sported with their lives. p. 6

Margin notes: The fickle river is indeed random chance, ceaselessly sporting with both our individual and collective life as mankind. To guide, this is our aim. As there is no divinity above to guide us, the divinity within must be the Virgil to direct the journey of our life, mankind's life through the ages.

Reade: A natural consequence of all this was the separation of the inventor class, who became at first the counsellors and afterwards the rulers of the people . . . a military caste. These allied themselves with the intellectual caste, who were also priests, for among the primitive nations religion and science were invariably combined. In this manner the bravest and wisest of the Egyptians rose above the vulgar crowd, and the nation was divided into two great classes, the rulers and the ruled. p. 6

Notes: A hierarchy, a system to guide our Power. We, powered by the divinity that is the mind within us, establish the system. We guide the priests, the military, and the inventors. We lead by not one hand, but a magnificent web of intertwined hands, the many hands needed for our human divinity to guide humanity.

Reade: Thus, when Nature selects a people to endow them with glory and with wealth, her first proceeding is to massacre their bodies, her second to debauch their minds. . . . She uses evil as the raw material of good; though her aim is always noble, her earliest means are base and cruel. . . . Having converted the animal instinct of self-defence into the ravenous lust of wealth and power, that also she transforms into ambition of a pure and lofty kind. p. 7

Notes: Moment by moment, our guidance will not always bring wealth or joy or beauty. The wars and hunger and suffering of one century will beget the fruitful harvest and hope of the next. We, the guides, must be strong against our conscience, to witness the misery we create in the present to guide humanity toward the beauty of its future. Our guidance must be the strongest, for so many of our members will live their entire short lives seeing only hardship and grief, having only a faith in our man-driven divinity to calculate and direct our fellow mankind toward prosperity. It feels an endless quest.

Reade: At first sight there seems little in the arts and sciences of Egypt which cannot be traced to the enlightened selfishness of the priestly caste. . . . It was necessary to overawe not only the people who worked in the fields, but their own dangerous allies, the military class; to make religion not only mysterious but magnificent . . . Above all, it was necessary to prepare a system of government which should keep the labouring classes in subjection and yet stimulate them to labour indefatigably for the state;

which should strip them of all the rewards of industry and yet keep that industry alive. p. 7

The Empire consisted of three estates—the Monarch, the Army, and the Church. There were in theory no limits to the power of the king. . . . But in reality his power was controlled and reduced to mere pageantry by a parliament of priests. p. 8

Notes: It is this balance we are to create and preserve. No feature of mankind's divided roles are outside our navigation. The instruments of government, the churches, and the military are directed by a solitary group of men. A group that directs not only one people and country, but all peoples and all countries. While there must be winners and losers in one time, the direction of the entirety of mankind is the aim.

Reade: The most powerful of the three estates was undoubtedly the Church. In the priesthood were included not only the ministers of religion, but also the whole civil service and the liberal professions. Priests were the royal chroniclers and keepers of the records, the engravers of inscriptions, physicians of the sick and embalmers of the dead, lawyers and lawgivers, sculptors and musicians. Most of the skilled labour of the country was under their control. In their hands were the linen manufactories and the quarries between the Cataracts. Even those posts in the Army which required a knowledge of arithmetic and penmanship were supplied by them: every general was attended by young priest scribes, with papyrus rolls in their hands and reed pencils behind their ears. p. 9

Notes: The strength of divinity is not limited at all by its creation in the minds of men. The yearning of mankind to create divinity came before our earliest forebearers in this group of guides, but we have harnessed the teachings of the divine and used the power of divine teaching to ourselves guide mankind.

Reade: In primitive times it is perhaps expedient that rational knowledge should be united with religion. It is only by means of superstition that a rude people can be induced to support, and a robber soldiery to respect, an intellectual class. . . . Theology is an excellent nurse, but a bad mistress for grown-up minds. The essence of religion is inertia; the essence of science is change. It is the function of the one to preserve, it is the function of the other to improve. p. 15

Notes: As we know religion to be mere fancy, we also know its useful role, a magnificent tool to influence the mind of the people. A great part of our guidance has always been and will always be the improvements directed by science, the change that will continue to better the lives of mankind and his right to understand his world and universe, a right that comes from the divine mind within. We will also preserve the guiding force of religion.

From "Religion":

Reade: All doctrines relating to the creation of the world, the government of man by superior beings, and his destiny after death, are conjectures which have been given out as facts, handed down with many adornments by tradition, and accepted by posterity as "revealed religion." . . . These doctrines are not in themselves of any moral value. It is of no consequence, morally speaking, whether a man believes

that the world has been made by one god or by twenty. . . .
There is a moral sentiment in the human breast which,
like intelligence, is born of obscure instincts, and which
gradually becomes developed. p. 64

Notes: Morality is encouraged by religion, but as Reade
rightly states, religion is not the pure originator of morality.
Morals arise within the heart, the instincts of man. We
must use the imagined divinity to guide the errant toward
this instinct for Morality.

Reade: As a single atom man is an enigma: as a whole he
is a mathematical problem. As an individual he is a free
agent, as a species the offspring of necessity. p. 66

Notes: We direct not individual men, but mankind as a
whole. We cannot foresee or direct the life course of one
man or a small number of men. We can only guide a state,
composite of states, of civilisations, of massive swaths of
humanity.

The work took almost a week, during which Molly never left her house. Relying on food in the fridge and delivery, she undertook no exercise, no emailing or texting, no responses to Roger or Samantha—nothing.

With each highlighted passage from Reade, upon completing her painstaking, letter-by-letter coding of ones and zeros into hexagrams, studying the King Wen sequence, assigning the Icelandic character, and translating the passages, she paused, walked around her house, and thought of the stark-raving majesty she was reading.

Molly couldn't yet discern the age of the group, the ancestry of this society, but they were harnessing a beautiful spectrum of influence to cross boundaries of time, of space, of class, government, religion, art, and technology, in order to direct not only individual human events but the entire course of human history. So many historical incidents and trends of the past that had verged on the precipice of dropping mankind into chaos or extinction they had strived through their influence to prevent, utilizing human institutions and frameworks to keep mankind's progress on a continuing path—not necessarily to good or evil, but on a path to continuance. To progress rather than the decay to which mankind was so prone.

29

MOLLY WONDERED whether to respond to Roger's emails and texts. He had been sending them periodically ever since she had arrived in Austria, and continued, pleading with her to get together and talk. The more time went by, the sillier their fight seemed.

Although she would never have admitted it at the time, now she realized she might have overreacted. She was used to people trusting what she said, whether they liked it or not. His insistent posture—sure he could convince her to take him along on her trip—was indeed annoying, and he should have been satisfied with what she said, but he wasn't. *Is that such a crime, really?* she asked herself.

Here and there, as she took breaks over the days of translation, she thought again about him and what they had said—or what they had shouted. At some point, everyone had fights, and she knew the old mantra that if you weren't fighting, you weren't really together. *But at what point does it outweigh the good parts of a relationship?* she questioned. *Especially one so new.*

Finally, Molly was pretty sure the good parts outweighed the fight. He had been the first man to pique her interest in so long. A few days after she completed the coding and translation, after she was satisfied with the result of her long hours of work and fascinated by what she had found, she emailed him back.

Dear Roger,

It's been a few days longer before I got back to you than it would have been if we hadn't parted on such nasty terms a couple weeks ago. Thank you for continuing to write to me.

I agree, let's let bygones be bygones and meet up and make up, ok, Rog? The only stipulation for the future is you just always do exactly what I say. That's all; no biggie!

Love,
Molly

Roger wrote her back immediately, and they made a date to meet up at a pizza joint beside his apartment building the next night. Roger ordered the pie, and Molly poured a glass of beer for each of them. They had greeted each other with a quick hug, but Molly pulled away from a kiss. She wasn't ready yet.

"Molly, I think we both overreacted."

"Rog, please don't say that. *We* didn't overreact. I feel justified in how I felt. Please just admit that I had my point. You assumed you could change my mind."

"And I couldn't. I now know that!"

"And you'll remember it." She smiled and grabbed his hand across the table.

"Time can heal, right?"

"Or at least make our previous anger fade."

She blew him a kiss across the table, and he leaned forward to get a real kiss over the beer.

"Funny," she commented. "I had a friend back in school who almost broke up with his fiancée, almost called off their wedding, after a quite heated argument—over an issue neither of them can even remember now, six years of happy marriage later!"

Roger laughed and drank more beer. "I'm sure it happens all the time. Heat of the moment, you know."

Their dinner continued in a pleasant manner, although she rebuffed his inquiries regarding what she had found on her trip and insisted that she still needed to put her findings together before presenting them. Roger reluctantly conceded.

Roger covered the bill, to Molly's protests but fairly quick surrender. *He did cause the fight*, she figured. "Hey, how about we go take a walk in the courtyard?" Maybe watching the young people running around would be good for me."

He winced. "I'm sorry for that comment about the sex in the stacks, Molly. I didn't mean to suggest that you're old. No one could ever think that about you. You're young and beautiful."

"Flattery will always get you points, Roger."

She took his hand as they headed out the door and sauntered up the street, then through large iron gates into a residential college courtyard. They sat on a bench for a few minutes until Roger leaned over to kiss her on the cheek, took her hand gently in his own, kissed it a few times, and then stood to lead her to his apartment. He nodded to his roommate, who was sitting in the living room, quickly introduced Molly, and without much hesitation ushered her into his bedroom.

She had never been in there and first perused his bookshelf, commenting on his interesting anthropology books. Roger didn't answer her. He locked the door and reached his arms around her belly from behind, holding her close, squeezing his chest against her back.

Molly smiled as she slowly rotated within his grasp to face him and plunge into a deep kiss, their tongues colliding as the embrace grew stronger and stronger.

The kiss was long, long and almost exhausting—but it did not exhaust Roger too much to lift Molly's red silk blouse over her head, exposing her ivory-white breasts nestled in a white bra. They continued to kiss, Molly moving to his neck as she began unbuttoning his fleece shirt, almost ripping it as she exposed his narrow chest.

Molly's loose, mid-thigh skirt fell easily, exposing her long, thin, smoothly contoured legs. Roger sat on his knees, rubbing up on her thighs as he kissed one, then the other, then the first again, rising up to nestle his hands along her tight butt cheeks, pausing only to lower his own jeans.

Their shoes had been flung off by the time Roger's hands managed—with slight delay and difficulty that made Molly squeal at his lack of dexterity—to unclasp her bra, letting it fall to the ground as he cradled her white breasts softly, lowering his head to kiss, lick, and suck at her nipples.

They simultaneously shed the rest, facing each other in a short, awe-inspiring, naked moment before collapsing into each other's arms and another deep kiss, walking sideways toward Roger's small dorm bed.

Molly was more satisfied than she had ever been before.

Fight over.

30

MOLLY SHIED AWAY from the university dining hall for breakfast, remembering the old walk-of-shame jibe from her college days, and they went around the corner to a coffee shop. Roger then headed off to class, and Molly returned to Stamford.

Back in her kitchen, scrolling through her credit card statements and incoming bills, Molly was dismayed to realize that she'd have to start on some paid consulting jobs to make ends meet while she continued to pursue her unpaid scavenger hunt of connected clues. Reluctantly, she sent a nice email back to a firm that had inquired about her looking into records of an 1870s mining deal in the Rockies. Seemed dull but perhaps easy. In every job, as she had told Roger several times, there were tiresome, tedious tasks that needed to be done.

Molly prided herself on her ability to concentrate on one task—an attribute seldom emphasized among the many geniuses of the ages. For instance, Einstein was no doubt outstandingly brilliant, but he was also able to work at a problem for days and weeks and months and years. That persistence was surely part of his success.

But now she struggled to avoid withdrawing into the confines of her ongoing, much larger and much more important (she thought) *secret* research project.

The words printed on the Carpenter's palm had been HIS WINE COOLER IS GUARDED BY OUR MAN WHO REGRETTED HIS MORTALITY. Interrupting her web search for the history of mining operations in the Western US, Molly Googled the phrase "wine cooler."

She received many Amazon links to buy wine coolers and kept searching.

Wine cooler could refer to a wine-based, summery beverage or perhaps to a contraption for storing and presenting wine bottles; she wasn't sure which. Nothing specific came up for the drink itself, so she tried to limit her search to the metal or wooden contraptions that were used to hold wine bottles in a generally ornamental fashion.

She stopped at a listing from Christie's auction house from 2012.[21] They had auctioned off a Sheffield-plated silver wine cooler, one of four that George Washington had bought for the President's House in 1789. The president gave one to Alexander Hamilton in 1797, and Christie's had auctioned the item on behalf of Hamilton's direct descendants. Washington had taken two with him to Mount Vernon upon his retirement.

"Guarded by our man who regretted his mortality," she repeated aloud. *Who regretted his mortality? Everyone.* But at that time, in the revolutionary period, one quote came to mind: "I only regret that I have but one life to lose for my country." Nathan Hale, a Yale graduate of 1773, had served as a soldier and gathered intelligence for the Continental Army. He was executed by the British in New York in 1776.

Did Hale, the person, physically guard the wine cooler during his life? All information indicated that Washington had bought the wine cooler in 1789, thirteen years after Hale's death. But there were pictures and statues of Captain Hale. *Could the wine cooler be adjacent to or underneath a statue of Hale? No, the wine cooler was sold by Christie's in 2012. Or was it?* There were originally four wine coolers. One was clearly given to Hamilton, and one was given to secretary of state Timothy Pickering.[22] But Molly couldn't find where the other two had gone. *Was the one sold by Christie's indeed the one presented to Hamilton, or was it replaced over the years?* Maybe a wine cooler was underneath a Nathan Hale statue.

The problem was twofold: there were several Nathan Hale statues. One, at the RFK Department of Justice building in Washington, DC, was sculpted by Bela Lyon Pratt, cast in 1930 and dedicated in 1948. Others were at Fort Nathan Hale along the east shore of New Haven Harbor, at the Chicago Tribune Tower, at the CIA headquarters, and on the Yale campus. The CIA one, she read, was a copy of Yale's, with the university's permission.

One wine cooler couldn't be at all these places. If only there was a way to know which one was used. *Any other clues I've read? Could I somehow survey the ground nearby and underneath these statues?* A metal detector could detect silver, but depending on how deep the cooler was buried, that might not work.

Molly sat back, stared up at her kitchen ceiling, and sighed. She spent a few idle minutes scanning documentation that the mine operation investigators had sent her, trudging through painstaking details of sites and acreage to get a rudimentary understanding of the locations they were looking at.

She definitely could not muster the enthusiasm she had for Nathan Hale statues and wine coolers at this point. Molly had to get a metal detector. *Maybe Roger can help.* He seemed to know all sorts of people at the university who might have ideas for her, perhaps in the Engineering Department.

She sent her boyfriend a text. Molly was always very reluctant to use that word until a man had really proven himself over several months, and in more ways than one, but Roger had finally earned that honor. He texted her back between classes—*Or, more likely for him,* she mused, *during a class*—and told her he was contacting an engineering friend he had. *Taking advice from grad students.* She laughed. *Better than nothing.*

A boyfriend certainly got back to her faster than the more senior research contacts she used. He asked her what she was looking for with a metal detector, but she said she'd tell him later. She knew she'd prevaricate until she found something on her own. Once again, Molly was a solo agent. Extra people on board were extra baggage to carry, even if it was a close friend or boyfriend.

Molly received a metal detector recommendation later in the day and went directly to the hardware store. She put the 250 bucks on her credit card, reminding herself as she signed her name that she needed to work on the mining project. Money was money.

Shying away from starting at such a secure location as CIA headquarters, Molly intended to begin her search at the Judiciary Department building in Washington. She went during a busy, tourist-infested day and walked back and forth around the statue, holding the metal detector at every possible angle yet finding nothing. She then drove up a busy I-95 to New Haven and tried the same at Fort Nathan Hale; again, nothing. The area around the Hale statue on Yale's Old Campus was closed off for maintenance, so she flew to Chicago and tried the statue at the Chicago Tribune building. This was getting disheartening.

She called a friend at the Pentagon and asked about the Nathan Hale statue at Langley but was told to steer clear. Security around that site was so intense that her presence, and particularly a metal detector, would light off more loud alarms than she could deal with. So, the Yale statue was next on the list—and her last hope if she wanted to avoid the year's worth of paperwork and intrusive background check the CIA would require.

Joining a campus tour to hide her intentions, Molly was pleased to see the maintenance workers still at work near Connecticut Hall, with huge trucks digging up and replacing underground piping about fifty feet from the statue. If she found something, perhaps this was an avenue for access.

Typical of all modern do-it-yourselfers, she had already watched several online videos of people digging underground tunnels, all of whom were exuberantly excited about the instruments they used and the progress they were making. She returned late in the day with her metal detector hidden in a large duffel bag and approached the statue, just feet away from the maintenance barricades.

The metal detector started beeping.

31

Now Molly couldn't deny that she could really use Roger's help. If he later failed as a boyfriend, at least he could be useful here and now!

When she gave him a call later that evening, he sounded excited to hear about what she was looking for, although he had perhaps imbibed a bit too much after dinner. She was out of town the next two days to meet with the mining company executives down in New York, but they made a plan to meet up after that, late at night on the Old Campus—and tunnel their way toward the site the metal detector indicated.

※ ※ ※

Not overtly dressed to conceal their identities but overall wearing darker shades, at around 2:30 a.m. the two approached Old Campus, holding hands, with Roger carrying the large duffel bag. They circled the statue with the metal detector and found the loudest, most reliable signal just to the left of the statue, almost directly lateral to Nathan Hale's left arm. Only two feet from the base of the pedestal. Hopefully, their dig wouldn't take them close enough to undermine the stability of the statue itself.

They took turns digging and keeping watch for police and students. A few times they had to suspend their work, throw a towel down over the hole, and walk around the block, holding hands to maintain the student-couple look while a police patrol came by.

"Cops are rotating through about every twenty minutes," Roger whispered on their next walkabout. Fifteen minutes later, on their next position swap, Molly took up the shovel again, and Roger began his usual patrol.

Minutes went by, and Molly grew tired, occasionally straightening to check for Roger. She could no longer see him. Her breathing grew heavy as she lifted smaller and smaller loads of dirt, digging deeper but still not finding anything. She tried the metal detector now and then and was still getting a signal. She prayed the device was not just picking up a metal pipe.

Twenty minutes later, she hit wood and began digging faster around the surface to reveal the edges of a lid. *Where the hell is Roger?* She was getting frustrated and upset and worried but continued to dig, uncovering a smallish box, about two feet long on each side. The soil to the sides of the box was looser, and she was soon able to get her long, thin fingers around it.

She crouched down to reach further along the sides of the box, and it moved under her fingers. Molly struggled to pull it up.

Suddenly she heard a whizz in the air and a tiny explosion of rock as a projectile hit the statue's pedestal, with a second one rapidly ricocheting against Nathan Hale's foot.

She ducked and cried out involuntarily. Soft pops, from silenced guns, now came from all directions. She tried to wiggle the box free while keeping her head down. "Fuck!"

Molly finally got hold of the box, ripped it from the ground, and gripped it tightly to her chest, sprinting toward the nearby Rosenfield gate.

Five men in black moved in through Phelps gate, with a second group of three approaching from the opposite side by Harkness tower. The men fanned out over the grass, unsure where the woman had gone.

"She must have gone toward one of the gates. Close them all off, now!" a man growled into a tiny microphone.

Roger turned to look back at the speaker, nodding and pointing toward the Harkness gate. Now dressed fully in black and clutching a black HK MP5/10, Molly's boyfriend was firing shots at anything that moved.

✺ ✺ ✺

Molly made it to the street and started running north, glancing behind her, hoping to see the police or a taxi. She thanked her lucky stars that her attackers hadn't found her until she was basically ready to flee. *But where can I run?* Whoever these men were, they were deadly.

A black van screeched to a halt on the street about twenty yards ahead of her, and men in black suits jumped out from the rear doors, well armed. They ran directly toward her. She heard the men behind emerging from the gate she had exited and spotted two figures leaving the other gate in her peripheral.

She pelted left, across the street, and a car careened off the road onto the sidewalk, narrowly missing her and hitting one of her assailants from the van.

Remembering the particulars of a small café nearby, Molly dashed over a cross street and dove downstairs to the underground door, ducking her head. She cautiously peered up through the wrought iron fencing and eyed the men in black moving toward her from the campus. With relief, she witnessed the second group start firing at the first set of men. Molly squeezed into a thin passageway alongside the café building, leaving the box in dark shadow just outside the enclosure.

"She can't have gotten far," one of the men muttered into his headset.

"She knows these streets too well," Roger replied. "She's a resourceful girl. I bet she had a getaway in mind when she started. And now these guys are on us!"

"And you know these streets well too, Soloview," the man almost shouted back, using Roger's call sign. "She never told you that plan?"

"Nope." Roger rolled on the ground under a tree and continued firing at the newer set of masked warriors. "We must get her. She's in too deep!"

"How the hell did we lose her?" another voice demanded over the joint radio frequency.

"Too dark in that corner of the campus," Roger replied. "But there was no way I could've convinced her to do this during the day."

※ ※ ※

Molly's defenders had seen where she hid, and four created a perimeter on the street, firing madly. Two jumped down into the underground passageway in front of the café, one grabbing the wooden box and the second Molly's arm, without a word pulling her out of her narrow hiding space as their black van spun around the corner and stopped on the sidewalk.

Men fired from the side windows. Molly's rescuer threw her light frame over his big shoulder and lifted her up toward the open van door, into the waiting arms of another man. The rest kept firing as they mounted a second van parked just behind the first, and then both screeched down the street, bullets scattering off the armored sides.

※ ※ ※

Molly lifted her head painfully off the floor of the van as one of the men pulled her up. Now on her knees, she sobbed hysterically.

"It's okay, Molly, it's okay. We got you." A man in a black suit turned to look at her from the front passenger seat. It was Nathan. He gestured for her to be quiet, and Molly clutched the box they had given back to her.

"Where's my friend?"

"We don't know. We don't know who was with you. He's the student you've been seeing?"

"Did they get him?"

"Maybe. We can't worry about that now." Nathan spoke calmly. "We're taking you home."

Molly cried, "How can I stay there? Who are these—"

"In time. In time, Molly. You'll know. We're watching you."

She sat silently in a seat they opened for her. Other than Nathan, the others stayed masked the entire ride, holding their guns but not speaking. They drove off the Stamford exit, found her little side road, and dropped her at her driveway. One of the masked men nodded to her, and Nathan shook her hand before she stepped out with the box. He opened the passenger window for some final words. "Molly," he said quietly, "we're watching you."

She said nothing, just turned and stumbled up the driveway to her door.

32

THE COLLIDING EMOTIONS in her head reminded her of her traumatic visit to the Ogilvies. She had had enough. Enough. She told herself she didn't care what was in that box.

Who were those people? Who are the other people? The first group of attackers clearly wanted her dead. The second group—Nathan's group—clearly wanted her alive. *But if they were watching me, why did they not do more? Where is Roger? Poor Roger.* She hoped he'd seen them and run. He was no athlete, but hopefully his stubby little legs took him out of danger. The mysterious attackers must have scared him away before they came after her. Molly called Roger's phone and left two messages but got no reply.

Molly did not want to open the box. That box might contain the answers to all her questions, and she still didn't want to look at it. It sat on her dining room counter. She would leave it there.

For a few minutes, at least.

The men who had assailed her were no doubt aware of where she lived, and despite what Nathan said about watching her, his group had yet to prevent the dangerous situations she kept finding herself in. She had no time to lose. After a dinner of kale salad and tomato soup and a healthy serving of Jim Beam, she stood from her kitchen table and approached the box.

The top was easy to open, just four mildly rusted, rotating screws, no lock; this box had been secured by its hiding spot, not by any feature of the box itself.

Molly held her breath as she pulled a hefty, hollow silver object out of the box and placed it on the nearby coffee table. A silver wine cooler. The inscription on the side of the cooler, she had read online, was a copy of the accompanying letter Washington had sent to his former military aide and Treasury secretary, Hamilton:

> *Mount Vernon, Aug 21, 1797*
>
> *My dear Sir,*
>
> *Not for any intrinsic value the thing possesses, but as a token of my sincere regard and friendship for you, and as a remembrance of me, I pray you to accept a wine cooler for four bottles, which Colonel Biddle is directed to forward from Philadelphia, where with other articles it was left, together with this letter to your address. It is one of four which I imported in the early part of my late administration of the Government, two only of which were ever used.*
>
> *I pray you to present my best wishes, in which Mrs. Washington joins me, to Mrs. Hamilton, and the family, and that you would be persuaded that with every sentiment of the highest regard,*
>
> > *I remain your sincere friend,*
> > *And affectionate humble servant,*
> > *Geo. Washington*

Molly sat back with a sense of wonder—and confusion.

What was the cooler sold by Christie's in 2012? she pondered. *A copy? One of the other three Washington had bought? This same one, later placed surreptitiously near the Hale statue?*

Molly spun the cooler slowly, peering in all sides of the inner bottle-holding chamber. Ostensibly nothing. But there had to be something. *Otherwise, why is this item hidden?* She raised the cooler over her head to look at its underside. A wooden plaque was fixed to the bottom.

As she turned the cooler upside down, a tightly bound scroll fell from within one of the chambers. Tiny, hand-inscribed ones and zeros appeared on both the opened paper scroll and the plaque.

Molly set the cooler back down, shuffled back into the kitchen in her blue sweatpants and light-pink socks, and poured herself another glass of Jim Beam.

On the sofa again, Molly copied the ones and zeros on the paper and then flipped the cooler over, holding it tightly between her knees, carefully transcribing the separate set of numbers onto a notepad. The decoding-and-translating saga had begun again.

This one took her all night.

※ ※ ※

What she learned through the messages and the subsequent research they led her to was that a man named John Honeyman had been George Washington's spy, a British informant posing as a Tory. He was also a member of Nathan's secret group.

In communication and cooperation with additional group operatives within the Hessian guard detail at Trenton, he contacted Colonel Johann Rall, the commander of the three Hessian regiments camped there. He managed to convince Rall that the Continental Army, after their defeats in New York and retreat through New Jersey into Pennsylvania, had such poor morale that there was no way Washington could attempt an attack on Trenton.

The Americans' ensuing surprise attack on Trenton in the early morning of December 26, 1776, and the resulting victory over the Hessian mercenaries, inspired American soldiers to fight on and inspired others to be recruited to the cause.

The second scenario referred to in this apparent coded message from Washington to Hamilton regarded the crucial battle at Yorktown in 1781. In September of that year, group operatives in the British camp in New York convinced General Sir Henry Clinton to send a letter to Lieutenant General Charles Cornwallis indicating that Cornwallis should expect reinforcements from New York. This message, in addition to further recommendations from Cornwallis's staff, convinced the commander to remain in Yorktown rather than fight his way out.

These same group operatives, working as officers on Clinton's staff, then convinced the general at a council meeting in New York that Cornwallis could not be reinforced until the British regained control of the Chesapeake.

Group agents who had infiltrated the engineering units of the British Army contacted the Compte de Rochambeau's engineers as they assisted American engineers in constructing the 2,000-foot trench that allowed the Americans to move their artillery within range of British defenses. These same pseudo-British engineers, earlier in July, had built fortifications at Yorktown that were strong against land forces but weak and susceptible to attack from the French naval blockade and siege.

The last sentence of the text—inscribed by Washington himself, she assumed—said, "A structure of Arden oak and Wilmcote stone witnessed the visit from stork carrying our man who brought magic to the Sea Venture's jetty."

It was almost creepy to think of such eminent founders involved with this clandestine group of conspirators, although the immediate result of their involvement certainly seemed to advance the development of representative government. Molly conceded to being a bit Americentric, but it was hard to argue that this wasn't, as far as potential group members at the time could have foreseen, a good thing for the world.

33

As a new day dawned, Molly set to work deciphering Washington's closing sentence, keeping Google open on her iPad.

After the London Company settled Jamestown in Virginia in 1607, the third shipment of settlers and supplies was sent aboard a seven-ship fleet under the flagship *Sea Venture*, which carried 500 to 600 people. The *Sea Venture* set sail June 2, 1609, from Plymouth, but encountered a strong storm July 24. The *Sea Venture* sheltered in Discovery Bay, in what later became eastern Bermuda, where 150 people and one dog were stranded for about nine months.

So the *Sea Venture*'s "jetty" (i.e., dock) was Bermuda. The "man who brought magic" there? Well, according to her research, this wreck was believed to have inspired William Shakespeare's *The Tempest*, probably written between 1610 and 1611, just afterward. In the play, the sorcerer Prospero—a magician!—lived with Miranda, his daughter; Caliban, a half-human monster; and Ariel, a light spirit.

The stork bringing babies was an ancient legend seen in folklore from Europe, the Americas, North Africa, and the Middle East, and most recently popularized by Hans Christian Anderson in a story called "The Storks."[23]

Another, slightly more involved Google search told Molly that oak from the Forest of Arden and stone from Wilmcote had been used to construct a house owned by John Shakespeare in Stratford-upon-Avon, Warwickshire, England, where his son, the presumed "our man," was born in 1564. A son named William.

Although there was no definite action indicated by Washington's inscription, the ultimate object of the words seemed to be the house itself. Perhaps something in it or under it.

Molly had to get to Stratford-upon-Avon.

She returned the wine cooler to its box and locked it in the antique wall cabinet in her dining room. If anyone wanted it back, no doubt they could easily enter her house and find it. There was nothing she could do for the item itself. But the information was hers now.

※ ※ ※

Roger called her later that morning. He had apparently seen the men in black and started running up a perpendicular street to get around them, but they were already in the Old Campus gateway when he rounded the corner. He couldn't get past them, and he didn't want to give away her position by sending a call or text to her phone, so he ran. In the wee hours after midnight, he had tortured himself over whether she was safe or not, before finally giving in and calling with the hope that she was out of danger and able to answer.

Molly sat on her couch and quietly listened. The moviegoer in her secretly wished he had done something more heroic but understood his position. This was real life, and these guys had real guns and real bullets. She had known this pursuit was dangerous when she invited Roger to get involved. If anything, she had failed to protect *him*.

Needing a change of scenery, she booked a hotel room in New York and invited Roger to join her for a quiet, isolated weekend in the big city. The two ate quietly together at a couple of good restaurants and sat through an excellent off-Broadway production of *Macbeth*. Neither said much about the treasure hunt. At one point, Roger casually asked if she'd found anything, and she said she didn't want to talk about it; he left it at that, holding her as they sipped martinis at an Upper West Side bar. She felt a little like he was tiptoeing around her, and she wasn't entirely sure why, but it made her anxious that he didn't push her on the subject of what had been important enough to send an army of gunmen onto a college campus to retrieve.

※ ※ ※

Back in Stamford, Molly reread *The Tempest* one afternoon, discovering nothing new. If an actual document—an early Shakespeare quarto, perhaps—was the target, perhaps she would find it in his birthplace, although she couldn't imagine that his home had not been examined and reexamined down to its foundations over the years. The clues left possibilities open but had yet to provide a clear direction.

Molly reluctantly changed into her workout outfit and trudged out to her car. She drove to the gym not out of duty or any regard for her health but to distract her mind. Standing on an elliptical and listening to indie music should help calm her jumbled mind.

She stopped on the way home to grab a take-out sandwich that would sufficiently cancel out her accomplishments on the elliptical and abruptly noticed two nondescript black sedans with tinted windows following her out of the parking lot. She eyed them in her rearview mirror as they followed her turn by turn back to her small dirt road. Then they continued down the road after she parked. She felt no less nervous as she got out of her car and watched them drive off.

34

MOLLY TRIED TO RELAX in sweatpants at her kitchen table, munching on her sandwich while emailing Samantha, whom she hadn't seen for a couple of months. No matter how up and down Samantha's friendship too often was, Molly appreciated and relied on it.

Yet Molly had always wondered in the back of her head whether this was in fact a real friendship. They usually had a good laugh and had gone out on double dates and even visited with each other's parents. On her good days, Samantha was great—fun, smart, the life of the party. But on Samantha's bad days, Molly felt that her awareness and expectations of who her friend actually was might be entirely wrong.

One of the more hard-to-believe discoveries Molly had made, after graduation and once Samantha had gone through nursing school and a master's program, was that Samantha had gotten married and divorced during those three years, all the while periodically emailing Molly from across the country and never mentioning it!

By the time Samantha returned to New Haven, she was divorced. She never spoke about her ex much, although she did finally mention to Molly that perhaps they would have stayed together if they'd had kids. But then again—so she said—he had been an alcoholic who had stolen money from her. Molly never learned more details. Samantha was great at superficial conversations.

Samantha then became a dating app queen, going on first date after first date, with no relationship lasting more than a few months, although she proudly proclaimed to Molly and another of their former classmates at a reunion event that she had been "almost engaged." Molly couldn't imagine what that meant. Did the guy get down on one knee, reach in his pocket, and then look up and announce he forgot to buy the ring?

Before landing her current job at the university hospital, Samantha had bounced from one private clinic to the next, at first enjoying her new workplace and then fairly quickly despising it and everyone she worked with, becoming more and more irritable, randomly not showing up to work, and then moving on.

Although they regularly spoke and emailed each other, Samantha's mood was a bit of a guessing game. Sometimes Samantha would greet Molly with fun and jokes. Sometimes she would just text back that she was having a really bad time and needed to be alone. Molly was a caring friend, listening to Samantha's perpetual gripes with coworkers, family, and old dates. Samantha, on the other hand, seemed to care little for Molly's work and life, seldom asking about her family or any guys she managed to see amid her endless work trips. And on the few outings Molly had been on with Samantha and her friends from the hospital, Samantha had driven her to the venue and then stranded her in the parking lot at the end of the evening to pop off and see some new guy she was dating.

Despite all this, Molly continued to regard Samantha as a sort of soulmate, a friend for life. She always offered to help. Samantha never offered the same.

The last time they had spoken, Molly had offered advice that she quickly realized was a mistake. Samantha was the type to be self-assured and confident that whatever she was doing was the correct and smart thing to do, no matter what common wisdom said. After only a few weeks of dating her latest prospect, the guy had moved into her house. She was in talks to buy a baby grand piano to convert her home office into a music room for him, they'd gone ring shopping, and she was planning on quitting her job and moving with him across the country in about a year to live closer to his parents.

Molly only suggested to her friend that this relationship was moving very fast and she should keep her head on her shoulders. Samantha became quiet and tersely told Molly that she had been through many relationships and could easily see that she had found the right man. She knew everything that was bad about him and could live with those things.

Molly, soon distracted by her various projects, as well as her occasional run-ins with random shooters, had not called Samantha since, and had heard nothing by text or email from her friend.

Until tonight.

Her cell chimed, and Molly was surprised to see Samantha's name pop up on the screen.

"Hey, Molly! What's up?!" Samantha's cheerful greeting was a stark contrast to the coldness with which she had responded to Molly's advice.

"I've been all over the place, Sam. Sorry I haven't called you, but work has been a mess. Often an exciting mess, but a mess."

"Not sure how research could be anything else."

"No need to go into it. What's going on with you? Work good? Things with Steve still . . . are things?"

"Oh yeah, Steve's great. I've finally found the right guy, Molly, I'm sure of it. And you? Oh yeah, Roger, right? That's his name? You still on that?"

"Yeah, that's still going. One of my longer runs."

"Me and Steve are the longer one! You proud of me? I found the right guy! And Roger seems good too, you say?"

"Yeah, I think so. He's a nice kid."

"How about we all go out? Double date? We've done a couple with Steve's friends. How about that same lunch place? Or do you have a dinner idea? I like Francis Café. Steve always suggests Wally's, but I don't like Wally's. Francis looks good. Yeah."

"When are you thinking? I need to check with Roger. His school schedule is, as you remember, always filled up. He does the—"

"Perfect, that's a deal," Samantha abruptly chimed in. "Let me know when's good. I'll send you some dates. Love ya, babe. Good night!"

The call ended before Molly could reply.

Surprisingly, for all that was on her mind, Molly fell asleep as soon as she hit the pillow. And slept well. No bad dreams. No good dreams either. Just sleep, the best sort.

35

She woke up without her phone alarm at seven and headed for her appointment at the hairdresser—more relaxation! But, dutiful as always, she had to get to work. The mining deal from the 1870s remained unexplored, so she returned to the library to delve into online databases of similarly arcane contracts, hoping the manuscripts section of the library had more general background on such operations in the Rockies in the mid to late nineteenth century.

"Good afternoon, Frank." Molly smiled as she strode up to the front desk. "Good to see you! How have the stacks been treating you?"

"Same old, same old. Got a new crop of undergrads poking around these days, so it's more of a police job than anything."

"Now? In midyear?"

"Yeah, the university is doing some exchange program, with students from other US and foreign schools coming around. They get all the ID access and everything, so this library is a den of secrets to them."

"I would have thought they'd avoid it. Folks I went to school with sure would have!"

"I guess it's a bit of a tourist thing. But nowadays kids know how to navigate the web better than the stacks."

"And they can get more off their phone in a lecture hall than they can get from the lecture."

"Imagine what you could have done with all this tech, Molly."

"I'm not that old, Frank!"

"Oh, yeah, sorry. But you use it a lot in your research now?"

"All the time. My Wi-Fi connection at home is basically my most vital professional expense these days."

"Tax deduction?"

"You bet. They tax us rotten elsewhere; we gotta seize on these escape hatches."

"Bit of politics in you? Yet you seem so rational," he said with a smirk.

"I'd say rational independent, basically. The nonsense from both sides basically forces me to the middle."

"That should be a political slogan!" He chuckled. "So, are you here looking for Rosicrucian stuff again?"

"Nah, I'm pondering mining contracts in the Rockies in the 1870s. It's my secret passion. Can't get it off my mind."

Frank laughed louder than he should have in a library and quickly cut himself off.

"But seriously, you know of any book-form catalogue of Western US contracts?" she asked.

"Not sure, but I'll see what I can find for you."

"Great. Take care, Frank." She turned and headed to the computer stations.

Molly explored data records online, periodically shifting over to her texts and emails on her laptop and taking an occasional break to search for info on Shakespeare's birthplace.

The house seemed like such a culled-out museum. Any treasure that might have been there back in the late eighteenth century, when Washington inscribed his plaque, was probably long gone. Of course, Molly was more aware than most people that hidden knowledge was out there. And so many of these clues led to modern places that somehow, unbelievably, still held hidden, ancient relics.

"Nothing is all good or all bad . . ." That mantra was often in Molly's head. The ability to have two browser windows open on a desktop was convenient, no doubt, but it meant the other task she

was avoiding was back there, popping up now and then to stare her in the face.

Beginning with the early 1830s, mining contracts were a maze of ventures, some successful, some dismally inept. The Southern Rocky Mountains had been a rich source of minerals as one of the first sites to be explored and exploited during US westward expansion. Although gold had been found by Native Americans and Spanish explorers in this region as early as the 1500s, the greatest boom occurred during the Great Pikes Peak Gold Rush of 1859, following the discovery of gold and silver in mountains just west of Denver.[24]

After poring through trite histories of several mining firms with owners based in the Eastern US who had ambitiously ventured westward, leading several gullible entrepreneurs, Molly started writing a short report but just couldn't take it anymore. The Stratford-upon-Avon websites ceaselessly beckoned to her.

As she emerged from the library, feeling lazier than usual, her phone rang. Samantha's name and face popped up.

Her friend rushed to the target of her call. "Hey, Molly! What's up? You free next weekend?"

"Sure, guess so. Roger and I haven't planned anything yet. I'll probably be heading out of town briefly this week, but next weekend's good."

"Great. I've a fun idea for Saturday. How about you and Roger, me and Steve? Dinner? Ask Roger now after we get off phone. Francis Café—I think dinner's better than lunch. What you got going on?"

"I—"

"Work's been a tiring mess for me too."

"I have a project I need to go to England for again," Molly managed to get out.

"You love England! Should be fun. We have a new nursing manager in the ICU; he's been a total creep with all of us. Can't let us do what we've already been doing without his constant needy advice."

"Sounds terrible." Molly was getting close to her car.

"But let's do Saturday. You check with Roger now. Love ya, babe!"

"Later, Sam. Have a good night."

Molly grabbed a pizza on the way home, enough to nibble at for a couple of days, and headed home after sending a quick text to Roger.

When she got home, he called.

"Hey, Molly! How are you doing, sweetie? Been working today?"

"Yup, it's been tiring, Rog. You good?"

"Got a couple mini-tests coming up, so I've been walking around muttering nonsense to myself all day."

Molly laughed as she sat back on her couch and grabbed a slice of pepperoni. She appreciated that she and Roger could have a quiet, easy chat without any fanfare on a tired evening when she just needed to relax and think of nothing.

"Samantha? Your friend the nurse? Yeah, a double date would be fun, I guess. I'm not sure I've ever been on one. It calls for a different sort of talking, right?"

"Yeah, it can be good or bad. I've never been a fan of the idea. Too much distraction, but whatever. Samantha is like double date or bust. Sitting across the table from just one guy is not good enough for her."

❋ ❋ ❋

After working two days in the library, collecting documents and beginning to summarize her findings, Molly received a call from a representative of one of the gold distributors who had hired her.

"Good morning, Mr. Joseph."

"Morning, Ms. McMurphy. Do we have any updates yet? It's been a few weeks, and our client wants to present your findings soon."

"Yes, we do. I'm putting a written summary together, which I'll send you hopefully in the next day or two. In the meantime, I can give you a brief idea of my findings. The most influential documents have actually been from the engineers. The ideas behind these mining ventures were more ambitious than the technology then available could support. In later years, that tech was developed, but in the meantime, much of the sales and purchases of the operations occurred when their yields floundered."

"Like we expected, but it will be good to have the details for our presentation. Anything else?"

"Nothing I can think of. Much of the findings are rather expected." Molly laughed lightly.

"For sure, for sure." Mr. Joseph cleared his throat. "Thank you again, Ms. McMurphy. I look forward to hearing from you."

Thankfully, it took only another half day for Molly to summarize and write up her rather mundane findings. Unusually, there really didn't seem to be any interesting tangents to be found here.

36

AFTER A BORING DAY taking care of household chores, Molly ran off to New York to take her flight to London. Although the narrow plane aisles were, as always, rough on her legs, Molly had never disliked air travel as much as most people. She was good at brushing off the merely irritating as just that, having long realized that what really bothered a person was not the nuisance itself but their own mind's fixation on it. This applied to dealing with other people too.

Her rental car sat in the same lane as the one she'd grabbed a few months ago. The two-and-a-half-hour drive to Stratford-upon-Avon was traffic-free and easy.

Upon her arrival, she perched on a bench across the street from the Shakespeare house, pondered the exterior, and then took the tour, making a floor plan in her head and with her phone camera.

This house/museum was, she was disappointed but unsurprised to find, painstakingly tightened up for tourists. It was a standard, clean, well-planned-out museum.

So where is it? With her prior clues, there had been some specific direction regarding where to search. At Fenham Barracks, she'd had a clue about which locker and which code. At the cemetery in Oxfordshire, she knew whose tomb to look for. But here she had nothing. There was no basement, but perhaps something was hidden in the foundation. *How can I scan the foundation? How do I get down there?*

Entering from Henley Street, straight ahead was the living room, to the left an old record room, to the right a museum. Behind the living room was the kitchen. Stairways to the second floor were located in the museum, in the old record room, and in the back of the kitchen. On the second floor, the birth room was directly above the living room, the library was above the museum, and an extra display room was above the kitchen.[25]

So many artifacts, a bed, fireplace, tables, chairs, floors, walls—there were just too many spots to thoroughly explore. Aside from the obvious rooms of interest, including the birth room and the library, there also seemed to be an unpublicized attic or crawlspace, given the height of the roof from the street and the ceiling height of the second floor.

Molly sat on the bench across the street again, staring at the house. She was almost sure no clue could still be here. *What was this trip for?* One day back and forth. Expensive, time consuming, and pointless.

Molly glumly drove back to London to stay at her usual hotel. She had a set few places where she stayed and ate in many cities around the country and world. When she was focused on her research, it was easier to not have to worry about where to go. As Molly liked to tell Samantha, she was adventuresome in a careful and organized way.

Over a gyro and hummus near the hotel, Molly's phone buzzed. It was the same clients from the Rockies, wanting a verbal presentation of her findings, in front of an audience. She reminded them this had not been in the initial agreement and there would be a cost for this added service, although she was happy to come and present for them. They quickly confirmed. Molly sipped her beer and smiled. *Nothing like letting these jobs grow.*

The next morning, Molly was on a flight back to New York and grabbed another flight, on standby, to Denver.

There was no way to make mining-venture contracts exciting, but she sprinkled in a few smiles and off-the-cuff jokes here and there to keep the audience of angry-looking men in suits and furious-looking women in pantsuits stimulated. *Why are they all angry?* They seemed like they were going through the motions. Everyone in the large room, including Molly, wanted to be elsewhere.

Molly relaxed in her airline seat on her return flight, closing her eyes, content that she was done with Western US mining contracts.

Now for Samantha's double date. Molly understood the purpose of these double dates; the idea was good, and everyone interacted. But it really depended on the four people and how much they each wanted to be there versus being alone with their significant other. During the few times Molly had ventured on a double date, it seemed like three-fourths of the group was annoyed to be there.

She hoped this one would be better.

37

THEY MET OUTSIDE the Francis Café. Molly and Roger walked over from Roger's apartment, and Samantha drove from Steve's place. Steve seemed polite and friendly. "Great to meet you, Molly. Samantha's said all sorts of good things." He grinned as he shook her hand. "Roger, I hear you're a student around here." He grimaced as he scanned the nearby college buildings.

Molly gave her usual greetings and hugged Samantha.

The café was sleek but warm, and the foursome was conveniently seated in a corner booth. "So, Steve, Samantha tells me you're in construction near here."

"Well, construction management."

"Steve isn't one of the grunts carrying the loads out there, Molly!" Samantha beamed as she leaned forcefully into Steve's side, grabbed him around the neck, and pulled him toward her to give him a firm "peck" on the lips and then a full french kiss.

Molly shyly diverted her eyes to Roger's curious, momentary frown.

"I used to do more actual design and materials acquisition work, out at the worksites, but now I'm back in an office, directing the others. Much easier on the legs and arms!" Steve began stroking Samantha's thigh.

"That sounds like a relief. Roger and I—"

"So Steve has more time in the office to text me all day!" Samantha laughed.

"Roger does . . ." Molly started and glanced again at her own quiet partner, reaching over to hold his hand and hoping that he would reverse his petrified silence.

"I study anth—" Roger stuttered and cut himself short as Samantha began sucking Steve's face off. He sent a nervous look to Molly and gripped her hand tighter. "Heading to consulting with McKinsey after school," he almost whispered.

"So, remind me, Steve and Samantha, how did you two meet?" Molly inquired, hoping they'd take a break from mouthing each other to mouth out a reply.

She waited through seconds of silence before Samantha finally purred, "Meeting Steve was the greatest thing in the world for me, Molly."

Steve managed to chime in, "Sam and I are an online dating success story. We should be on commercials for these sites. You know, they say thirty-nine percent of couples are meeting online nowadays. That's almost half!"[26]

Samantha grunted as she unbuttoned the top button of Steve's shirt and stroked his chest. "Steve reads so much and knows so much. I used to go to Google for random facts, but now I go to Steve!"

"You ever tried Bing?" Roger quietly asked, and Molly snorted, patting his hand. Samantha was too distracted by Steve's chest hair to notice Roger's joke.

The rest of the dinner continued like this, and Molly was relieved that she could stomach her quite-good roasted chicken. She liked the place. She and Roger would be back, she was sure.

Roger had arranged for the four of them to attend a musical at the nearby university theater afterward—*Sweeney Todd*, by Stephen Sondheim. Luckily, there were two separate sets of seats, so each couple sat together.

"Good." Roger gave Molly a kiss on her cheek. "Now you and I can enjoy the play without the distraction of softcore porn."

Molly giggled and kissed him back.

"Yeah, that restaurant is really . . . stimulating, eh?" She mock-frowned at him. Roger chuckled as the lights came down.

Samantha and Steve remained in their seats during the intermission, and at the end of the play, Molly and Roger eventually discovered the two lovebirds had flown the coop without saying good night. Roger held Molly's hand as they roamed the theater in search of their compatriots. Molly imagined he was trying—in vain!—to compete with the pseudo-affection with which he had been bombarded over dinner.

Out on the street, starting back toward Roger's building, he hummed a song from the musical, murmuring the words, "Green finch and linnet bird, nightingale, blackbird . . ."

"How is it you sing?" Molly finished, kissing him on the cheek. The two of them hummed the song together all the way back. "Funny you remember that song, Rog." She squeezed his hand. "Not the most prominent of the play, but clearly beautiful."

"I just love the singsong nature of it. The lyrics are so pretty."

As they entered the foyer at Roger's place, Molly gave him a hug. "That's what I like so much about you, Roger. None of that showmanship and aggressive courtship and—"

"And rubbing my you-know-what along your leg as we walk."

Molly smirked, then turned soft and serious. "You're just a sweetheart, a sweet soul." She kissed him on the cheek again as they entered his apartment. She had planned to go home and be back at work early tomorrow, but plans changed sometimes.

38

According to the museum's website, in the mid-nineteenth century, Shakespeare's birthplace was bought by the Birthplace Committee, later called the Shakespeare Birthplace Trust. Extensive renovation of the property ensued from 1855 to 1862. These efforts included removal of the properties on either side of the main house, removal of a brick facade on the portion of the property that had been used as the Swan and Maidenhead Inn, and replacement of the gables, which had previously been removed from the property. The plans to cover the house with a glass roof were never carried out.

An act of Parliament in 1891 gave legal protection for the committee to gather a collection of Shakespeare-related objects, books, pictures, and manuscripts in addition to the original collections from the Birthplace Museum, located in the Swan and Maidenhead portion, which held such curiosities as mulberry souvenirs from "Shakespeare's Tree" and a 1598 letter to Shakespeare from Richard Quiney, who served Stratford-upon-Avon as alderman and bailiff, basically a mayor.[27]

Molly took close account of the objects on display in the house. The Falcon Inn chair—also called the Bidford chair, located in the exhibition room—was once thought to be the chair Shakespeare had occupied during a drinking game at the Falcon Inn, at Bidford-on-Avon, after which, the story went, he fell asleep under a tree on his way home. Although this relic indeed dated from the early seventeenth century, the date was later discovered to be closer to 1630, about fourteen years after Shakespeare's death.[28]

No objects in the house were definitively known to be Shakespeare's personal belongings. A late-sixteenth-century oak-boarded chest was located in the birth room. An earthenware cooking pot known as a pipkin hung in the kitchen. An oak cradle in the birth room was likely similar to one owned by John and Mary Shakespeare. An oak-boarded stool sat in the hall. The only object that might have been in Shakespeare's actual house was the famous second-best bed, which he left in his will to his wife, Anne Shakespeare (née Hathaway), but this was now located at Anne Hathaway's cottage.[29]

The contents of the house had surely changed since Washington inscribed his message to Hamilton. Following this clue, she had no idea how she could find anything.

However, whoever this group of people were—*Or are*, she thought—they no doubt were powerful. *Could they have held on to and replaced any items? Could they have replanted a message for me or someone else to find? Could any of the period objects currently in the museum have been originally owned by Shakespeare, unknown to current scholars?*

Molly had made so many rapid plane reservations recently that her info on the travel website filled in automatically as soon as she typed *M*. In a matter of days, she was on her way back to London.

※ ※ ※

Sitting at her customary bench across the street from Shakespeare's house, there was no way Molly could have seen the two heads, both wearing baseball caps and windbreakers, emerge from the scattered shrubbery behind her. The two men casually ambled over to another bench about fifty yards past her, one holding a camera with telephoto lens—which he twice raised to take a quick shot of the back of Molly's head.

The two joined Molly on one of the tours, neither uttering a word to each other or a question to the tour guide. At least one of them always kept an eye on her. They returned to occupy a different park bench after she had made her latest rounds of the house.

One of them spoke softly into a button on his shirt cuff while they sat.

"Viper continues scouting property. Examining the walls, focused on the fireplace. Has not been close to house pieces," he muttered.

"Seen the item?" the firm voice on the other end demanded.

"No. It remains covered against wall. Not seen."

"No pause to look?"

"No."

"Any pause in the room?"

"No."

"Guide is same?"

"Yes."

"Keep standard."

The firm voice was Roger's.

Joining every tour group was not giving Molly time or access to find clues, and she was sure the guides would start to recognize the tall, thin, silent girl who kept showing up.

She hung around the museum until it closed, observing from a casual distance as the evening security guard took over. He seemed, from what she could see through the windows, to merely sit at a table in his office and read his tablet.

Molly returned to her nearby hotel and mused over a dinner of canned pot roast and a soda in her room. The only unfettered access to the house would be at night. The daytime was fairly impossible.

As she flipped through channels on the TV, a knock came at the door. She had told no one other than Roger she was coming to England and had not called the front desk.

"Hello?" Alarmed, she peeked through the peephole and saw a doorman from the lobby downstairs.

"Ma'am, this is hotel service request."

"I didn't—"

"Ma'am, there is a water leak on the second floor. We need to survey several of the third-floor rooms."

Molly couldn't be sure there was no one else in the hall, but she slowly opened the door anyway. The man was short and polite, came in for only a moment, and took a cursory look at her bathroom sink and shower.

"Thank you, ma'am. Sorry for the disturbance." The man nodded quickly to her and headed down the hallway. Molly heard him repeating the same exercise at two more rooms adjoining hers and then heard the stairway door slam. She turned the TV back on.

※ ※ ※

"All secure," the doorman said into his cell phone as he walked down the stairs. "Molly is fine. Room unmonitored internally, and neg signals detected."

"Good," a woman grunted on the other end. "Maintain post."

"Aye." The short doorman paused on the landing and then emerged to return to his post in the lobby, helping a late-night arrival with his bags.

※ ※ ※

Molly spent the next two days furthering her research on the contents of the Shakespeare house and the history of its renovations, and attempting to watch—from a safe distance—the habits of the evening guard, an ordinary middle-aged man who napped during his shifts. He appeared to be the only one on the job, although she didn't know if that would change in a day or so. On her tours, she hadn't seen any video monitoring, but she knew there had to be cameras somewhere. In addition, she could detect from the habits of the departing day staff that the doors and windows were locked and alarmed.

In her hotel room, she mused over schemes to distract or remove the security guard from the scene. Molly chuckled as she watched James Bond movies from the bed, wondering if she could pull off one of 007's tricks on this guard. The thought again came to her that if a group of powerful individuals wanted her to find something in this house, they could at least come along and help her.

Molly called Roger.

"Hey, babe, what's up?" The grad student sounded tired but happy to hear from her. "Everything going okay over there?"

"Yeah, same old drudge," she muttered. "Getting tired, though, Roger."

"I wish could be there with you, sweetness," Roger purred into the phone. "You know what I say . . ."

"I know, I know. I wish so too, Rog," Molly chuckled weakly. "Are things good with your paper?"

"Oh yeah! That's done—handed in yesterday."

"Nice." Molly leaned back and smiled at the ceiling. "Didn't even need me to proofread it for you," she laughed. "I had so much fun with that last one."

"Nah, this was easy. Prof basically just told me what to say." Roger stammered a bit, then laughed as he went on to list off the conclusions of his paper and tell her about a party from two nights ago.

"See, Rog? If I dragged you out here, you would have missed that bong 'n keg and your party peeps."

"Oh, the party wouldn't have happened at all, Mol. No me, no reason to be there!" he quipped.

The two chatted until late, and Molly thought about the Shakespeare house as she closed her eyes, planning a late morning.

✺ ✺ ✺

One ambitious idea Molly had while munching on a sandwich on the park bench was to drive her rental car in front of the house a few times and purposely get into a bad accident that might distract the guard into opening the door and running out while she ran in.

But that would only work if she didn't die in the car crash.

Wow, Molly thought. *My research job has entered a whole new sphere these days.*

Another sinister plan was to start a fire outside the house. But even if she was then able to find this clue, she had no intention of endangering this house or people nearby.

Molly continued to ponder as her sandwich digested. She stared down at her stockinged legs.

Stockinged legs.

That was it.

39

Although pretty, Molly had never been a seductress. But it was time to learn. She went shopping.

At 7:30 each morning, the day crew arrived at the house, and the overnight guard unlocked the facility, puttering around for a few minutes as the newcomers took their positions for the museum to open at 8. The guard seemed friendly with the crew and typically strolled out just before the doors opened. Molly shadowed him for a morning to follow his walk to a nearby parking lot and his car.

The next day, Molly positioned herself across the street and ambled over to casually intercept the guard just before he reached the street corner. She hadn't spotted a wedding ring, so either he didn't wear one or he was single. She just hoped he was the susceptible sort that girls like Samantha preyed on.

Molly wore a tight set of jeans that complemented her figure—at least, she had thought so in the store dressing room. A form-fitting blouse and a push-up bra accentuated her features as well. So, attractive, but not too much for an early-morning stroll.

"Excuse me." She infused as much urgency and sweetness as she could into her words. "Excuse me, sir."

"I'm sorry, miss?"

"Oh, please, sir, I'm looking for the way to—"

"The Shakespeare museum is back there." He pointed over his shoulder. "And the shops are a five-minute walk to your left," he hurriedly said, without taking much of a look at her.

"Oh, but"—she managed to squeeze her phone out of her pants pocket—"do you know where this place is?"

He looked annoyed but slowed down enough for her to catch up with him while he peered at the photo on her phone.

"I'm not sure . . ."

"My friend told me it's here. There's supposed to be great coffee."

"Uh, I think it's near the park. Not this park here." He pointed at the park behind them where Molly had spent days sitting. "The park by the walkway downtown."

"Really? Oh good!" She began striding in step with him. "You look like you work in the area; it seems nice!"

He looked a bit uncomfortable as he crossed another street, heading toward his car. "Well, I do. The Shakespeare theme is the thing here."

"Of course! I gotta check that out. I just drove in from London. I'm from California."

The man began to grin as he flitted his eyes between her and the ground in front of him. Molly was almost a head taller than the man, but she made eye contact every time he looked toward her.

"Great. I hope you enjoy our town." He stepped into the parking lot.

"You know . . ." Molly skipped a step to keep up with him as he hastened toward his car. She took a chance and patted his upper arm. He looked down at her hand and at her as she continued with a sweet smile, "This is nuts, but you look like you know this area so well! How about I buy you a coffee or a tea? It looks like you're getting off work? Couldn't you use a coffee?"

"Oh, ma'am, I—"

"Miss, please." She grinned at him.

"Uh, miss, I shouldn't . . ."

Molly rested her hand on the roof of his car. Samantha would be shocked at her flirtatiousness!

"I . . . uh . . . I guess a coffee wouldn't hurt. Maybe you can enlighten me a bit about the Western US."

"Of course! It'll be fun." She touched his arm again, and he began to lead the way. "As I've always said, if you don't do fun stuff in life, why live at all?" She tried a giggle and could swear she detected a glimmer of a smile or smirk as she gently rubbed her arm against his on the way up the street. "Oh, this is the place my friend said!" She smiled at him.

"Right here around the corner. I stop at this place a lot," he muttered, directing her into the shop.

They both ordered small coffees and sat across from each other near the window.

"So, what do you do . . . Oh wow, I never asked your name! I'm Molly!" She reached her hand across the table to shake his.

"I'm Raymond. Nice to meet you, Molly." He leaned back and seemed to relax. "Actually, I work a night shift, so this is basically dinnertime for me."

"I've always wondered what a night schedule would feel like. Never tried."

"It's boring but quiet. I do security for the Shakespeare house."

"Ah, yes, that's the main thing to see around here. It's definitely on my list—hopefully for later today."

"Oh, you should. It's real nice. My wife has gone on the actual tour, but, funny enough, I never have. I spend all night in there, so I've of course seen everything."

"You get to walk around?"

"Whole place is open to me. It's small."

"You like it there?"

"It's alright. As I said"—he took a long sip from his coffee—"it gets boring."

"I imagine. Lot of phone surfing time, I bet." Molly laughed and winked at him. "You're cool, Raymond. You're a nice guy. I'm glad I ran into you," she purred.

Raymond chuckled and looked down, taking another sip. "What's your story, Molly?"

"Recent grad, doing the Europe backpacking thing."

"Must be fun."

Raymond's smile became more and more generous, Molly was happy to notice.

"Most of the time. It's good to get away from it all for a while, after being locked up in school."

"Nice. I never made it past half of high school."

"Security since?"

"Nah, garage stuff, custodian. I've roamed around the jobs. My wife is a cook at a local lunch spot. That's where I met her."

"Nice." Molly hoped to steer the conversation away from his wife. "Raymond, you know, I've met lots of people on this long trip of mine. I can tell you're one of the good ones."

He chuckled. "Well, Molly, I—"

"This is nuts; I can't believe I'm saying this," Molly gently laughed, rubbing her thigh casually. "Raymond, you think you could show me the place?"

"What?"

"The Shakespeare house? I'd rather you show me, just two of us, without all the tourists."

"I can't let—"

"Oh, Raymond, c'mon. Remember the line: if you don't have fun . . ."

"I wish I could, but I can't, Molly."

Molly struggled to produce her most coquettish smile, hoping she had succeeded. "I won't touch anything."

"It wouldn't be right."

"I'm not saying right or wrong, Raymond." Molly reached across the table to take his hand and squeeze it. "I'm just passing through. Why not? You could show me all around." She winked.

"I . . ." He trailed off, having apparently run out of the energy to protest. Molly pounced.

"What time should I knock on the door?" She winked again,

rubbed his hand, and made a slight groan of impatience, as if she couldn't wait to be alone with him.

"I can't . . . I should . . . Molly, I just met—"

"You just met me? That's the idea, Raymond. You get to really meet me."

He nervously gulped his coffee and blurted out, "Eleven."

"Eleven? Be there at eleven?"

Raymond made a minimal nod, staring at her. "Eleven. Knock at the west window, not the door."

Molly giggled and shifted in her chair to show him more leg.

After walking him back to his car, Molly brushed Raymond's arm slightly as he got in. "See you later, Raymond," she whispered in his ear. "Sleep well today; be ready for me tonight." She took another chance and gave this man she had just met a light kiss on the cheek. As she turned to walk back to her hotel, she was pleased to see Raymond shed a sheepish grin. *Night watchmen probably dream of this kind of thing every night!* she figured.

Molly sat in her hotel room for the rest of the day, not even eating lunch or dinner, just obsessing over how she would approach things that evening.

40

IRONICALLY, FOR ALL HER MENTAL preparation, Molly slept through her alarm clock and only managed to rush out of the hotel at about 11:45 that night, decked out in shiny, black high heels, a miniskirt, sheer black hose, and a tight pink blouse. She rushed down the street to the Shakespeare house and scrambled behind the bushes outside to tap on one of the side windows, only hurrying to the front door when she heard it open.

Molly snuck her hand to her thigh to tug down on her skirt as she transformed her face from fear to a beaming smile and entered the house. Raymond quickly shut the door.

※ ※ ※

Two men wearing baseball caps were hiding in the shadows of the trees across the street. "Viper inside. Viper inside. Copy."

"Got you," Roger answered. "Monitor windows at the room. Second, control perimeter."

※ ※ ※

Molly had been followed at a distance by the doorman, complete in his livery, who had rapidly abandoned his post. As she went inside the Shakespeare house, he ducked into a bush across the street.

"The guard let Molly in. Don't know what's happening. She's inside. Haven't spotted counter-shadows." The doorman had failed to follow her to the store and had no clues as to her intentions.

"Maintain post," Nathan's voice said through the doorman's earpiece.

❀ ❀ ❀

Molly decided to make her intentions clear from the start. Once the door was firmly closed, she rushed to Raymond, threw her arms around his neck, and plastered him with a broad kiss, which he did not hesitate to reciprocate. In Molly's mind, a married man who was ready to cheat was not looking to just continue flirting.

"Thanks for seeing me, Raymond," she whispered into his ear. "I've been anxious all day for your little tour." She cradled that last word like a kitten.

"Mmmm," the security guard moaned back at her, "never thought I'd do something like this." He began stroking her back. "You got me, Molly. Your smile and looong legs got me." He continued to stroke her back, bringing his hand lower and lower. She let him. Pulling her close to his desk, he reached blindly to his side to flick off the video monitoring system.

After Raymond fully embraced her presence in the house, Molly managed to move toward her real goal.

"Show me the place, the bard's place, your place." She kissed him.

The challenge now was to seductively drag Raymond through the house while taking as close a look as she could at the pieces on display. Not easy.

She started with the famous Falcon Inn chair, pulling the man to the floor as she sought to examine the back and underside of the piece. Nothing. The earthenware pipkin in the kitchen was a relatively easy and quick examination. There were so many surfaces of the chest in the birth room to cover that she had planned out in her mind the contortions she would need to lead Raymond through. Rolling under the guard posts surrounding the item, she noted that the carvings on the chest centrally featured a bird. A thought jumped into her mind, right there as she lay on her back: Nathan had mentioned a bird.

Continuing to whisper absolute nothings in Raymond's ear, Molly forcefully held him down while climbing onto his back, rolling back and forth and keeping him face down each time she whipped her phone out of her blouse to capture a rapid pic off the notifications screen of her jailbroken phone—a nifty trick Roger had taught her!

Once she could swear she had captured shots of every surface, Molly got them to their feet and guided the security guard back to the front entrance.

※ ※ ※

"She has a sex racket going," one of the baseball-cap men whispered into his mic. "The guard let her in there."

The response was terse. "You have to get that phone."

"No way it leaves town with her," Roger added. "No way."

A long silence followed as the two men watched her exit the house after giving the guard a long parting kiss. The watchman looked frustrated and frazzled.

Roger said, "Watch for shadows. I'm sure they're there. Phone is target. She is sec—"

"Eliminate. Eliminate her. Too much is out," the first voice interrupted.

"Follow. It's done."

As Molly rounded the street corner heading back to the hotel, Roger's men trailed after the doorman, who followed her closely.

She went into the hotel lobby, and the two men in baseball caps stopped to observe from across the street as the doorman hurriedly followed her inside.

"She has a tag. Not sure how many others are here."

"Don't risk a scene," Roger quickly replied. "Watch her till we can isolate her."

"I'm not sure we can," the other man grunted. A long silence followed. "Agree we need to isolate, but—"

"Follow her closely," Roger continued. "We'll find a time. She has tags at airport and on plane. We've seen them."

"Monitor hotel from outside."

The men followed their orders, hours later trailing Molly by car as she drove directly to the airport. The doorman and a second ally from the parking garage followed.

Molly made haste onto the highway. The two men in baseball caps swiftly angled their car directly behind her, but a second car, driven by the doorman, followed them closely, flashing his lights and pulling along their right side.

"We're following her, but we're closely followed too. They're here! They're here!" one of the men in baseball caps barked into a mic.

"Pull back," Roger shouted in reply. "Don't make a scene. Pull back and keep watching. Just make sure there's no real handoff. Follow her all the way to her house, but no contact as long as she has shadows."

The other man's voice jumped in. "So when are we—"

"As long as she does nothing with her findings, we're fine." Roger spoke slowly. "We follow."

"Why can't we—"

"No. Not now," Roger growled.

"When can we step in again?"

The radio went silent for a minute, then Roger continued, "I will follow. She won't break through."

"Hasn't she already?"

Roger was curt. "She won't break through. We keep following. I will follow."

41

Arriving home at eleven at night, Molly could not bear to sleep. Moneymaking and ordinary tasks could no longer distract her. She ignored two emails from Samantha and Roger and set directly to opening her scattered and haphazard photos from the Shakespeare house. The bird, she again noted, featured prominently on the wooden chest carvings in the birth room. A bird with a short, conical beak. She carefully transcribed the scattered long and short branches surrounding the bird and making up its nest, some branches so tiny that she struggled to magnify the images using a photo app on her laptop.

This time, she had little sense of where a coded message might begin or end, but she could map out a binary code from within the long and short lines, which, making a long translation, might yield a sense of where a message led.

Molly worked all night and much of the next day at her kitchen table, in a sweatshirt and sweatpants, with no whiskey. No attention even for that. Finally, she had a short paragraph in front of her.

> *This righteous stone harbor brought the divine proclamation of the Virgin to the West. This same wonderful harbor provided honor to the seven arts of the mind. To harness together the beacons of the spirit and the beacons of the cognizant has been the eternal mission of our men. The notions of the heart and spirit are crucial tools for directing humanity. Question the serpent held by logic.*

A long message. And a packed one.

Nathan had pointed to a bird in the trees as he sat next to Molly at the pond. "You know, it almost looks like that bird—we see them back in Europe . . . a bird that likes hemp."

She Googled what birds might fit those parameters and discovered that finches, which had short, conical beaks, liked hemp. They came from the family Fringillidae and had a phylogeny that included Hawaiian honeycreepers, Eurasian rosefinches, bullfinches, grosbeaks, African canaries . . . and the linnet.

"Green finch and linnet bird, nightingale, blackbird, how is it you sing?"

Was it chance that took us to Sweeney Todd*? Or does he know something? Is Roger directing me? . . . Who is Roger?*

Molly began to cry.

42

"THIS RIGHTEOUS STONE HARBOR brought the divine proclamation of the Virgin to the West": Molly rolled the sentence over in her mind. The Virgin, she quickly presumed, was the Virgin Mary. Mary had not been central to church (i.e., Catholic) doctrine until the thirteenth century and was first sculpted in stone on the western facade of the Cathedral at Chartres—a "righteous stone harbor." This facade was built during the second reconstruction of the church beginning in 1134, after it had been twice destroyed by fire during the tenth and eleventh centuries.[30]

Chartres as a place of worship was even more ancient than Christianity itself. Julius Caesar had believed there was a Druidic site there, and this was later confirmed; parts of the foundation were indeed that old. The town and its religious sanctuaries had undergone many stages of destruction.[31]

Chartres was the first church to display secular carvings, also on the western facade, representing the seven liberal arts: grammar, rhetoric, dialectic, arithmetic, geometry, music, and astronomy. The "seven arts of the mind." At the time of the church's design and creation, these liberal arts were not a part of Catholic doctrine, and thus their inclusion in a church program would have been considered heretical. These carvings may have been a response to a movement to diminish the use of classical writings in the study of theology.[32]

Near Chartres was a religious school for monks and clergy known as the School at Chartres, whose chancellor at the time of the presumed dating for the sculptures, 1145 to 1155 AD, was Thierry of Chartres. These divine and secular themes may have reflected the curriculum there. Thierry had in fact written a treatise on the liberal arts between 1120 and 1150 AD.[33]

The target of this opening clue was elegantly worded but clear. The Cathedral of Chartres. The sentence "Question the serpent held by logic" would require more reading. She was not sure what the message was here, but logic was clearly related to the liberal arts.

And from what Molly had already seen, both divine and secular thought were essential to this mysterious group's mission to guide human history.

43

Molly's phone chimed Sam's ringtone. Knowing Sam would complain about her ignoring the emails she'd sent, Molly reluctantly answered and struggled to be friendly.

"Hey, Sam, what's kickin' with you? How's it with . . . that guy—the guy?"

"He's history, Molly. You know I'm picky. But I've got a new one on the burner. That's what I'm calling about. Another double date? Last time was so fun! You and whatshisname still okay, I hope?"

"Roger. Yeah, sure we are." Molly fell silent as she continued to scroll through websites on her laptop, looking for tidbits on Chartres, until she heard Samantha whistle for her attention and ask where they'd all go this time.

"Can't, Sam. I'm just too busy. Too many projects."

"C'mon, don't you and Roger need a night out? More than just a one-on-one, babe? He liked it last time."

"I know, I know. I'm just too busy. How about this? I'll call you when I can go, okay?"

"Molly, you gotta be there for me!"

"I'm sure you've got everything under control, Samantha. You always know exactly what to do."

"Fine, be that way." Samantha made some pithy remarks about people who annoyed her at work and then hung up. Molly was relieved; she wasn't in the mood for more porn action.

Remembering Roger humming that linnet bird song and then realizing the finch was a beacon for this recent clue left Molly with a pit in her stomach. Nathan's reference to the bird who liked hemp was no doubt a message; he of course knew too much, likely much more than he had ever told her. *But was Roger saying something too?* She was sure many people loved that song. After all, it was beautiful, and the musical was popular. It could definitely be a coincidence. It had to be. Roger was just an innocent anthropology student who happened to like Molly a lot. And happened to also like that song.

Molly shook her head violently and tried to stop thinking about it.

She spent time returning emails for other projects and paying bills.

Then she called Roger.

"Hey, babe, what's going on?" Molly asked. She had always liked to hear his voice but now was curious to hear his tone.

"Not much, Mol. Just same old school stuff. It's getting tedious. Your work good?"

"Yeah, it was a good trip to England. Found some interesting stuff, I think."

"Nice, nice. Were you in London? I've been to the city but never out in the country. It's probably nice."

"Oh, it's lovely. Yeah, I was pretty much just in town."

"Right, yeah."

The two had a relaxed, lazy conversation. He sounded tired, and Molly was exhausted. They agreed to meet for a quick dinner in Stamford that evening, and Roger stayed the night at Molly's house, making the drive back up to New Haven in the morning for a late class. Molly was glad to lie on her couch and then bed with him. He was totally the same goofy guy she had grown so fond of over the months. Perfect for her, at least for now; Molly never took anything about the future for granted. Hopefully McKinsey wouldn't change him too much.

Roger called Molly after his day of scattered classes, a pleasant interruption to her afternoon of chores around the house she seldom spent much time in anymore.

"You getting up to some new projects these days?"

"I've got one brewing—an interesting one."

"Not just looking at Ancestry.com and stuff?" he laughed. "I know, I know. You do more than that."

"More than pay a subscription service and have them organize findings I could make on the internet myself? Yeah, I do more than that."

"Any trips?" She heard him washing dishes in his sink.

"Probably, probably," she muttered as she buttered toast in her own kitchen.

"Great! This is the one where I come and act as your intern, right? My maiden voyage!"

"Nope, nope, not now or later. You got—"

"Where to? Hopefully it's something like Antarctica, or somewhere cool like that so I can carry you over mountains!"

"Nope, just France. Nothing exciting, nothing for you to pine over. Although I will send you a postcard! With little hearts on it," Molly purred into the phone. Thoughts of his singing of linnet birds were slowly evaporating from Molly's mind. Slowly evaporating, but not gone yet.

"France, nice. Paris?"

"Yup, just—"

"Romantic!"

"Yup, just staying in the city, nothing else. Seeing the sights there."

"Cool, so when we leaving?"

"Roger, I've told you—"

"I'm off from school soon. It's the perfect time!"

"I can't."

"Yeah, you can, Mol! Please! I'll totally stay out of your hair when you're working. You go do your work, and I'll just sit in the hotel or wherever we are, and we just hang out in the evenings. It'll be fun."

"It's a big thing to go on a trip together, Roger."

"I know. We're ready, Molly. I promise you. And you'll see I can keep my word. I'll totally leave you to your work—no questions, no bugging you, just fun. We'll have dinner and coffee in Paris. C'mon, it'll be cool."

"Roger, I don't know how this work trip is going to pan out. I may be busy in the evenings."

"How long are we going to be over there?"

"That's the thing, Roger. With these trips, I have no idea how long things will take."

"Don't you have a plan?"

"Of course I do!" She felt a tinge of annoyance with him. It felt like she could never truly relax into the relationship before he started getting pushy again about her work.

"No problem. Remember, I'm off in a couple days, after my semester paper is in. Then we're all clear."

"Until graduation."

"That's a couple months away! We can do it. If you have to stay, I'll just come back on my own."

"So that's what you want to do?"

"No, of course not! I want to come back with you, but just in case."

Molly stayed silent on the phone for a while. She was not always sure she knew exactly what he wanted.

"Okay. I hope I'm not going to regret this, but okay."

"Fantastic, we'll have fun!"

"You'll keep your promise and let me work however and whenever I want? No questions?"

"None. Remember, Mol, one day I—"

"No questions?"

"Okay. None."

The plans were set. Molly hadn't forgotten her concerns about Roger, but it all seemed so natural. She wouldn't harp on it now. Molly was very selective, so her boyfriends were few and far between, and she never rushed.

Roger and Molly met up two days later on the airport shuttle, climbing into the van's back seat together. Roger grabbed Molly's hand and didn't let go the entire ride to New York.

"She's on airport shuttle," one of the men in a car tailing the shuttle reported. "Boyfriend with her."

Nathan quickly replied, "Keep tailing them. Regular handoff at security."

A second car in the right lane also closely followed. The two teams of agents followed the travelers to security, the second set escorting Molly and Roger from a distance onto the plane, then sitting behind them.

44

MOLLY AND ROGER joined the line at the rental car counter in Paris.

He smiled. "Not a bad flight."

"Not bad at all. Everyone stayed nice and quiet."

"No babies!" He grinned, leaning over to kiss Molly on the cheek. "So, so, so glad you let me come, sweetie. It'll be great. From that time you told me about your Austria trip, I knew I wanted—"

"Yeah, we'll work it out. We'll have fun in evenings, I hope." His enthusiasm was a little overwhelming.

"When you went to Cornwall, all I could think of was going to some London pub kind of place with you!"

Molly laughed and took his hand in hers.

Then she stared up at the ceiling with a slightly perplexed smile.

Cornwall had been a while ago now. Molly hadn't met Roger yet. She had never mentioned Cornwall to him.

"I'm sure we can find some nice café here." She continued to hold Roger's hand, struggling to not change her loving expression. He gave her another smooch as they moved up to the counter.

With Roger holding the keys to the rental car, Molly excused herself to go to the ladies' room, walking around the corner with her bag while Roger waited by the baggage carousel.

Molly stepped into the large restroom and stood staring at the mirror.

Roger couldn't know about Cornwall. Roger sang of the linnet bird . . .

She had to lose Roger, right now.

The gunmen in masks had grown in dedicated ferocity as rapidly as her curiosity for the clues and the secrets they hid had grown in her mind. She knew Nathan was watching her, likely helping her. The man at the Ogilvie house and men at Yale campus were clearly trying to kill her.

But who is Roger? Who is he with?

She carried nothing that could be used as a disguise and had no time for one. Peeping cautiously out the door when another woman entered, Molly didn't spot Roger or anyone else in the small side hallway. She clutched her bag tightly and dashed out, scurrying in the opposite direction of baggage claim and running up a flight of escalator stairs. Her eyes scanned the overhead signs. She rushed— but didn't run, to avoid alerting security guards in the terminal— toward the public transport train linking the airport to the city.

Hurrying down a second escalator, she rummaged for her wallet and had her internationally authorized credit card ready to purchase a train ticket to Paris. She sighed as the doors closed behind her and the train started along its underground ramp.

※ ※ ※

Two men in airport baggage claim came together. "Did you see her come back to rental?" one whispered.

"No. Haven't seen her. Let me . . ." He spoke into a lapel pin.

Nathan's voice answered. "Nothing at bath?"

"Bathroom is cleared."

"Back toward main concourse?"

"I've been watching north escalators. No."

"There must be south too." Nathan sounded angry.

The men stood silent, then: "There are only two of us."

"Scan main concourse. One of you. Now."

Roger muttered into one of his polo shirt buttons, "She's not back. I just sent cleaning staff into bathroom. No one there."

"Is she upstairs?"

"I'm heading there now. I need backup. I need backup!" he hissed.

※ ※ ※

By this time, Molly was a few minutes out of the station and on her way to Paris. The minutes ticked by excruciatingly slow for Molly on the short ride. Emerging with a quick glance at the nearby map in the Paris station, Molly scouted her direct path to the closest rental car outlet. The line of two people seemed way too long, but without much delay, she was pulling the mini car out of the lot and following directions to Chartres, a small village fifty-five miles southwest of Paris.

※ ※ ※

"For Chrissake, we need backup!" a man shouted into Roger's earpiece as the young man tore up and down the main concourse, looking in every store and side hallway for Molly.

"I'm going directly to Arc now," Roger whispered into his button, more and more agitated. "Need backup, lot of backup there. Not here. She's flown from here!"

"How do we know that's her tar—"

"That's where she went; I'm sure of it. She insisted she's only coming to the city. The tomb is her target."

"The Arc clue is not well stated! If anything, she's on a path to Char—"

"No, meet me at the Arc. She's not leaving Paris!"

"But shouldn't we send a second team?"

"No. All with me. Now," Roger sputtered into his microphone as he hurried toward the rental car pickup, still grasping the key.

※ ※ ※

Nathan likewise directed his scattered agents in Paris toward the Arc de Triomphe, sure that Molly had managed to find the clue sending her there. The value of the prize buried beneath the monument was too precious for her to bypass, and its clue was too clear, as far as he was concerned. Leaving nothing to chance, however, he sent a separate small team to watch the cathedral at Chartres.

45

Molly made the drive at a good, nervous clip, arriving in just over an hour. Wanting to minimize contacts with anyone in Chartres, she headed directly to the cathedral, leaving her car in the tourist parking lot and starting on a long walk in the woods along the highway. At the end of her journey, she huddled beside the trunk of a large tree and began to cry, all at once feeling so alone and so scared—but also utterly committed to waiting until nightfall to approach the building itself. She hoped her phone battery would last as she continued to read about the western facade sculptures.

The west wall was divided into three portals, along the bottom of which were sculptures of kings, queens, and saints. Above these sculptures was a frieze interrupted by three large doors displaying scenes from the lives of Mary and Christ. Above each door was a tympanum with surrounding scenes called voussoirs forming an arch around it, or archivolt.

The north tympanum showed a scene of Jesus's Ascension. Surrounding this, the associated archivolt showed signs of the zodiac and months of the year. The center tympanum showed Christ with animal representations of the four gospels, with the surrounding archivolt showing twelve angels and twenty-four elders holding musical instruments. The south tympanum showed Christ's early life and him and Mary enthroned in heaven with a surrounding archivolt displaying allegorical representations of the seven liberal arts alongside the most prominent author of each.

Along the left aspect of the south portal was the personification of dialectic (i.e., logic). In one hand, this sculpture held an unidentified object, which may have been a torch or scepter or flower. The other hand held a small creature. Some scholars thought this creature was a dragon, one a scorpion, and some suggested a serpent.[34]

"Question the serpent held by logic," she recalled.

Molly sat on her knees and closed her eyes, trying to rest before her nighttime explorations.

When night fell, she anxiously watched the cathedral staff saunter to their cars for the night. She waited another hour, closely watching the building and its surroundings to make sure no one remained.

If she had guessed wrong, it would take a long time to reevaluate the clues in the sculpture, so for now, she headed directly for the left aspect of the south portal. Using her phone flashlight, she had trouble clearly identifying the creature held by the dialectic statue.

She was not sure how to "question" this serpent, so she touched it, feeling mere stone. She pushed the serpent. Nothing. She pulled at the serpent's head . . . and the entire personification of dialectic began to rotate on creaking hinges, revealing a thick wooden box.

※ ※ ※

Meanwhile, Roger had angled his rental car into a spot directly facing the Arc de Triomphe and approached the edifice on foot, keeping a careful eye out for Molly and finally taking a seat at a nearby café where he could watch the monument and speak with his agents. Two pairs of agents radioed him that they were taking up position.

He stared down at the picture of Molly on his phone screen as he scanned for messages from the two sets of agents who were scouring the great monument. "Hold our positions," he grunted into the microphone.

"Why not check Chartres as well?"

"I want our full force ready for her here. Another couple hours. No doubt she's trying to avoid us. She's figured who I am. If we don't find her, then Chartres—"

"Why is she not—"

"She's not. She's told me her plans. They are clear. Maintain your positions and follow my lead." Roger angrily pulled away from the microphone, grasping his phone, which still showed Molly's picture. He then stared at the Arc de Triomphe, slowly shaking his head back and forth.

A furious woman spoke through his earpiece. "We should have put that digital tag on her. You insisted—"

"We have a hierarchy here, Diamond." Roger pursed his lips tightly as he spoke. "We had no chance to place one without her noticing."

"But you were—"

"We had no chance. Enough. We watch. The prize here is greater than Chartres, and she knows it."

"We need her."

"We will have her," Roger whispered. "You stand your post and follow me."

※ ※ ※

As Molly headed back to her car after removing an envelope in the box and scanning the stone enclosure for other clues, she heard the sculpture pane slowly rotating shut, quickly replacing the box before she left. The box had a simple wire latch, no lock. Like the box by Hale's statue, its location had been its security. Whoever placed it behind the statue surely expected it would not be found. She couldn't help shaking her head at the astonishing ingenuity she had been witness to on her journey.

The walk back seemed longer. Emerging from the bushes into the rear of the parking lot, she noticed two black cars parked out on the highway shoulder but did not stop to look at them.

Roger had to be avoided at any cost; she was now certain. She'd had former relationships fail, but usually for stupid reasons, not life or death!

Although she knew there would be no flights out until morning, Molly drove straight to the airport, luckily finding the rental car return open. She was ready to hop on any flight with a standby seat.

Reading further about the cathedral she had just visited by night, Molly was struck by its clear, close ties with Freemasonry. While Thierry no doubt had a role in the creation of the west facade, the master mason—as architects were then known—who had been responsible for the Chartres Cathedral now standing was unknown.

The cathedral had been designed utilizing simple geometric patterns reiterated and expanded upon to form the final complex structure. The proportions of three, four, and five—those of the Pythagorean right angle—were present. A square, circle, and rectangle were at one end, with a semicircle at the other.

The five-pointed star, the pentagram, considered to have magical powers in Freemasonry, was used to make the pointed arches atop the slender windows, while the seven-pointed star controlled the interior structures. The seven-pointed star had been a symbol of the seven Amesha Spenta, or "Bounteous Immortals," of Zoroastrianism, an ancient Persian religion. It also symbolized the seven colors of light in the rainbow, which in turn represented the seven liberal arts taught in the fellowcraft degree of Freemasonry. The sculptures along the west facade focused on human knowledge. Priscian was sculpted as the holder of grammar, Cicero as that of rhetoric, Aristotle of logic, Nicomachus of arithmetic, Euclid of geometry, Pythagoras of music, and Ptolemy of astronomy.

Three tables were carved on the Chartres floor, one square, one circular, and one rectangular. The rectangular table was in a proportion of two to one, the proportion of King Solomon's Temple, the ancient bastion which played a central role in the symbolism of Freemasonry.[35]

※ ※ ※

Molly made a conscious effort the entire trip back home to not answer her phone. She knew from the vibrations that she was missing calls but did not want any messages marked as read for several hours. In her kitchen, she finally opened the message app and saw tons of worried notes from Roger.

46

You okay, babe?

Missed you.

Where you at, Mol?

NUMEROUS missed calls from him.

Molly dropped her head and shook it forcefully. Even after her extreme move of abandoning him in France, she had doubts about her doubts. But he couldn't have known about Cornwall. She was sure he couldn't. Molly sat at the kitchen table and drank her last can of seltzer water, racking her brain. She always avoided detailed discussions of her work, for her clients' sake. Especially the trips she had made for these arcane clues—she'd never spoken of them. Cornwall was an ancestry search at first, but by the time she knew Roger, she had found the disc. She would never have mentioned it.

She regarded the neatly folded parchment paper from the envelope. Experienced with running across ancient paper and manuscripts, Molly knew she should wait and take this to the responsible curators at the rare-book library. But instead, after a second's pause and rapidly cleaning her large kitchen table, Molly began to slowly unfold it herself.

Her phone continued buzzing as she worked on the parchment. Molly finally brought herself to listen to Roger's urgent, worried voicemails. He spoke as if missing her coming out of the bathroom were his fault, saying he might have missed her when he ran to the men's room himself, that he had notified airport security to look for her. He begged her to call him back and sounded worried sick.

"Fuck," she whispered as she put down her phone, repeating one thought in her head like a mantra: *Roger couldn't have known about Cornwall.*

A map, remarkably well preserved, revealed itself after almost an hour of careful unfolding. It measured about four by six feet, entirely covering Molly's table. She had seen this map at the Yale library. This was the Martellus map.

It had been thought that Yale owned the only surviving copy of this map, made by Henricus Martellus in about 1491, but evidently they didn't.

She learned that a copy of this map had likely been used by Christopher Columbus in planning his trip across the Atlantic, suggested by two historical facts: that Columbus and his son had written of sailing west from the Canary Islands to search for Japan in the region where it appeared on the Martellus map; and that Columbus believed the island would run north to south, as it appeared on the Martellus map but not on any other surviving map made at that time. This map later influenced another German cartographer,

Martin Waldseemüller, whose map in 1507 was the first to use the term "America."[36]

On this copy of the Martellus map, two separate reams of short and long lines had been etched over the coastal waters of Africa, the two coded phrases appearing, to Molly's eye, to have been written by two separate inscribers.

Molly continued to angrily ignore Roger's texts and voicemails as she copied the lines and unfurled the translator chart she had developed for the coded texts. But he knew where she lived. And the Roger she had known would not hesitate to come here. The Roger she feared certainly would not hesitate to come here. *Damn.*

It would take many hours to translate these lines, and she couldn't afford having him show up with the Martellus map strewn over her kitchen table.

"Roger," she began, her tone muted.

"Molly!" Roger shrieked into his phone. "Ohmigod! Molly, I lost you! What happened?"

"I-I wasn't feeling well, Roger. I went to the ladies' room. When I came out, you were gone."

"What? No, I was right there, by the rental counter, the whole time. I—"

"Not sure where you went . . ."

"Well, I did run to the men's room for a second at one point. I've gotta go too, Molly, sometimes," he chuckled, although she cut him off before he could add a cute, flirtatious sort of laugh.

"No, Roger, you left." Molly remained very serious.

"Molly," he said quietly now, "it was a misunderstanding. We just missed each other in that big airport. All the hallways look the same in there. You probably just—"

"You weren't there, Roger." She had to maintain the guise that she'd never left the airport in France. "I was sick, and you weren't there, Roger."

"So, did you ever make it?"

"No. My whole project fell apart. I never made it anywhere. After a few hours of looking for you—"

"Molly, you never called! You know I have a phone. Remember, you put that international card on my phone. Why didn't you call?"

"I said, Roger, I wasn't feeling well."

"Who doesn't call, just a quick call, even if you're not feeling well? Oh, baby, if I had known you weren't feeling okay . . ."

"You would have done what, Roger?" Molly knew she had to lose him completely. It agonized her, but she didn't trust him. *God, I hope Nathan's men are watching somehow.*

"I would have come and helped you. We could have just flown back together, or I could have helped you and we could continue. That's what normal couples do on a trip. Happens all the time, Molly!"

"Roger, I can't talk to you about it now."

"You sound so different."

"You seem different now to me too, Roger."

"How am I different?"

"You just are. Please, give me a few days, Roger. Just give me some space. A few days. Then I'll call you."

"Can I just come over?"

"Please don't, Roger. I don't want to see anyone."

"I'll bring you tea, Mol. Please. I love you, Molly. I love you." He sounded so earnest. "Please, sweetie, I love you."

"Do you?" After a pause she repeated, "Roger, I just need some time. I need some space."

"Oh, baby, please." When she said nothing else, he stammered, "Can I call you, in a couple days?"

"I'll call you, Roger." Molly was curt, then ended the call.

❋ ❋ ❋

Roger sat on his bed, holding the phone.

He nudged the earpiece in his right ear. "Agents," he said firmly, "stand down. I repeat. Stand down. I'm watching her. I'm on her. All is fine. We have her controlled. She's found nothing." He waited for words of assent from three different agents.

He stared down at his phone screen, at the picture of the tall girl with gentle features and a dignified, sweet smile.

※ ※ ※

I should have stocked up on nonperishables, Molly thought. She was starting to run out of cans of tuna, beans, and lentil soup.

The translating came quicker and quicker, though. She knew this code inside and out. The lines on the map were interspersed with Roman characters, coming together in a final message:

> This treasure gift bestowed on Columbus by his true hidden patrons. Bjarni Herjolfsson sailed west of Greenland and sighted a land where his countryman later set foot. Follow the men of the north on their occidental passage and bright harbors will you possess. Our men were with Herjolfsson and Eriksson. Our men are with you. Castile's bounty was milked by our men at court.

Pytheas saw our home. Our home is heart-shaped.

47

THE FIRST PASSAGE was a message to Christopher Columbus. This group of people had given him the map he used to plan his voyage and worked to capture the sponsorship of the Catholic monarchs of Spain to fund his venture. Nearly five hundred years before that, or so this passage indicated, this same group had supported the ventures of Leif Eriksson to the New World.

She learned that the Norse sagas included two accounts of Eriksson's arrival in North America. The first had him crossing the Atlantic in error after sailing off target as he made his way from Norway to Greenland. A *Saga of the Greenlanders*, on the other hand, described a voyage that was not by accident but rather followed the story of a previous Icelandic trader, Byarni Herjolfsson, who had accidentally passed by Greenland and come within sight of North American shores about a decade before Eriksson's voyage.[37]

Moreover, this group of individuals not only supported but also possibly guided Columbus on his ultimate "discovery" of the New World. In the biography of his father, Ferdinand Columbus asserted that Christopher had sailed to Iceland:

> In the month of February, 1477, I sailed one hundred leagues beyond the island of Tile [Thule], whose northern part is in latitude 73 degrees N, and not 63 degrees as some affirm: nor does it lie upon the meridian where Ptolemy says the West begins, but much farther west. And to this island, which is as big as England, the English come with their wares, especially from Bristol. When I was there, the

sea was not frozen, but the tides were so great that in some places they rose twenty-six fathoms and fell as much in depth.[38]

Molly searched for information on Thule. In about 330 BC, the Greek explorer Pytheas had sailed north from Marseilles, looking for a source of amber. In Britain, he heard of an archipelago even further north called "Thule," which was now thought to be a Celtic name referring to the Shetland Isles. Over time, as known geography expanded, this site, known as "Ultima Thule" in poetry, moved further north, from the Faroe Islands to Iceland, and eventually became Greenland.[39]

Perhaps it was no coincidence that the code this group had translated their messages into was Icelandic.

"Our home is heart-shaped," she repeated aloud, adding "heart" to her search terms. The Eskimo settlement at the base of the rock at Thule, Greenland, known as Mount Dundas by British explorers and currently known as Thule Mountain on North Star Bay, was called Umanaq—which meant "heart-shaped."[40]

Thule, Greenland, had to be her target. Molly was crystal clear on this one. Whoever these people were, their aims and methods were earth shattering. This clue did not suggest a further clue. In a roundabout way, they suggested this clue led to "our home."

Amid Roger's numerous calls and texts, one came through from Samantha and one of Samantha's friends, whom Molly had briefly met. Ignoring those was easier than avoiding Roger's missives of feigned despair.

48

THE AIR ROUTE to Thule Air Base went by a DC-8 aircraft run by Air Transport International, which would depart McGuire AFB in New Jersey on Wednesday night, then transfer via Baltimore-Washington International, departing on Thursday for a six-and-a-half-hour flight to Thule.[41] Molly doubted she'd find these tickets on Expedia.

She sat in her house, eating her last cans of pinto beans for two days straight as she waited to begin her Wednesday drive to meet the flight in Baltimore.

She wanted to be able to lose whoever would be tracking her on her trip to the airport. She told no one when or where she was going—certainly not Roger. It scared her to think that someone could be monitoring her internet usage, in which case they could have seen she had searched a flight path to Thule, but hoped that hadn't happened.

Driving her own car all the way, they would obviously know how to follow her. Arranging a rental car would be the same. Taking a limo service was both slow and she would be easily followed.

Molly had changed a lot since her initial foray into this avenue of research, dating from her meeting with Dr. Samuels. What she was finding was bigger than everything she had ever read about. It might end with her getting arrested or killed, but she realized she would do anything to pursue this to its end. She would lose her house, her work, her friends. She would definitely lose Roger.

Aside from her normal suitcase, Molly packed a diverse set of tools into her trunk. Her uncle had been a car mechanic before his early death in a car accident, and she had learned a few things from him. At least he had taught her how these tools worked, which was a big part of the challenge with such jobs, she knew. She hoped she wouldn't need to use them.

If she missed this flight, it would be another week before she could make the trip, a week during which she had no idea what might happen. She was eager to leave early, heading off in her car at 3 p.m.

As she rolled down her small driveway, Molly scanned the roads around her house and saw no cars watching or following her. *Maybe they've given up on me. Maybe Nathan somehow intervened to make them all go away.* Still, she was prepared. Two days of sitting alone in her house had led to many, many assorted web searches. In her desperation, Molly had memorized scattered parking lots in highway-adjacent restaurants, hotels, and gas stations.

※ ※ ※

As Molly took the ramp onto I-95, two black sedans quickly pulled in behind her at an unobtrusive distance. Roger's men were committed to not letting her get to any train or airplane. She had seen too much and knew too much. They knew, however, that they in turn were being shadowed.

※ ※ ※

"Close tag. Leave no distance," Nathan said. "She knows we're there; no need to hide ourselves anymore. Their cars are to your left. Keep them away from her."

The five cars drove like this without pause or communication for almost an hour and a half, making it beyond New York.

※ ※ ※

"I think she's heading to Newark," a woman said through Roger's earpiece. "You said your communication was intact with her."

"It is," he replied. "She has told me nothing. Maybe the Arc. She now figured it right. We follow."

"No," the woman continued. "Soloview, your methods have failed us. She should be dead by now. I'm assum—"

"Assume nothing. I am command here."

The two men in the front seats did not turn to look at him when he spoke.

"There is only so long this can continue," the woman hissed. "Their goal is exposure, and she is achieving it. It stops now."

"I am command."

"You are rem—" She cut herself short. One of the men in the front seat turned, pointing a gun at Roger.

"We have new orders," the young man said. Roger stared without blinking at the gun barrel but accepted the message, dropping his hands to his sides, leaning back into the leather seat.

"What is wanted?" He coldly glared back at the man. "I'm with you, following her, aren't I? We're following her, she is going nowhere, and we are isolating her."

"This should have ended long ago. You have been delaying the inevitable," the man relayed from the voice in his ear.

"The measures Scorpion wants are not needed yet at this point."

"Scorpion has taken command; we follow. This target knows too much."

Roger fell silent, staring back at the man.

"You will be confined to reorientation," the man with the gun said tersely.

They continued for another twenty minutes, until they were within about fifty miles of the southern border of New Jersey.

Then a car passed closely on the left. For a scant instant, the man holding the gun diverted his eyes to the passing car, and Roger lunged forward, throwing the gun to the right as the round fired, narrowly missing his head. Roger incapacitated the arm.

※ ※ ※

"Gunshot!" one of the men in the sedan just behind and to the right shouted.

"Divert them!" Nathan yelled into the earpiece. The sedan sped and collided into the right rear doorframe of Roger's car, violently angling it into the left lane as the driver struggled to stay on the road.

※ ※ ※

Molly had sensed she was being followed not long after getting on the highway. Three similar cars seemed to always be in her view when she glanced in her rearview mirror. "Crap," she muttered, rubbing an itch on her nose and leaning her head back in the seat, stretching her arms straight out in front of her. She dared not even move out of the center lane.

Scattered pops of gunshots sounded off behind her, and sweat erupted across her forehead. Molly began speeding ahead. Two sedans accelerated to engage each other, a total of four vehicles violently angling back and forth across lanes and sending several other cars careening off the highway.

A bullet shattered her right rear window and created a gaping hole in the right dashboard.

Should have invited Roger on this trip and had him sit in the passenger seat, she thought with a hysterical giggle as she accelerated as fast as the old car would take her.

She merged into the right lane, and the four cars fell back amid the mayhem. Molly knew there was an exit about two miles ahead. Her hands shaking, she managed to veer onto the exit ramp and made a quick left to park on the side of the road under the highway overpass.

There was a rest stop about four miles further on, but Molly guessed it was better to be on foot than in her well-known car. She grabbed her backpack out of the trunk and snatched a few items from her small suitcase, then looked up past the overpass. It was time to put her high school varsity track-and-field experiences to good use.

There were local roads that paralleled the highway, and with her backpack tightly strapped to her, she began straight out running, glad she'd worn sneakers as the squealing cars passed her position, continuing south.

❊ ❊ ❊

"Do we have eyes on Molly?" Nathan demanded.

"No, no visual. Her car disappeared," a woman in one of the cars shouted back. "We're still engaged."

"Keep driving. Hopefully she escaped off highway. Accelerate to make them chase both your cars! Divert them off at an exit."

"One of their cars has crashed onto median. I repeat, one car has crashed onto median. Being pursued by one vehicle now. Still firing rounds."

"Good," Nathan growled. "They want you. Make them pursue, then divert."

❊ ❊ ❊

Molly ran up the grass hill to the highway rest area, complete with restaurants and gas station. She breathed heavily, scanning the scene before making her way directly to the tractor-trailer parking station at the far end.

She sat along the barrier bordering the rear of the parking area, away from the highway.

"One of these trucks must be shipping through BWI," she whispered to herself. No time to wait, she hand-combed her hair and marched toward the trucks.

She tried to be calm as she asked drivers if they were heading for Baltimore-Washington International. No one said they were, and most seemed very uninterested in talking to the girl in jeans and a sweaty T-shirt.

She waited for a while, watching as more drivers came out from the restaurant.

"Yes, I'm to BWI—at least, a storage facility right near BWI," one older gentleman replied.

She was surprised he'd responded but smiled and asked if he would let her ride with him.

"Miss, I wish I could. I used to hitchhike a lot when I was younger too." He gestured toward her evident itinerant apparel. "It's just my job—"

"Please, sir, please. It's personal, but I have no way to—"

"There are Uber sorts of things will pick you up."

"Please, sir. I can't explain, but I need to leave right now."

"On the highway, they'll be here fast." He shrugged, shaking his head. "I'm sorry. I wish I could."

"If it's money, sir, I can pay."

"No, no, no, definitely can't do that." He started chuckling. "My boss would hate me even more if you paid me!"

"But are you planning to see anyone else between here and there?"

He paused, looking thoughtful. "Well . . . no."

"My lips are sealed. I wouldn't tell anyone. Don't even tell me your name. I won't look at your license or anything."

The man continued thinking, shifting his weight back and forth, stopping to look at Molly and what she knew was a pained, desperate expression, the sweat pouring from her forehead in the midday sun. He looked back at the restaurant and gas station, shaking his head again.

"Okay," he muttered. "Get in. Just quickly get in, and we start right away."

Molly didn't hesitate to climb up into the truck as the man held the door for her.

She was somewhat disheartened to realize they still had about a two-hour drive to BWI. She spoke little, and the man spoke little, but he seemed like a nice sort.

She had been careful to deactivate the location services on her cell phone before she left her house. She was on airplane mode and would stay that way throughout. But although she believed there was no way her stalkers could be tracking her in this unknown tractor trailer, Molly remained anxious the entirety of the drive.

Approaching BWI, finally, the man had to drive to a storage facility, but he kindly asked Molly where he could drop her.

"Could you please take me along one of the fields adjoining the airport, where the ground crew works?"

Oddly, the man did not ask questions. "Remember, miss, I don't know what you're doing here, but please, please, you never saw me."

"Of course. Thank you. I promise I have good aims. I can't tell you, but I promise," she said, nodding to the truck driver as she climbed down, clutching her small backpack.

Now the big challenge. Darkness had fallen. She walked along the perimeter of the airport on a side adjacent to one of the terminals but far from the passenger exits. Watching the ground crew, she soon determined which crew members had which jobs and kept an eye out for the luggage transport crew. She finally identified the small metal shed that was their base.

Searchlights scanned the perimeter, but she had at least three minutes of relative darkness to work with. The bolt cutter she'd lugged through her short run and long drive was out and ready. Waiting for the searchlight to pass before quickly crawling up to the fence, she cut the chain fence material along its right inferior corner, making a small opening that she could fit her thin frame through without leaving too visible a defect. Two sensors were positioned higher on the fence, and she avoided those.

Her tools and bag would have to be left behind—too large. She tucked them under a dense bush before squeezing through the fence.

Molly made her way to the shed, hiding behind it in a patch of ratty grass, in almost complete darkness. She heard crew members still inside the shed and waited for them to leave the small outpost empty, then dashed in and rapidly grabbed a loose jumpsuit, neon jacket, helmet, and visor. She scrambled back onto the grassy patch to don the suit and wait for another team to enter the shed and then leave. She had seen manifests lying on the simple desk and figured she could find the DC-8 Thule flight from there.

She kept her face hidden and moved rapidly so no one could notice in the dark that her face did not match the ID badge she had stolen with the suit. Molly again hurried into the shed when it was empty to scan the manifest, quickly finding the Thule flight, which would leave in one and a half hours.

She waited just behind the shed, standing as if she were a member of the crew waiting for her orders, her helmet and visor covering her face, and listened for the number and name of the Thule flight.

The crew set out toward the DC-8, and Molly followed. No one seemed to care she was there, and she began assisting as they moved boxes toward the cargo hold of the aircraft. Molly waited until a good portion of the cargo had been loaded before dashing into the hold while the crew headed back to their vehicles to gather more cargo. Squeezing behind the boxes, pulling one with a folding lid over her, Molly remained as still and silent as she could as the crew spent another five minutes finishing up. She only allowed herself to breathe fully when the cargo door slammed with a hollow metal clang and fastened shut.

※ ※ ※

Six and a half hours spent kneeling and crouching in one position while straining not to move as turbulence shook the plane was not easy. The touchdown at Thule was, she could swear, the most painful jolt she had ever felt. *It's remarkable how cushioned airplane seats are*, she thought. Everyone always complained about flights, but they had no idea!

The ground crew at Thule mercifully opened the cargo door and, after moving several boxes out, left to get another truck while Molly crawled quickly under the plane, running toward the passenger terminal. Ditching the ground crew uniform behind a small equipment shed, Molly scrambled into the indoor stairwell leading up to the terminal.

The few passengers and crew inside the air base were in uniform, and Molly walked as quickly as she could to the exit, praying no one would stop the odd individual wearing a T-shirt and jeans amid frigid outside temperatures. She stopped at the small airport store and bought a sweatshirt, to at least look foolish and tough rather than crazy.

Thule was small, and Molly easily found the main street and a physical map showing the clear and short walk to Mount Dundas. She licked her lips as she walked, her tongue keeping them warm. Thule seemed like it could be a quiet, nice place to visit once all the clues and targets nonsense was happily behind her. She hoped to live long enough to return.

Molly's walk was straight, and it would take only a few minutes to cover about a mile and a half. She hummed some old jingle to herself, hoping to find a clear clue at the base of this mountain to direct her more precisely.

As she headed down the street, momentarily heedless, a hand slapped over her mouth, and her head was grabbed from behind, the unseen force yanking her painfully into a nearby alley. She felt the sting of a needle in the right side of her neck and fell unconscious to the ground.

49

MOLLY SQUEEZED HER EYES, shaking off a faint headache. The blurriness soon cleared. She was sitting in a wooden chair, her hands fastened together behind her back by a hard plastic device. Molly squinted at her surroundings, wanting to cry. The air was cold. Large ice bricks around her formed a circular room, and she looked up at an icy dome. It was a very large, modern igloo.

Molly realized she was wrapped in a thick wool blanket that was tied at the front. She wore a wool hat that came down low on her forehead, making her itch; she wished that were the worst of her problems.

The headache returned.

A man dressed in black walked from behind, positioning a chair directly in front of her. He sat and looked at Molly with a calm but serious expression. It was Roger.

"Hello, Molly."

His left arm was in a black sling, and a gash on his right cheek was bandaged.

"How are you feeling?" he quietly asked.

Molly whimpered, looking away from him, then turned her head back to glare at him desperately. "You bastard." She began crying as she shook her head, tears streaming down her cheeks. "You bastard," she faintly screamed.

He half stood, using a white cloth to wipe her tears. "Molly, we need to talk."

"You're one of them." Molly continued to cry, stammering, "You're one of them." She both couldn't believe it and had long known it to be true. "You would kill me. I opened myself to you, and you—"

"Yes, Molly," Roger interrupted her gently. "Yes, Molly, you did. You opened your heart to me."

"You bastard!" she hissed again.

"Please, listen to me, Molly. Let me speak."

Molly replied with only silence and an angry stare.

"You tied me up," she eventually gritted out.

"To protect you from yourself." He shook his head as she continued to cry, and he rose twice again to wipe her tears. "What is your sense of what you know, Molly?"

"What do you mean?" she demanded.

"All the places you've been, all the objects and documents you've seen. What does it all tell you?"

Molly said nothing, just shaking her head. He stared at her for what seemed like an hour. She stared back. "I know what's going to happen," she growled. "I hate you. I hate you, Roger."

Roger stared down at the igloo floor. "I'm sure you do."

"I'm going to tell you, and then you will kill me," Molly stated simply.

"Let me know what you know, Molly, and then we will talk. I would untie you, but I don't know what you would do and what I would have to do. We need to talk."

"No, you need to die! That is the only way I make it out of here."

"Let me hear you and you hear me. You will explain. I will explain. What have you found, Molly?"

"You're not that . . . that silly student."

"No, I'm not. But I looked the part, eh?" Roger managed a weak grin. "I will explain. First you tell me what you know or think you know."

Molly stared at the ceiling, breathing deeply. He allowed her to sit silently.

"You people . . . whoever you people are. I don't know who you are, but—"

"It's fine you don't know who we are." Roger relaxed back in his chair. "We are no defined entity. We are no defined group. We are above that."

"You are controllers. You control events and people."

"Yes," he interrupted her. "But control is a firm word. Guide. We guide people; we guide events."

"You do. It's scary."

"We guide large-scale events and large-scale groups of people. Yes, we do."

Molly stared at a spot on the ice wall, unsure of how much she could really talk with and learn from this man who had so savagely betrayed her. "Centuries. This has happened for centuries."

"Yes, many centuries." Roger nodded. "Even we following this path today don't know how long we have been doing this."

"The earliest evidence I found was . . ." She thought back through the clues and evidence jumbled in her mind.

"The earliest evidence and documents you have found are no doubt far newer than how ancient this effort has been."

"But why? Why are you doing this? Who are you to want to do this? Do this to everyone?"

Roger sat thoughtfully for a moment. "Sometimes, Molly, even I don't know that. I'm not sure any of us do. We just know we—whoever we are—have been guiding mankind for centuries."

"You just keep doing it?"

"We just keep doing it."

She frowned at him. "What I don't understand is there seem to be two groups of you people, fighting each other."

Roger nodded. "Yes, that's the problem here. That's what I need to tell you about, Molly. For about fifty years now, as you no doubt can see, there has been a schism in our group and in our efforts."

"Who are you? Who are they?"

"There are those like me, like my father and my grandfather before me, who have harbored this cause, who continue to harbor this cause. Our efforts are secret, but we are the defenders of a bastion that has, as you have seen, stood for centuries. Guiding mankind. Guiding countries, banks, the church. Guiding all avenues of human existence."

"Who is Nathan?" Molly pushed, hoping he wouldn't react to the name.

"Nathan turned."

"He turned away?"

"Yes. He and many others. You have met one of his minions, Father Stevens. He is safe, you should know. A renegade faction began to question our methods and our purpose. They began to question the very need for our existence. They can better explain to you who they are and what they stand for."

Molly frowned again, more uncertainly. "So, you're going to let me leave here?"

At that, Roger stood to begin untying her.

"Yes. I will now take you to them. And they will kill me. Nathan doesn't know who I am. He and his people departed way before I embraced this cause. He only knows he has to kill those who are loyal, like me."

"So why are you taking me there?" Molly demanded. "You can leave and run and tell Nathan to find me."

"No, Molly. My time has come."

"Can't you—"

"Molly. Watching you work, watching your findings, thinking of you, I realized . . ."

Molly gawked at the almost dreamy expression he now wore.

". . . Nathan and his people are right. Let me take you there now."

She shook her head, confounded. Roger released her hands and removed her blanket, giving her a large parka. He helped her stand up and stood in front of her.

"Where do we go, Roger?" Molly murmured.

"Not far. A very short walk. Let me say something else so you understand me completely when we meet with them."

"Okay." Molly meekly stared at the man she had loved and who she was sure should have killed her by now.

"I met you to direct you, to guide you away from this path that Nathan sent you on. We rely on utter secrecy, and we would do anything—anything at all—to preserve that secrecy. I came to know you in order to kill you if we needed to." He said this with kind eyes but no emotion in his tone.

"You would have?"

"I would have followed my orders, yes. But more and more, as I came to know you, I only desired to deflect you away from the path of knowledge you were following."

"So why didn't you kill me?"

"I came gradually to realize that in the show I was making for you, the act I was putting on, the geeky anthro guy, that I deeply meant every word I ever said to you. I wanted to be that boy. I wanted to be that real young man who cared for you, who loved you."

She couldn't stop from gasping, "You did?" She hated that her heart fluttered at his words.

He looked her firmly in the eyes. "I did and I do."

Molly hesitated a moment, allowing Roger to reach out and touch her hand.

"Roger, I still don't know who you are."

Roger gave her a faint grin. "Let us take a walk, Molly."

He took Molly by the hand and led her out of the igloo.

The parka kept her comfortable along the dusky walk toward Mount Dundas. They approached the stone base of the mountain, and he twisted a portion of the rock face to the right to reveal a fingerprint and retina-detection apparatus, which he used. He glanced at Molly.

"The instrument's data still includes all our identifiers, but Nathan's people took this place over." A man's voice came through quietly, and Roger said who he was and that he was "bringing a peace offering, a prize."

Roger covered the detector apparatus, signaling to Molly to stand still and wait. They stood there for about five minutes.

A larger aperture in the rock face slid open, and Roger led her down a narrow stone corridor into the mountain. After a long, silent walk in dim light, they stepped into an elevator and began to descend.

When the steel elevator doors opened, Roger and Molly emerged into a massive, cathedral-like chamber. Although frightened, she marveled at her surroundings. The stone walls glittered under the lighting of an enormous chandelier, which cast its glow across ancient tapestries on the walls, large wooden tables and leather-lined chairs, and several gigantic stone fireplaces, all lit. The two of them padded over Persian rugs to a sitting area and just stood, waiting for what seemed an eternity.

A door to the side of the fireplace directly before them opened. Nathan entered in his gray suit and stood in front of them, looking first at Molly, then at Roger, before smiling.

"How are you, Molly?" Nathan strode forward to hug and give her a perfunctory kiss on the cheek, as if they were meeting for dinner at a cozy restaurant. "It is good to see you. Are you well?" He stepped back, taking another long look at Roger. "And who is your friend?" Roger opened his mouth to speak, but Nathan gestured for him to be silent. "Please, Molly, I want to hear your voice."

"This is Roger. You probably recognize him as my supposed boyfriend. He captured me, Nathan. But he also has protected me and did not hurt me. He has been kind. I don't know his intentions, but I know that."

Nathan felt along the arm of Molly's parka. "Did he give you this coat? It's very nice—warm." He smiled faintly at Roger, stepping back.

An aide hurried forward—Molly had not previously noticed anyone else in the room—and took Molly's coat, as it was not needed in the warm hall. Another individual came forward to hand glasses of wine to Molly and to Roger.

Roger finally spoke. "Nathan, sir. I am Roger Parkson, an agent of the loyalist camp. You may remember my father and grandfather."

"Yes, I do. You have been following our Molly, accompanying her, trying to stop her." His expression was mild and unaccusatory.

"Yes, I have. Yes, we have."

"She knows too much for your liking, I imagine." Nathan nodded toward Molly. "Yes, my dear, you now know a lot, don't you?"

Molly smiled uncertainly. "Yes, I have seen and know too much, I think."

Nathan turned back to Roger. "I have seen your efforts, Roger. You would have killed our Molly to protect your secrets."

"Our secrets are your secrets, Nathan."

He continued to regard Roger with his calm gaze.

"Please, let us sit." Nathan gestured to the large leather chairs, and they sat, Roger at Molly's side. "And, Roger, you are here now to . . . ?"

"As I hope you realize, Nathan, through watching Molly, watching how she has learned of our efforts, I have come to see that you and your camp have the right vision."

"I see." Nathan's gaze remained inscrutable as he relaxed into his seat, sipping a glass of pale-yellow liquid. He stared back and forth at Roger and Molly, then addressed Molly. "My dear, what is your understanding of what you know?"

Molly paused to think. "I know that there has been an effort by a group of individuals for centuries to guide"—she emphasized that word and glanced at Roger—"mankind. Be a guide to mankind's relations with each other, among and between societies, with regard to utilization of resources and acquired learning, to guide mankind, I believe, along a beneficial course. Sometimes, those efforts prevented actions that could have led to catastrophe, or at least further catastrophe. For instance, your people tried to stop MacArthur from advancing into China and expanding the war with a larger power."

"Yes, yes." Nathan nodded, sipping at his drink again. "We feared expansion of a world war. We contained the conflict. And who are we?"

"Roger told me you are unnamed." She paused. "My research at Chartres showed me a connection to Freemasons—"

"We are not the Freemasons," Nathan interrupted her. "We are not the Illuminati. We are not the New World Order." Nathan put air quotes around these names. "We are not even Skull and Bones." He chuckled.

"Well, I am." Roger smiled weakly.

"We are not a government. We are not a church. We are not mere rituals." Nathan paused to take a longer sip. "Molly, we are all of them. We have, for centuries, utilized these societies, these organizations, these brotherhoods, these churches and their religious devotions, these political structures, these leaders and these followers, these armies and these missions of peace, these diplomatic entities between nations, these social interactions and exchanges between nations and societies—we have used these structures as tools for our guidance. What greater tool to guide mankind than the church? Of course, we did not create religion or mankind's ancient and ingrained belief in a higher divine entity or entities. That was developed over eons. But we used it."

"So you own—"

"We own nothing. We guide through these entities." He steepled his fingers together in front of him, resting his elbows on the arms of the chair. "So, how did this arise? Well, as you know, mankind has long believed, long before such firm structures as Judaism and Christianity and Islam existed, that a divine intelligence guided mankind." He paused. "Long ago—we know not when or where—a group of individuals realized that there was no real, or at least no consistent, divine guidance. The belief in a higher, divine entity was not doubted or rejected, nor is it rejected now, but the notion that mankind could fully rely on such guidance to progress and flourish as a society or larger set of societies was erroneous."

"You replaced religion?" Molly asked.

"Not at all. We simply found ways to utilize structures that mankind had already created. In some cases, it is true, we influenced certain individuals to create these structures, in order to use them as tools."

"Along my path of learning, so many of my clues were found in writings by such figures as Sir Arthur Conan Doyle and Sussmayr."

Nathan nodded. "And Mozart too."

"Were these tools of influence?"

"Yes and no. These persons, whether government figures such as George Washington or writers such as Shakespeare, were tools of influence as well as influencers themselves."

"They were part of your group?"

"Yes. Many of them. Part of our camp, our group of guides. These individuals realized, or at least were invited to know and to realize, that their exquisite talents in music, in writing, in speaking, in leadership, could aid the advancement of civilization. These were people who deeply yearned for the best for their country and their society. In turn, we invited them to join us in guiding mankind toward the best for all societies."

"And I'm sure I know what you'll tell me here: your mission of guidance was toward the good?"

"Yes, ultimately toward the good." Nathan leveled a steady gaze at Molly. "Sometimes positive developments, for social structures, technological advances, and such; however, such positive developments originate as a reaction to negative events, catastrophic events even."

"War is a great driver of medical advances," Molly agreed.

"A very good example. And those advances in response to dismal human events can have even larger scope and ramifications."

"So, do you—I hate to think of this—do you guide mankind toward these negative events?"

"No and yes. How to say this?" Nathan gestured to Roger that he could join in. "We at least direct these events and the response to these negative events so that they, in many ways, lead to positive developments. Sometimes, it is true, we . . ."

"We generate conflict," Roger jumped in, "with the outcome and its subsequent responses and resulting circumstances in mind. For instance, would the League of Nations have arisen without the catastrophe that was the First World War? I'm not saying that we created that awful war. But could the response to it, could Woodrow Wilson's response, have been guided, at least in part?"

"Yes," Nathan continued. "Roger suggests a good point to discuss. Different individuals in human history and over the course of human events remain individuals, unique despite any of our desires for guidance. Some are more easily guided than others."

Roger chuckled humorlessly. "I personally know that for sure. Some are not guidable at all!"

"Yes, part of the art of this effort is and has been based in psychology."

"But what is the nature of this schism that Roger mentioned to me?" Molly asked.

"Ah, it's good Roger has introduced you to why he and I are currently sitting at opposing sides of this effort." Nathan nodded, and an aide refilled his glass. "A schism there has been." Nathan sipped his drink and asked Molly and Roger if they wanted anything to eat. Molly was hungry but in no mood to eat. "Well, Molly, a way to think of it is this: what was the reason that this ancient set of individuals decided that mankind needed intelligent guides? Intelligent human guidance?"

"I don't know. Maybe they were concerned that without direction, mankind would merely . . ." She gestured vaguely, searching for the words.

"Collapse into randomness," Roger finished. "They believed that without divine or human guidance, the structures of mankind would proceed randomly, disorder would beget disorder, conflict would beget conflict, times of peace would produce complacency that worked against progress. They thought—they still think—that without guidance, chaos will reign."

"And we agree with the notion that human endeavors, that human history, is dominated by chaos. Do you know the chaos theory of mathematics?"

"I've read of it briefly. Cloud structures, that sort of thing."

"Yes," Nathan continued. "Chaos theory does have a societal manifestation. And that chaos arises both by human and natural causes. For instance, Molly, think about this: Adolf Hitler was a corporal on the lines in World War I. Think of how many poor men died in that war. Imagine this. A bullet flying through the air toward the German lines. A tiny gust of wind could adjust the course of one of those hundreds of bullets just inches to the right or left—to penetrate straight through a young Adolf Hitler's brain or heart."

"Yes. But that can't be directed."

"No, of course not. What I mean here is that our forebears knew that chaos reigned in human history. Bullets hitting or missing Hitler. A baby Winston Churchill being exposed or not exposed to a deadly infectious agent sitting on a table inches away from his young hand when he played in his nursery. The fuel injector of a rocket malfunctions. A single, isolated individual, powerful or not, on his or her own, could influence events. Any of these tiny events could drastically alter human history."

"For better or worse," Molly interjected. "Of course they could."

"So this ancient group believed that chaos would beget chaos and more chaos if a benevolent, intelligent set of *human* hands did not guide mankind through these waters."

Roger said, "Then, some within our group, such as Nathan and now me, realized that this chaos—"

"Could never be avoided entirely. And had never been avoided, despite all our strenuous efforts. Moreover, we realized that chaos does not always, as humanity progresses through the ages, lead inexorably to more chaos."

Molly nodded. "Attractors."

"Yes." Nathan smiled. "You know chaos theory better than you said. Exactly. As mathematical chaotic systems have a set of values toward which they evolve, so does—or so my team of renegades began to postulate years ago—human society. Chaos does indeed reign, but against that, the forces of mankind's virtues, whether they be good or bad, altruistic or selfish, passive or aggressive, themselves become the attractors that keep mankind on a progressive course, a course that is broad but broadly defined and, we say, human-nature directed."

"And that direction is no doubt not always positive." Molly looked toward Roger, and he nodded.

"But the direction of mankind will not always be in a positive direction. It may one day be positive, but not over short periods of time," Roger added. "Just as our own efforts could be characterized."

"Is your focus on directing individuals?"

"Yes and no, again." Nathan maintained his pleasant smile. "We guide individuals in order to guide much larger sets of individuals. We can't definitely direct the course of one person's life but rather are directing large societal structures. I'm sure you remember, Molly, what Sherlock Holmes said about Winwood Reade: 'He remarks that, while the individual man is an insoluble puzzle, in the aggregate he becomes a mathematical certainty.'"

"But back to this chaos and attractor talk—where does that leave you in your schism?"

Roger continued, "The traditional adherents of this group of individuals continue to believe that without guidance, without often forceful guidance that can sometimes be ruthless toward one group of people in order to direct the larger segment of societies, disorder will reign."

"You believed this?" she asked.

"Yes, I did. Perhaps part of me still does, to a degree."

"I continue to partly believe this too," Nathan agreed.

"But the renegades, like Nathan . . ." Roger stopped short as Nathan gestured that he wanted to speak.

"Those, like me, who feel that human proclivities will create many directions within human societies to direct an overall course within chaotic structures feel that we need to pull back."

"You mean stop all these efforts."

"No," Nathan continued. "It's very nuanced and has different implications in different situations, but we think we can take a more . . . relaxed, almost back-seat approach to our guidance. But always be a force for good. When we can guide positive, healthful developments for human societies, we should. The nature of our power would be an awful waste if we did not do this. But, at times, we should be more passive. When bad events occur, whether they be war or illness or famine, we feel we should step back from fostering these under the excuse of directing them toward a more fruitful future."

"You want your efforts to be more positive."

"The effort was always for positive goals. But we were more ready to promote and tolerate injuries in order to create trends of healing. We want to adjust that focus. Show concern for the individual who suffers as well as the whole."

"So how was it thought to be beneficial for me to go on this . . . this scavenger hunt?" She couldn't help chuckling at the absurdity. "Why did you want me to find all this?"

"Well, I'm sure you've often been frustrated by these ventures—"

"That I wasn't paid for!"

"Yes, yes, we'll talk about that." Nathan shrugged. "We wanted you, an independent observer, to find all this because we no longer want to remain hidden and anonymous."

"My group, on the other hand, has been fiercely committed to secrecy, so much so that I was directed and programmed to kill you if you found too much."

Despite his supposed change of heart, his words sent a chill through Molly.

"My team of renegades has long sought an avenue to expose this group's efforts. My faction found you and sent you on this path. We thought," Nathan continued, "that if an independent individual learned about our history from actual evidence and documents, rather than our just telling you—"

"In which case I would have thought you were a crazy conspiracy theorist."

"Yes, you would have. We thought if you learned about us and wrote about us for the larger world, we could, in a way, more reliably augment the telling of human history by including these forces of human guidance. Add a new, overarching human guidance to the course of the history of mankind, as opposed to only a divine notion of guidance."

"So, is that where I fit in now, to write you up?"

Nathan smiled. "You sound like you're arresting us."

"Thought of it, actually." She smiled. "And why me?"

"We knew that this researcher had to be suitable to join our efforts. From what we've seen of you, Molly, and by reasons of family connections that you do not yet know of, we chose you."

Molly couldn't even begin to delve into this new bit of information, having long thought that her ancestry had been lost to history. She sat silently, considering her next steps.

"Can we set a table for dinner, Molly?" Nathan pointed toward a large wooden table. "Broiled chicken and noodles good for you?"

"Love it." Molly rubbed her starving belly. "I've been hungry. It's been a long trip." And she didn't just mean the flight to Greenland.

"Perfect. And some pineapple for dessert." Nathan directed Molly and Roger toward the table, where a fine dinner was served. "Where you come in is to write about what you have learned, with further details that we will share with you."

"And then?" Roger asked tentatively.

"And then, Molly becomes—has to become, given what she knows now—one of our number."

"She's a fine addition." Roger sent Molly an affectionate smile before taking a seat next to her. "She's very smart, Nathan."

"I know. She is better than just smart. Molly has a good heart."

"Hopefully she will be a force for reason and goodness as your efforts go forward, Nathan."

"I think you mean to say, Roger, our efforts. I didn't know what to think when you captured Molly and brought her here to us, but now I believe that you can be loyal to our efforts as well?" He cocked his head inquiringly.

"Affirmative, Nathan. Thank you." Roger dropped his head and whispered, "Thank you."

"And now"—Nathan smiled and held up his glass in a toast—"to the chicken!"

REFERENCES

1. Loudon, I. "Why are (male) surgeons still addressed as Mr?" BMJ 2000 Dec 23; 321(7276): 1589-1591.
2. The Royal Lancers (Queen Elizabeth's Own) Association: [http://theroyallancers.org/17th-lancers/]
3. Manchester, W. American Caesar: Douglas MacArthur 1880-1964. Back Bay Books 2008: 546-7.
4. Manchester, W. American Caesar: Douglas MacArthur 1880-1964. Back Bay Books 2008: 556.
5. Manchester, W. American Caesar: Douglas MacArthur 1880-1964. Back Bay Books 2008: 556-7.
6. Manchester, W. American Caesar: Douglas MacArthur 1880-1964. Back Bay Books 2008: 565.
7. Edwards, Paul M. Korean War Almanac, Infobase Publishing, 2006: 470.
8. Manchester, W. American Caesar: Douglas MacArthur 1880-1964. Back Bay Books 2008: 583.
9. Manchester, W. American Caesar: Douglas MacArthur 1880-1964. Back Bay Books 2008: 586.
10. Manchester, W. American Caesar: Douglas MacArthur 1880-1964. Back Bay Books 2008: 596.
11. Davenport, E. The plumbat affair. Lippincott 1978: 28.
12. Eyles, A. Sherlock Holmes: A Centenary Celebration. Harper & Row 1986: 11-12.
13. Fleming, JV. "Winwood Reade and the martyrdom of man." *The Princeton Independent*, 2003.
14. Wertheim, M. "Radical dimensions." Aeon website: [https://aeon.co/essays/how-many-dimensions-are-there-and-what-do-they-do-to-reality]; Bayley, M. "Alice's adventures in algebra: wonderland solved." New Scientist, 16 December 2009: [https://www.newscientist.com/article/mg20427391-600-alices-adventures-in-algebra-wonderland-solved/]
15. "Faust: the legend of Faust from the renaissance times. the end of civilization.": [https://www.faust.com/legend/alchemy/].
16. Blockley, RC. "The romano-persian peace treaties of A.D. 299 and 263." Florilegium 1984, 6(28): 30-1.
17. "The End of an Era: TV Enriches the Majors and Impoverishes the Minors.": [http://www.mikeroer.com/bridgeporthistory1950.html]
18. Ray, JL."Lou Gehrig." Society for American Baseball Research: [http://sabr.org/bioproj/person/ccdffd4c]
19. Sadie, S. "Reviewed works: requiem, K. 626, by Wolfgang Amadeus Mozart, Richard Maunder; Mozart's requiem: on preparing a new edition, by Richard Maunder." Notes, Second Series, 46(4); Jun. 1990: 1052-1055.
20. Cossey, A. "On Leibniz and i-Ching." 2015: https://annecrossey.wordpress.com/2015/11/05/on-leibniz-and-i-ching/
21. Christie's. "George Washington's wine cooler presented to Alexander Hamilton: [https://www.christies.com/lotfinder/Lot/george-washingtons-wine-cooler-presented-to-alexander-5525820-details.aspx]; "George Washington's wine cooler could be worth a cool $600,000.": [https://www.paulfrasercollectibles.coOpm/blogs/memorabilia/george-washingtons-wine-cooler-could-be-worth-a-cool-600-000]
22. It's Hamiltime!: "Hamil-swag Friday: the ultimate wine cooler." September 30, 2016: [https://itshamiltime.com/2016/09/30/hamil-swag-friday-the-ultimate-wine-cooler/]
23. Bryce, E. "What's behind the myth that storks deliver babies?" LiveScience website: [https://

www.livescience.com/62807-why-storks-baby-myth.html]; Kolb, A. "The Tempest". American Heritage website: [https://www.americanheritage.com/tempest#1]

24. "The teacher-friendly guide to the earth science of the northeastern US.": [http://geology.teacherfriendlyguide.org/index.php/78-southwestern/mineral-sw/609-mineral-region3-sw]

25. [https://www.bing.com/images/search?view=detailV2&id=BB5DFB-03171DA66B2383804F137909EFFF2224CE&thid=OIP.p9Y5vT02UXep-wxCBJO3OsQHaLn&mediaurl=https%3A%2F%2Fi.pinimg.com%2Foriginals%2Fa7%2Fd6%2F39%2Fa7d639bd3d365177a9c3108124edceb1.jpg&exph=894&expw=570&q=shakespeare%27s+birthplace+stratford+upon+avon+floor-plan+diagram&selectedindex=0&ajaxhist=0&vt=0&eim=0,1,2,6]

26. Shashkevich, A. "Meeting online has become the most popular way US couples connect, Stanford sociologist finds.": [https://news.stanford.edu/2019/08/21/online-dating-popular-way-u-s-couples-meet/]

27. Shakespeare Birthplace Trust. "Reinventing the House.": [https://www.shakespeare.org.uk/explore-shakespeare/shakespedia/shakespeares-birthplace/reinventing-the-birthplace/]; Shakespeare Birthplace Trust. "Letter from Richard Quiney to William Shakespeare." Shakespeare Documented: [https://shakespearedocumented.folger.edu/exhibition/document/only-surviving-letter-shakespeare-letter-richard-quiney-asking-shakespeares]

28. Shakespeare Birthplace Trust. "Collections Items on Display.": [https://www.shakespeare.org.uk/visit/shakespeares-birthplace/collections-items-bp/]; Arts Council England. pdf "Falcon Inn Chair.": [http://collections.shakespeare.org.uk/search/museum/strst-sbt-1865-5]

29. Shakespeare Birthplace Trust. "Collections Items on Display.": [https://www.shakespeare.org.uk/visit/shakespeares-birthplace/collections-items-bp/]; Shakespeare Birthplace Trust. "The Second-Best Bed.": [https://www.shakespeare.org.uk/explore-shakespeare/shakespedia/william-shakespeare/second-best-bed/]

30. Knitter, BJ. "Thierry of Chartres and the west façade sculpture of Chartres cathedral." Thesis presented to Department of History of Art, San Jose State University. Advisor, Anne Simonson. August 2000: 2-4: [https://digital.library.pitt.edu/islandora/object/pitt%3AFC-SP11250210; http://www.medart.pitt.edu/image/france/chartres/chartres-cathedral/Portals/westfacade/general/FCSP1-General.html]; Hutchens, RR. "Chartres cathedral and freemasonry."

31. Hutchens, RR. "Chartres cathedral and freemasonry."

32. Knitter, BJ. "Thierry of Chartres and the west façade sculpture of Chartres cathedral." Thesis presented to Department of History of Art, San Jose State University. Advisor, Anne Simonson. August 2000: 3-4.

33. Knitter, BJ. "Thierry of Chartres and the west façade sculpture of Chartres cathedral." Thesis presented to Department of History of Art, San Jose State University. Advisor, Anne Simonson. August 2000: 4-7.

34. The art story: gothic art and architecture: [https://www.theartstory.org/movement/gothic-art-and-architecture/artworks/]

35. Hutchens, RR. "Chartres cathedral and freemasonry.": [https://www.facebook.com/GrandLodgeScotland/posts/chartres-cathedral-and-freemasonryby-brother-dr-rex-r-hutchens-of-tucson-arizona/1909624225789816/]

36. Miller, G. "Uncovering hidden text on a 500-year-old map that guided Columbus." Wired 9/15/2014: [https://www.wired.com/2014/09/martellus-map/]

37. Kavenna J. "The lost land of Thule: a legend melts away." NYT Feb. 15, 2005: [https://www.nytimes.com/2005/02/15/opinion/the-lost-land-of-thule-a-legend-melts-away.html; "The Viking explorer who beat Columbus to America.": [https://www.history.com/news/the-viking-explorer-who-beat-columbus-to-america]

38. Ruddock, AA. "Columbus and Iceland: new light on an old problem." The Geographical Journal June 1970; 136(2): 177-189.

39. Gilberg, Rolf. "Thule." *Arctic:* June 1976; 29(2): 83-86.: [http://pubs.aina.ucalgary.ca/arctic/Arctic29-2-83.pdf]
40. Gilberg, Rolf. "Thule." *Arctic*: June 1976; 29(2): 83-86.: [http://pubs.aina.ucalgary.ca/arctic/Arctic29-2-83.pdf]
41. "Getting to Thule air base.": [https://cloud1.arc.nasa.gov/oib/docs/thule_rot_flight.pdf

www.ingramcontent.com/pod-product-compliance
Lightning Source LLC
LaVergne TN
LVHW041909070526
838199LV00051BA/2549